A Bean to Die For

Also available by Tara Lush

Coffee Lover's Mysteries

Live and Let Grind

Cold Brew Corpse ✓

Grounds for Murder ✓

A Bean to Die For

A COFFEE LOVER'S MYSTERY

Tara Lush

NEW YORK

Published in the United States by Crooked Lane Books, an imprint of The Quick Brown Fox & Company LLC.

Crooked Lane Books and its logo are trademarks of The Quick Brown Fox & Company LLC.

Library of Congress Catalog-in-Publication data available upon request.

ISBN (hardcover): 978-1-63910-545-8
ISBN (ebook): 978-1-63910-546-5

Cover illustration by Brandon Dorman

Printed in the United States.

www.crookedlanebooks.com

Crooked Lane Books
34 West 27th St., 10th Floor
New York, NY 10001

First Edition: January 2024

10 9 8 7 6 5 4 3 2 1

To my bestie, Heather.
I should've listened to you in
the beginning when you suggested
I write mysteries.

Chapter One

Ever since my mother handed me that first mug of java at the tender age of thirteen, I, Lana Lewis, have measured my life in coffee cups.

My high school days were marked with frothy, sweet drinks. In journalism school at university, I tried to show I was tough by consuming it black. While working at my first newspaper in Miami, I didn't have time to spare between crime stories, so I downed shots of Cuban coladas that were like thimblefuls of jet fuel.

And now, as a thirty-something divorced woman and the co-owner of Perkatory, the best café on the island of Devil's Beach, Florida, I drink what my mother did: house blend, a splash of cream, a scant teaspoon of sugar. Simple and classic. I want the richness of the beans to shine, need to savor the aromatics and enjoy the acidity of the coffee—all with a hint of sweetener to make it bloom.

But not today. Today I wasn't savoring anything. I was hustling out the door with my best friend Erica Penmark while making sure my dog, Stanley, wouldn't follow us out.

"It's a shame he can't come with us." Erica pushed out a sigh as she slid a pair of Ray-Ban Wayfarers over her eyes. "I mean, it's a community garden. What the fluff does Darla think is going to happen if we bring the doggo?"

Darla Ippolito was the elected president of the garden, and as far as I could tell, not a fan of dogs. "She's worried the dogs will poop everywhere or dig up the plants." Feeling terrible for my sweet shih tzu, I quickly shut the door and locked it. A whimper from behind the closed door tugged at my heart. I hated leaving him alone.

"We'll be back soon, buddy. Go play with your tennis ball."

"You don't think we should wait for Peter?" Erica leaned against the house and ran a hand through her short, jet-black hair. With her lanky frame, she looked like something out of an ultracool eighties music video. How she'd landed on a tropical island in the Gulf of Mexico as opposed to some fog-shrouded city was still a mystery to me. About a year ago, she sauntered into my family's coffee shop, looking for a job. Because she was the most talented barista I'd ever met, I hired her—and we became best friends.

"No. Dad's probably overslept. Or woke up and smoked a joint and is running late. He'll meet us there." My father, Peter Lewis, was a well-known hippie around the island and had a Florida medical marijuana license so he could buy legal weed. He claimed it was for his "eye pressures" and "stress," but I suspected otherwise, because his vision was like a hawk's, and he was the most laid-back guy I'd ever met.

As if on cue, an older, weathered Prius came chugging up the street, the sound of bass and something else—air horn, I think—barely contained inside the vehicle.

"There he is." I waved as Dad slowed to a park in front of my house.

Dad killed the engine. The music stopped and silence reigned once again on my beautiful, bungalow and birdsong–filled street.

"Sorry I'm late." Dad did a little boogie by my manatee-shaped mailbox, then jogged up the walkway. He was wearing cutoff jeans, ratty sneakers, and a neon-green T-shirt that said "CLÜB LÏFE." I had no idea what that meant, or how to pronounce it, but I suspected it had something to do with his newfound love of electronic dance music. It was a hobby that I'd been trying to ignore because I hated the stuff.

To my knowledge, Dad hadn't been to any clubs lately. But one never knew with Dad.

I gave my father a quick kiss on his cheek. "Glad you made it. Nice goatee. Goes well with the ponytail."

"Silver fox." Erica pretended to shoot him with finger guns, and they both made little pew-pew noises back and forth. Both were ridiculous, and I adored them.

"Hey, did you remember to bring the tools?" Dad asked.

"Got 'em right here." Erica slapped her duffel bag, the spades and mini shovels clanking.

We were headed to look at the plot and discuss our plan for the coffee crop. I'd gotten the idea that perhaps we could grow local coffee and sell the beans to customers. Although Florida didn't have a mountainous climate like Jamaica or Guatemala, wild coffee plants did grow here. Those weren't edible, however, but other varieties were a possibility.

I'd recently read an article about University of Florida researchers saying that because of climate change and temperatures warming, the state could become the next big coffee-growing locale.

My family's café and Devil's Beach were in southwest Florida—and we were ready to test the researchers' theories with some coffee seedlings sprouting in a makeshift mini greenhouse in my backyard. It was the cutest little contraption, one that I'd bought online. It looked like a domed, plastic raincoat for a raised planter, and had zippered access so I could water and tend to the seedlings.

As we walked, Erica and Dad chatted about what they needed for the plot. I strolled a few paces ahead so I could check my texts. It was a

Sunday, and my boyfriend, Noah Garcia, had a long-standing brunch date with friends from college. It was my day off from the café, and the one day that both Noah's schedule and mine didn't mesh.

I hate not seeing you in the morning at Perkatory, he messaged. *Ruins my entire day.*

This made me smile. Something had blossomed, and it wasn't only the seedlings I was about to plant in the community garden. This week was a monumental milestone in my relationship with Noah.

I was meeting his mother in six days.

Ileana Garcia was scheduled to arrive on the island Saturday morning and would stay through Monday. Not only that, but I was cooking dinner for her, Noah, and Dad at my house. I had to contend with impressing Mrs. Garcia with my culinary skills, but also had to navigate conversation between my father, an avowed peacenik, and Mrs. Garcia, whose late husband was a Tampa police captain.

Noah was the chief of police here on Devil's Beach, and while he and Dad got along, Dad also was trying to talk Noah into retiring and embarking on a new career in hopes of getting him out of law enforcement. He not-so-privately thought Noah shouldn't "work for the man." I had mixed feelings about that, and generally felt that Noah should follow his heart.

Dad thought Noah would be happier in a lower stress job.

I secretly agreed with him on that point but hadn't told Noah this. His career was his business, and who was I to butt into something he'd done for decades? After all, Noah was nothing but encouraging to me when it came to Perkatory.

"Hey, guys?" I looked up from my phone and twirled around to face Erica and Dad. I bounced a little as I walked backwards for a few steps. "What do you think of lasagna for Saturday night?"

We all fell into step together on the sidewalk. Erica screwed up her face. "That's labor intensive. Do you want to be sweating in the kitchen all day? I'd help, but I agreed to work the booth at the Funnel Cake Festival."

"Good points," I grumbled, wondering whether Noah's mom was planning to visit the festival, which was famous statewide because, well, who didn't love fried dough covered in sugar?

"I love a good lasagna. And you've made showstopper lasagna before." Dad offered.

This was true. I had made an incredible, six-layer version last month, and both Noah and Dad had raved about it. "I still haven't figured out the menu, and I'm starting to worry. I want everything to be perfect. I'm thinking tiramisu soaked in Perkatory house blend espresso, so we could do the Italian theme for every course."

"You've got plenty of time. Six whole days," Dad pointed out.

"Why not get something catered from Joey's?" Erica asked. Her boyfriend Joey Rizzo owned the Square Grouper, a popular restaurant in town. "He's making a ton of stuff to sell at the festival. I'm sure we can set aside some trays for you. How about funnel cake topped with strawberries and whipped cream for dessert?"

"Lana hates strawberries." Dad shook his head in mock sadness, as if I'd disappointed him deeply.

"I need to wow Mrs. Garcia. Who, apparently, makes the best arroz con pollo this side of Havana." In truth, I was a little intimidated at the prospect of meeting her. A couple of weeks ago, Noah had visited her in Tampa and returned with a dozen homemade guava pastries. Called *pastelitos*, they were so flaky, buttery, and sweet that I was convinced my cooking skills were subpar in comparison.

"Maybe I need to do something more local? Fresh-caught, pan-seared grouper and key lime pie for dessert?"

"You're really stressing this. Look at you, little miss housewife. Next thing you know, Noah will have you barefoot and pregnant," Erica teased.

A snort erupted from my nose. "Hardly. One can be a feminist and love the domestic arts, missy. And Stanley's the only baby in this family."

"You'll figure it out, munchkin. Listen, I need to go over a few details about the garden plot before we arrive." Dad's voice took on a serious tone.

Laughter bubbled out of Erica's mouth. "You say this like we're being inducted into a secret society."

"Peas on Earth is no joke, kiddo. It's a serious, nonprofit business, and those of us lucky enough to get plots don't mess around."

That was the name of the community garden. *Peas on Earth.* Like many community touchstones around Devil's Beach, it was founded by a group of hippies who settled here back in the 1970s and '80s, back when it was a remote spit of land in the Gulf of Mexico. Dad and Mom had been among the hippies, and over the years had helped usher in a tourism renaissance on the island. Now the place was less hippie and more hipster, but the old-time families like ours still clung to our counterculture roots in our tropical paradise.

Mom, who passed going on four years ago, would be appalled at how upscale the place had gotten—but she would've adored selling coffee to the hordes of tourists coming into Perkatory, that's for sure.

"We wouldn't dream of making fun of such a weighty matter, Dad." I stifled a snicker. "For a bunch of nonconformists, this garden sure has a lot of rules. I was looking at the rulebook the other day. It's a fifty-page PDF."

"It didn't used to be like that. The garden used to be much more free-form. Casual. Your mother used to run a meditation session there during wildflower season. But none of that happens these days because Darla's really laid down the law. You definitely don't want to cross her."

Chapter Two

Darla Ippolito was a newer Devil's Beach resident, a few years older than me. According to what she'd said one day while getting coffee, she moved here about three years ago from somewhere up north, while I was working at the paper in Miami. When I was laid off and returned to run Perkatory, my family's coffee shop, I got to know Darla as one of the many regulars who adored our coffee, and we'd become friendly acquaintances.

She worked retail, like so many of us on the island. She was a manager at a popular saltwater taffy joint a few blocks from Perkatory. Ye Olde Taffy Towne was in a small pink building, and it was a must-see on the tourist circuit of the island, along with the sugar-sand beaches and the plethora of tiki bars. Everyone raved about the taffy, and Darla received plenty of satisfied reviews online for her attention to detail with the candy.

I couldn't stand the stuff, but she was always giving me free samples. Good thing Noah liked it, although sometimes he begged me to hand it off to someone else, because he couldn't stop stuffing his face.

Darla was also, apparently, the supreme ruler of Peas on Earth. As annoyed as I was about Stanley not being able to come with us, I understood. Working behind the counter at Perkatory had given me a new appreciation of rules. More than anyone, I knew that if you let the public do whatever they wanted, chances were they'd probably muck it up somehow. And I only witnessed the situations involving drink stirrers, sugar, and milk; I couldn't imagine how people would bend the rules with metal gardening tools.

Homicide would ensue, most likely.

"How did Darla lay down the law?" I asked Dad.

"Well, you know about the no-dog edict."

"Which I think is absolute rubbish," Erica interjected.

"So does Stanley, and so do I."

Dad ignored both of us. "We can only use organic fertilizing methods. No planting in buckets or pots. Oh, and if you create non-organic waste, pack it out. Darla's worried about the critters."

Erica arched an eyebrow. "Critters?"

"Raccoons, possums, squirrels." Dad shook his head. "Now there are the giant lizards to contend with too."

Erica visibly blanched and shuddered. "Please don't say that word. I cannot even."

The biggest news on the island recently was that a father of four had spotted a three-foot-long lizard scaling his window screen. The man had done what any self-respecting Floridian would do in that situation: filmed it for social media.

The video showed him banging on pots and pans. It scurried off, and wildlife officials feared it was a monitor lizard, a non-native species that could lay waste to the lush green foliage that blanketed the island.

The video went viral and the lizard was still on the run. Locals had dubbed it "Larry." The residents of Devil's Beach took their giant prehistoric critters in stride.

"Yeah, let's not scare Erica away. We need to keep her around." Although she seemed fearless, reptiles were my best friend's weak spot. Even the mere mention of a cold-blooded, scaly-skinned creature was enough to make her gag. I'd seen her knees buckle at a mere glance at a snake.

Dad nodded. "Okay, back to the dos and don'ts of the garden. Don't plant beyond your plot's boundaries. Use non-GMO seeds. And whatever you do, don't ever fail to put away the hoses when you water. That's a major infraction, not putting the hose away."

"How many major infractions before you get booted? I'm not great with rules," Erica said.

"Hoses, two strikes and you're gone. If you're caught smoking, you're booted immediately. So don't toke up." He stared at Erica. "Take an edible instead. And if you use nonorganic fertilizing methods, you will be publicly shamed on the garden message board and thrown out."

Yikes. I didn't smoke weed or take edibles, and I certainly didn't want to be publicly shamed. Maybe I was in over my head. "Harsh. I'm shocked you were able to pull strings to get us in here."

"Well, there were a few factors that contributed to you getting a plot. Mostly it's because I've been giving Darla some of my mint crop. She's fond of her mojitos." Dad looked at me over his glasses, as if I was supposed to infer something important in his statement. "She likes you a lot, too, Lana. That helped."

"My charming personality wins again," I quipped.

"Hey, I know a weird detail about Darla," Erica piped up.

"She likes saltwater taffy?" I countered.

"You're weird for not liking that," Dad said, and I made a face at him.

"Darla remembers things mne . . . mene . . . mnemonically. I can barely pronounce it."

"Huh?" I often marveled at what Erica knew about people. She often wrangled the strangest details out of our customers. I considered it a superpower.

"She uses acronyms to recall things. She said she taught herself how to do that while in jail."

"Oh, I know about this. I saw a documentary on it. A lot of doctors use it to remember details in medical school." Dad gestured with his hands excitedly. "SCUBA is one. Do you know what that means?"

"No," Erica and I said at the same time.

"Self-Contained Underwater Breathing Apparatus. Isn't that interesting?"

"Wait, why are we glossing over the fact that Darla was in jail? I didn't know that. What for?" I asked.

Erica shrugged. "Dunno. Didn't ask."

Only a non-journalist wouldn't think to ask the crucial details. "It is interesting that she uses acronyms to remember things. And it's fascinating that Darla's brain works like that. It's so foreign to me. I think in images." Whenever I'd written a news story for the paper, I'd have to visualize everything in my mind before, and during, the writing process. Like a movie. I recalled details better with visuals and couldn't imagine trying to come up with an acronym to help with my memory.

"Anyway, Dad, what are you planning on doing with all that mint, anyway?"

He'd been growing a giant crop of mint for a while now. It started a few months ago, and what I thought was a mere hobby had turned into something closer to an obsession.

Dad stopped walking, which meant Erica and I did as well. He made a sweeping arc gesture with his hand in the air. "Paradise Perk Pops."

Nodding, Erica repeated his words.

"And those are?" I asked.

"I haven't wanted to tell you until they're perfected, but it's time, because I'm close. I've been tinkering with a mint and coffee–flavored popsicle. Kind of like a mint mocha popsicle. Or, to put it in a different way, an iced mint mocha drink in popsicle form. Perfect for the long, hot Florida summers. I'm thinking of going statewide, then national. Maybe even global."

Sometimes Dad's tastes ran toward the unusual, and his dreams were just that—fantasies. This, however, was intriguing. It also sounded hella tasty. "You're planning on selling these at Perkatory?"

We all continued trooping down the street. Dad nodded. "First a small freezer for the café. Then I was thinking of a popsicle cart with an umbrella. Maybe a boom box, so I can play some tunes while selling Paradise Perk Pops by the beach. I'm working on a logo now. Thinking about a palm tree and a popsicle, but so far, the popsicle looks like a rocket ship, or something more salacious. It's all wrong."

Erica and I cracked up.

"Don't you think you might be biting off more than you can chew? Pun intended," I asked.

"What do you mean?" Dad replied.

"Well, with Perkatory, and your monkey activism. Don't forget your meditation, and yoga, and reiki." Dad was a social butterfly with his New Age groups, and heavily involved with trying to save a troupe of local wild monkeys from being relocated out of an island park. He'd even been arrested not long ago for a sit-in at the police station. Thank goodness the charges had been dropped by Noah and the county prosecutor.

The monkeys were still living on the island, but it wasn't clear for how long. The primate saga had dominated the headlines in the *Devil's Beach Beacon* in recent weeks.

"No, I've got help with the popsicles. An angel investor, if you will. Someone who knows both coffee and small business."

I frowned. "Who's that?"

"It's not important right now."

"Don't get caught up in a scam, okay?" I'd been a crime reporter for years and had covered all sorts of fraudulent schemes targeting the elderly. They were prevalent in Florida because of the state's large population of oldsters. That was one of the many reasons I'd moved back here, to help Dad as he aged. Not that he needed my help—in many ways, his social life was far more interesting and fuller than my own.

But Dad was such a mystery sometimes. He knew everyone on the island, and it wouldn't surprise me if someone did want to invest in his eccentric popsicle plan.

And setting aside the obvious question—why Dad wanted to make popsicles when he could be sliding into retirement and chilling on the beach—I didn't think it was such a bad idea. "Sounds like a great addition to the café. When can we taste test?"

"That's what I'm talking about." Erica nudged Dad with her shoulder. "I've always thought this place needed a good popsicle shop. I like that new ice cream truck, Give Me Chills, but sometimes you want a lighter frozen treat without dairy, y'know?"

We all nodded in agreement.

"I have a batch freezing at the house right now. I'm going to harvest more mint today and try a new, more caffeinated version." He slapped a crossbody tote slung around his chest. It appeared to be a repurposed burlap coffee bean sack held together with rainbow straps.

Dad and Erica lapsed into a discussion of whether freezing coffee lowers the caffeine content, while I pondered what this meant for the store. Mom had started the café about a dozen years ago, and when she passed, Dad kept it afloat, but barely. Although he'd been a successful realtor when I was growing up, as a small businessman he wasn't all that organized. He had great ideas but lacked the executive function to make a shop thrive. Mom had been the planner and the organizer.

When I moved home, he decided I should co-own the place, and since I'd been back, it had blossomed. I'd found new purpose and passion, and was slowly letting go of my old life as a journalist. It hadn't been easy, though, and I'd had so much change and chaos in the past couple of years that I yearned for tranquility in the coming months.

Dad was an integral employee, and not only because of his eternally sunny disposition. He worked a lot of late shifts. If he was out selling popsicles at the beach, I'd have to find a new employee to take his place. The last thing I wanted was for Dad to work himself to death. Hiring a new barista was a task, too, since I had a great crew of four and didn't want to upset the easy, friendly balance we all shared.

Still, none of this was imminent, and it sounded like a problem for future me. This week was far too jam-packed to take on any more duties.

Six days until the dinner.

We rounded the corner of Magnolia and Oak. This street was lined with old bungalows and squat, full palm trees. Many of the hedges were flowering hibiscus shrubs, and today they were a riot of red and pink flowers. It was one of the prettiest blocks on the entire island, and the homes here had weathered hurricanes and a depression, along with the changing tides of growth in a booming state like Florida. Even tourists loved to stroll down this street and gawk at the green foliage and Old Florida beauty, snapping photos along the way.

Today it was quiet, though, a welcome respite considering how many people I saw every day at Perkatory.

We were only a block from the community garden, which sat at the end of the cul-de-sac, and less than a quarter mile to the beach.

Up ahead, I spotted the charming, weather-beaten seafoam-green sign with the words PEAS ON EARTH in fat, white letters.

In addition to being an experiment that could help Perkatory, gardening was my latest effort at having a hobby. Pursuing things for pleasure was something I'd long neglected when I was a journalist. I'd been wanting to test a coffee crop, and this seemed like the time and place to do it. Sure, I could've planted in my backyard, but something about being part of a community garden spoke to me. I was trying hard to be more extroverted, and when Dad said a plot had come available, I jumped on it.

Come to think of it, Dad had never answered my question about the plot.

"Dad, you never told me whose plot I'm getting. Last I knew there was a yearlong wait, and then suddenly Darla approved me. What happened?"

Dad's expression pulled into a grimace. "It's a wild story."

Erica chuckled. Dad always had wild stories, and by the way he pulled on his silver goatee, I could tell he was about to launch into telling us every juicy detail.

"Do you remember Jack Daggitt?"

I shook my head. "Doesn't ring a bell."

"The town gadfly, always going to meetings and talking during public comment. Sometimes he quotes Robert Frost. Environmentalist. A little eccentric. He wears Birkenstocks, sometimes talks about his prostate."

"Uh, that literally could be any man over the age of fifty on Devil's Beach."

"He's an old-timer like me, really involved in environmental issues. When you were little, he was instrumental in beach cleanup efforts."

"Was he part of the Beach Brigade?"

"What's that?" Erica asked.

"Dad and a bunch of other parents thought the Girl and Boy Scouts were too pro-establishment, so they formed their own group for the kids. We cleaned up the beaches. It was essentially free labor, like prison inmates would do, but they gave us good snacks."

"Seems like a reasonable trade-off." Erica shrugged.

"We stopped when our group found a few bricks of marijuana washed ashore."

"Only in Florida," Erica said.

"No, Jack was part of the cleanup crew even before the brigade," Dad continued. "And he had a plot at the garden for many years, was one of the original founders."

"What happened to him? Did he pass away? Is that how Lana got his plot? She took a dead dude's garden spot?" Erica asked.

"No. Worse. He was kicked out."

"Yikes! Drama in the community garden," I joked, which made Erica dissolve into giggles. I loved hanging out with both her and Dad at the same time, because it was like a running comedy hour.

"You know it. Jack and Darla had a dust-up. The cops were called."

"Wait, what? I didn't hear about any of this." Then again, Noah didn't tell me about every incident on the island, and unlike when I was in Miami, I didn't have the need to cultivate sources inside the department. Still, gossip traveled far and wide on the island, and I was surprised this tidbit hadn't filtered to me.

By now we were at the garden, and Dad was fiddling with the electronic lock at the gate.

"Hang on, I can't talk and remember the code at the same time."

Erica and I exchanged glances with raised eyebrows. Dad was notoriously tech averse.

Finally, the lock beeped and disengaged, and we walked through the gate.

"Man, look at this, it's so cool," Erica said, stretching her arms wide. "I've walked by here a hundred times and didn't know how awesome it is. Check out those pineapples."

I went to stand next to Erica. It was a vast garden, obviously well tended. It seemed like every plot had either flowers or veggies bursting from branches. And there, on the far side of the garden, taking up what looked like two plots, were three neat rows of spiny pineapple plants.

"Whoa," I cried. "Love this."

I forgot all about Dad's tale of garden drama while Erica and I walked slowly through the rows, remarking on the plants. I envisioned us growing more than coffee here. Maybe herbs to use in unusual coffee drinks. Edible flowers for iced lattes. Herbs that I could dry in picturesque bouquets.

"Do you really think the coffee will thrive in here?" I still had my doubts.

Erica clicked her tongue against the roof of her mouth. "It won't be Jamaican Blue Mountain quality, but I believe it will grow. Everything I've read said coffee can be cultivated in Florida."

Offering a locally grown bean in a small batch for our customers would set us apart from Island Brewnette, the other coffee shop on the island. Plus, tending to a garden seemed like a solid adult hobby. I'd started to roller skate for exercise, and now could imagine adding another pastime to my repertoire.

"Where's your plot, Dad? And my plot?"

"Down here, they're close to each other," he called out, pointing at the back end of the garden, which was partially obscured by what looked like two mango trees. The entire place was a much larger space than I envisioned, probably a double lot that was worth a tidy sum in this hot real estate market.

"Those are Mrs. Ryan's mango trees; they were here before the garden. She cares for them, along with her pineapples."

I came up to Dad. "Why can't she have the pineapples in her own yard? That's an odd thing to grow in a community garden."

"She sells them at the market, and she has a vast garden at her home. She's really into orchids. Orchid people can be a little . . ." Dad made a so-so motion with his hand. "You know."

"No, I don't. Orchid people are what?" I asked.

"They're a little odd. C'mon. The plot's down here. See all my mint?" Dad pointed to a lush, green thicket.

"Whoa, that looks unruly." Unsurprisingly, Dad's plot was the most chaotic of all. It was a mass of mint that came up to my hip. It was pretty rich that Dad would call orchid people odd.

"It grows incredibly fast. In fact, Jack, the guy who had your plot, was pretty upset that my mint grew into his plot a couple of months ago. In my defense, it spread in a weekend. If left to its own devices, the mint would take over the entire island."

I laughed, imagining Devil's Beach covered in a carpet of aromatic, verdant leaves.

We stopped and I ran my hand through the waist-high mass of bright green, serrated leaves. A fragrant scent filled the air, and I took in a huge lungful. "Smells incredible, though."

"Only the best heirloom seeds. It's a true spearmint, sweet and pungent. Here." He snapped a sprig off one bushy plant and held it up for me and Erica. We plucked the leaves off and popped them in our mouths.

"Wow, that is minty," Erica said. "My breath is going to be fresh all day. This might take away the worst coffee breath."

"I can totally imagine this with mocha. You're onto something, Dad." More than anything, I was proud of the way Dad had, over and over again, managed to find new things to love about life since Mom died.

I made my way onto the main, gravel-lined walkway, with Erica in tow. "So, you say my plot's over here?"

"Yeah, I'm not sure Darla even cleared out Jack's tomato plants. We might have to do that. Jack ended his time here on such a bad note . . ."

Dad continued talking about Jack's crop, and I walked on. Sure enough, there were some tall vines snaking up wire trellises. The spicy, earthy scent of tomato plants hung in the humid, heavy air. Maybe I'd get some free tomatoes out of this situation. Was that unethical, to take the previous guy's fruit?

It was March, which meant the Florida growing season was in full swing. Unlike up north, it's impossible to cultivate anything in Florida in the summer. I still didn't fully know what this meant for my small coffee plants sprouting in the makeshift greenhouse back at my place. Would they grow as well as these tomatoes? I sure hoped so.

I was about to round the corner and walk along the last, long row of my plot when I stopped. There was something unusual lying on the ground.

Feet.

"Uh, guys." Black sandals and white socks came into view, with the toes pointing to the sky. I leaned forward, unsure if I should proceed further. "Hello? Are you okay?"

Erica slammed into my back, probably because she was looking at her phone. "Hello! What? I'm fine!"

"Not you. Him. There's something other than tomatoes here," I said in a shaky voice, pointing in front of me.

There, sticking out between two tall plants bursting with fruit, were the sun-beaten, motionless legs of an elderly man.

Chapter Three

Dad was still muttering about tomatoes when he approached me and Erica. We were rooted to the ground in horror. The man wore a wide, frozen expression, not one that was natural or indicative of the living. I knew that much from covering crime in Miami for years. And from seeing more than a few dead bodies in my time.

"Did I ever tell you that as a young man I went to Spain for a tomato throwing fes . . . yikes, what's Jack doing on the ground?"

"He's not doing much," I said, still staring at the body.

"He's on the ground because he's dead." Erica's tone was mechanical, like a robot.

"Hopefully not." I shot Erica a dirty look and pulled her away, out of sight of the body. "I'm calling Noah."

"I'll check for a pulse." Dad knelt and disappeared behind the tomato bushes.

My hands were shaking so much that I couldn't locate the cell in my duffel bag. Eventually Erica shoved hers toward me and I tapped out Noah's digits that I'd memorized. It rang. And rang. And rang some more.

"Come on." I looked around. The molecules in the air seemed to slow and shift. This had happened when I'd discovered another dead body on the island, but that time, I was well acquainted with the victim. It had been a Perkatory barista, deceased in the alley behind the café.

Back then, I thought I was so unsettled because I'd known Fabrizio and liked him. Turns out that seeing any dead body in a place where it shouldn't be—really, anywhere outside of a funeral home or the morgue—was enough to give me the shakes.

"He's not answering." I jabbed at the cell screen and a close-up photo of a tattoo in an unknown place on a body filled the screensaver. I suspected it was Erica's boyfriend Joey, and I didn't want to know more. "I need a minute."

I walked toward the gate, wanting to catch a lungful of fresh air, away from the now-oppressive scent of tomato plants and possibly dead body. Although this was the second deceased person I'd found on Devil's Beach, it was now the fourth untimely death I'd been involved with since I'd moved back home. Things were getting weird around here.

Or perhaps they'd always been weird, and I hadn't noticed because I'd been in Miami all those years.

I could hear Erica and Dad talking in loud voices, but the words didn't hit my brain with any meaning. A dizzy feeling overtook me, and I started to shuffle back toward them. There was a bench flanking the main path through the garden, and I slumped onto it. I blinked a few times, hoping to clear my head. The thought of a dead man among the tomatoes was almost too much to handle.

That's when I saw a glint in the dirt. It stuck out like foil, something shiny in a world of organic matter. Bending over, I studied the object. It appeared to be a piece of jewelry. I glanced up and was about to call Dad and Erica over, but they were arguing about whether to take Jack's pulse on his wrist or his neck.

I picked up a large wood chip and poked at the sparkly object. It was a gold earring, a teeny replica of a watering can. Could that be evidence? Or did someone unrelated to Jack lose a treasured piece of jewelry?

I still had Erica's phone in my hand, and I snapped a photo. Interestingly, it was a clip-on earring, not the kind for pierced ears.

She walked over to me. "Your dad's strange."

"I know. Hey, watch out for that thing in the dirt. It might be a clue. I used your cell to take a photo." I pointed toward the jewelry, and where I'd planted the wood chip sticking straight up to mark the area. "It's an earring."

Erica sank next to me on the bench and grabbed the phone from me, ignoring everything I said. "I'll call 911. Probably better to do that anyway, because Noah's going to lose it when he finds you're involved with another dead body."

"Yeah, yeah, you're right." I stood and paced a few steps while carefully avoiding the earring. Needed to check on Dad, make sure he was okay. He wasn't used to dead people at all.

I found him pressing his fingers to Jack's Adam's apple.

"Dad, I don't think that's where the pulse is."

He looked up, still crouched. "Really? Then where? He seems awfully cold. I was also checking his chakras."

Dad and his New Age woo. I flapped my hands in the air in a nope motion, fanning my face, and walked back to Erica.

"Bernadette?" Erica yelled. "Can you hear me? You're on speakerphone."

"Get stuffed," came a shrill voice.

"Sorry, sorry. I have the bird with me today. It's take your pet to work day. How can I help you?" Bernadette, who had the voice of a pack-a-day smoker, owned a well-known, foul-mouthed parrot named Max. The last time I'd seen the bird was at Perkatory when he cussed out the mayor.

Erica and I swapped glances. This was turning into a farce. While Bernadette sputtered, I eyed Erica's earlobes, something I'd never paid attention to until today. She had pierced ears, with tiny safety pins in the lobes. It was absurd to think she'd wear a twee watering can as jewelry.

"Bern, this is Lana. From Perkatory," I hollered.

"What? I can't hear you."

I took the phone from Erica and brought it closer to my face, repeating myself while yelling.

"Oh hi, Lana, I haven't seen Noah in a while. It's his day off. It's Sunday."

"I know."

"He's having brunch, like he always does. He's supposed to be on his way back, he called to check in a while ago. He also had that church function."

Right. Church. I'd temporarily forgotten that detail. "That's okay, Bern, I don't need him. Well, I do. We need someone here. I'm not calling for him exactly, I'm calling because I found a body."

"A body? A human body?" The way Bernadette said the words, it was as if she was personally offended. "Are you sure it's not one of those blow-up things for Halloween?"

"It's March. Yeah, a man. A dead human man." Erica shouted, rolling her eyes. "We're at Peas on Earth, the community garden. Apparently, it's a guy named Jack."

"Jack Daggitt? Why would he be there? Darla had a restraining order against him. He wasn't supposed to be there at all."

I contorted my face into a grimace and Erica tugged me in the direction of the body, pointing at Dad. He was holding his hand over Jack's forehead, like he was taking his temperature. Oh dear.

"I dunno, Bern, but Jack's here and he's obviously dead. This is an emergency. Can you send someone?"

"Of course I will. Right away. And I'll get Noah on the radio and tell him you're there."

I glanced at Dad, who had a solemn look on his face and appeared to be shutting Jack's eyes gently, like he was in a war movie or something. He mouthed what appeared to be a little chant and pressed his thumb on Jack's wrinkled forehead.

"And, Lana, listen, don't touch the guy, okay?"

Too late for that, Bern.

* * *

It took officers and paramedics mere minutes to arrive, probably because Devil's Beach is relatively small and nothing much happens on a Sunday morning.

Noah wasn't far behind the emergency workers. He came careening up in his unmarked Crown Victoria, siren wailing, lights flashing. Unlike most days, he wasn't wearing his uniform—today he was looking handsome in a sharp, cobalt blue suit and expensive-looking brown leather shoes. That's when it all came back to me: he hadn't only eaten brunch. He'd also been scheduled to give a talk about public safety at a local church after this morning's service.

I watched him stalk through the gate and into the garden, pause to talk with an officer, and head straight for me with a stern look. When he was in police mode, he looked so official, so serious. When he was off duty, he was silly, geeky, and gentle.

I adored everything about the man.

"I feel like we're in deep doo-doo, from the look on your boyfriend's face," Erica whispered, which would've made me giggle if the situation wasn't so dire. She had broken open a granola bar.

Noah stopped in front of me. "You found a body? Another body?"

"Hello to you, too." I folded my arms over my chest despite my stickiness. Thank goodness I'd worn a floppy straw hat today because it sure seemed unusually bright outside.

"Where is the deceased?" Noah was speaking in police talk.

I gestured with my head, and the leopard-print scarf tied around the hat fluttered in the air. Nearby, Dad was chatting with two paramedics. He and Noah waved, then Noah walked to the body, peeled back the white sheet covering the face, and carefully arranged it back to where it had been.

Noah scratched the back of his head. "Lana, were you the first one to see Mr. Daggitt lying here?"

"Yes. Dad was at his mint patch." I waved in that direction, "And I was walking, with Erica behind me, to my plot. Which used to be Jack's plot. That's when I saw his legs." I gave a few more details, including the time we arrived at the garden.

I pointed to the earring still on the ground. "That might also be something."

"Good eye, cupcake," he said, softening his tone and scooping it up into a small plastic evidence bag.

Noah looked around, hands on hips. "So you were coming here to prepare the plot for the coffee plants." He said this in a low voice, as if he was reminding himself.

"What was Jack doing here if he had a restraining order?" I asked.

Noah turned to me. "Who told you about that?"

"Bernadette." Erica, who was standing at my side, bit off a piece of a granola bar and nodded at her own statement.

"Well, considering Jack's age, this is likely a situation of natural causes. But Vern's on his way, so we'll wait for the official report."

Vern was the county's medical examiner and one of Noah's friends from college. In fact, he was one of the regulars at Noah's Sunday brunch on the mainland. Although we'd socialized with

Vern and his wife as a couple, I also knew him from the three previous, and quite recent, homicides on the island.

"In the meantime, let's get your father over here. I want to find out what you all know about Jack."

"Why? Thought you said it was probably a natural death." Erica slid her sunglasses down and eyed Noah with suspicion.

"You know me. Due diligence is my middle name." He called out to Dad, who was still talking to the paramedics.

"I thought it was Arturo," I quipped, hoping to lighten the mood.

"Is it really Arturo?" Erica whispered. "That's so cute."

I nodded, and Noah shook his head. "You two."

Dad loped over and clasped Noah's hand in his. "Sir. Good afternoon. Sorry we have to see each other under these circumstances."

Why Dad felt the need to be formal with Noah in public like this, I had no idea. It must be out of respect for Jack.

"Indeed," Noah sighed. "Listen, what can you all tell me about Mr. Daggitt?"

Erica and I shrugged. "Nothing. I didn't know him. Did you know him?" I looked at Erica, and she shook her head.

"You did too. He came into Perkatory sometimes," Dad said. "Well, maybe only when I was working. Yeah, come to think of it, Jack liked to drink his coffee in the afternoons. It sure fired him up, though. He loved to talk politics with anyone who would listen."

"Okay, so that's one thing. What else?" Noah turned his full attention to Dad.

"He was the kind of guy who thinks the sun comes up just to hear him crow."

Noah, Erica, and I stared at Dad with slight frowns, letting his assessment of Jack soak in. Noah blew out a breath, his cheeks puffing. "Well, then."

"Jack left the garden under some rather unfortunate circumstances." Dad's tone dipped to a low octave, and he emphasized the word *unfortunate.*

"Tell me about those."

I suspected Noah already knew everything—how could he not, if Darla had gotten a restraining order?—but Dad's eyes glittered at the prospect of sharing some juicy gossip.

"It all started when Jack used a new fertilizer on his tomatoes. He insisted it was organic, but Darla claimed it was a banned substance. It really blew up between the two of them. Then Darla accused Jack of stealing two pineapples, which is a huge no-no here. You don't touch anyone else's crop unless you get written permission."

"Wait, written permission? Like a note?" I interrupted.

"We have a Google doc for that, it's a release form." Dad tossed this out there like it was the most normal thing in the world, but I was still stuck on the fact that Dad seemed to know what a Google doc was. Until recently, Dad texted random sloth emojis to me. And by *recently*, I mean *yesterday*.

"Go on," Noah said.

"Well, Jack changed his story and insisted he didn't steal the fruit. And he kept using his fertilizer. Then Darla claimed that Jack was really using the most toxic kind, can't recall the name now. But that particular brand is a massive breach of trust."

"Something doesn't add up. How would they know what substance Jack was using for his plants? Did he bring the toxic fertilizer here?" This story was already annoying me because it embodied the worst of small-town gossip.

"That's the thing. Jack brought the stuff in an unmarked container. That was their first indication. Then they swiped some and snuck a sample to a lab."

Erica and I stepped back in tandem and turned around while Dad and Noah continued to chat.

"These gardening people are intense. Imagine swiping some guy's fertilizer and getting it tested at a private lab. So wacky," I whispered.

The corner of Erica's mouth quirked up. "Any wackier than the rest of Devil's Beach?"

My gaze went to the emergency worker Dad had been chatting up. He was sporting mirrored shades, a handlebar moustache, and, I believe, lip gloss. It was as if he was channeling a 1980s *Miami Vice*-Boy George vibe in a paramedic jumpsuit. He also had a glorious blonde mullet that practically glinted in the sun.

"Probably not," I sighed.

Chapter Four

Once Noah cleared us to leave the crime scene, Dad, Erica, and I booked it back to my house to grab Stanley, who was overcome with doggy joy when he saw us.

Then we collectively decided that we needed a jolt of caffeine after the shock of the day, so we strolled over to Perkatory with the dog, trying to talk about anything but the fact that we'd just found a dead body.

Normally Stanley wasn't allowed in the café—stupid local health department rules—but since we'd recently put a few tables on the sidewalk, I figured we could have a leisurely drink and snack there. The dog would happily snooze in the shade. Plus, I could get some paperwork finished.

As we approached, my phone buzzed. I handed the dog's leash to Erica and answered. It was Mike Heller, the editor-publisher of the *Devil's Beach Beacon*, the local newspaper. He didn't even say hello.

"I have a favor to ask you."

"Mike, how's it going? Please tell me you're not calling to ask me to speak to the middle school kids again." The last time we'd done this, right after I was laid off in Miami, I'd depressed the entire class by telling them horror stories of my dismal salary, pay cuts, and layoffs in the exciting world of newspapers. The kids had hoped to hear stories of celebrities.

Mike laughed. "No, no, nothing like that. I heard you made an interesting discovery today."

"Ahh, the Devil's Beach grapevine. Gotta love it."

"Want to do an interview about what you found?"

I let out a little strangled groan. Of course I wanted to help Mike, since the *Beacon* had been my first internship, and Mike my first editor. In many ways, he was the one who started me on my career path as a journalist. Well, Mike and my parents, who had helped me get the internship one summer in high school. They'd hoped that the part-time job would help lift my spirits after my best friend Gisela disappeared shortly before the end of our freshman year.

Instead, the newspaper internship strengthened my resolve to poke around, be nosy, and write crime stories.

Gisela was never found—her case is still considered a disappearance here on Devil's Beach, the only one in the town's history—and I was still intrigued as ever by secrets and mysteries. Still, that didn't mean I wanted to be on the other side of the notebook. Not today.

"An interview? Ugh, Mike. I'm not sure. Jack had a heart attack or something in the garden. I think it feels a little intrusive. It's not newsworthy, is it?"

"Lana, between me and you, it's a slow news day. We don't have a lot going in the paper tomorrow, and our website's main story is about next weekend's Funnel Cake Festival. A well-known local guy turning up dead in public is big news, however he died."

"Okay. Well. Still." I hedged, not wanting to be quoted in the paper about something so unseemly. I had to be mindful of that as a small-town business owner. This was a thing I hadn't known as a reporter. Back then I'd been relentless about seeking quotes from anyone—especially those who found dead bodies.

Now I had mixed feelings about the entire process of crime journalism.

Yet I empathized with the dreaded slow news day. "Can we at least wait until Noah releases some information about the death, so I don't come off as disrespectful? Doesn't Jack have a next of kin? Shouldn't we wait for them to be notified?"

"Sure, that's fine. I'll touch base in a couple of hours. We've got time before we go to press."

"Good deal. We're all headed to Perkatory if you want to join us." Mike and I hung up, and up ahead, I saw Dad, Erica, and Stanley near the door of the café.

I took Stanley back from Erica, and she went inside to grab some drinks. I poked my head in to make sure everything was cool.

My gaze swept around my family's shop, which occupied the better part of the bottom floor of a four-story brick building in downtown Devil's Beach. Inside, exposed brick on one wall and windows on two sides gave it an open, yet cozy, feel. The place was decorated in what I liked to call "beach shabby chic," with distressed, white wood furniture, mismatched chairs, a shelf with Florida coffee table books, and robin's-egg blue accents that included overstuffed pillows, and, most recently, a glorious secondhand wicker chair that I'd placed in a reading nook in the back corner.

Today, an elderly woman was in the chair, blissfully sipping and reading. I wished I was living her life right now.

Everything looked tranquil, with about half the seats filled—normal for this late in the day. The strains of Robby Dupree's 1980 hit "Steal Away" lilted through the air, which instantly made my muscles relax a little. Yacht rock had a way of doing that to me, and to the customers—several online reviews said they adored the 1970s and '80s vintage tunes. It seemed that people on vacation liked the oldies but goodies.

"All copacetic inside," I declared to no one in particular as I shut the door.

Dad took over an outdoor table and unloaded the contents of his backpack. A notebook, an iPad, and a phone, along with a pack of rolling papers and an assortment of pens littered the table by the time Erica came out with our drinks.

I picked up a bottle opener sporting the words "FLORIDA MAN," with an illustration of a shirtless guy holding a machete, then set it atop the rolling papers.

"Classy. What's all this?" I slid a container of breath mints out of the way to make room for our coffee.

"Command center," Dad replied in a brisk tone, clicking a pen like he was ready to kick off an important business meeting.

Erica plopped in a chair and took a slurp of her iced coffee. "What are we commanding?"

I sat opposite her and poured some water into a collapsible bowl for Stanley. He lapped it up noisily while I grimaced in anticipation of Dad's answer.

"Jack's death," he said.

I allowed my head to roll back. "Dad, come on. Why? Jack was how old? Eighty? I'm sure he died of natural causes, like Noah said."

Dad pointed his pen at me. "But why was he at the garden when he wasn't supposed to be there at all? He was banned. Darla had a restraining order against him."

"Maybe he was there picking his tomatoes? He seemed to have a lot of fruit on the vine and I'm sure it was upsetting that he couldn't harvest. There were a few tomatoes on the ground, near his hand."

His cold, lifeless hand. I shuddered, thinking of the body. "Anyway, it's terrible what happened. I didn't even know the guy and I feel bad for him."

"On the other hand"—Erica wiped her mouth with the back of her hand—"he died in a place he loved."

Dad nodded in agreement, and I checked on Stanley. Sure enough, he was sacked out on his side, the light breeze ruffling his golden fur. His coat was getting long, and I wondered if I'd have to take him to the groomer soon. Maybe before next weekend's dinner, even.

I was about to ask Erica her opinion on the matter when Barbara, one of our baristas, burst out the door wearing her branded, ocean blue Perkatory apron. Her long, silver hair was tied back into a ponytail. She was around Dad's age, and had been my mother's best friend for years.

Barbara's presence in my life had been a constant since I was little, and now that we worked together, I appreciated her gentle demeanor and her laid-back attitude. She also loved to gossip, and knew she'd be eager to join the conversation about Jack. Thank goodness our other barista, Heidi, was at the counter serving the last few customers of the day.

"I can't believe you all found Jack Daggitt dead!" Barbara was positively breathless. "Bernadette from the police station called to tell me."

"Of course she did."

"Did you know Jack?" Erica asked.

Barbara shrugged. "A little. He used to come into the café and order black coffee. Kind of gruff, frosty guy. Got real wound up after his coffee and liked to talk about state government. I ignored him. He gave good tips, though. What do you think happened?"

"We're trying to figure that out now. Have a seat and we'll go over some theories," Dad said, clicking the pen a few times.

"We have no theories," I offered.

"Speak for yourself," he said.

Barbara nestled into the one vacant chair, holding a cup of iced coffee in one hand and a stack of tasting cups in the other. Even though she was technically on duty, dinner hour was slow at Perkatory on a Sunday, and the café would be closing soon.

I leaned toward her and Erica, hoping to change the subject from a man's untimely death and pointing to the iced coffee. It was impossible not to stare at Barbara's earlobes. She sported a pair of small, pierced gold starfish. I had to forget about that found earring clue because it probably held no significance.

"These ice cubes were an excellent idea, you two," I said.

Barbara and Erica had been working together one day last week and decided to freeze espresso in small, ball shapes. They'd started putting them in certain iced drinks, and the result was outstanding—because it was so warm in Florida, the ice in the cold coffee almost always melted and diluted the drinks.

Nobody liked that watery mess left at the bottom of an iced coffee. That problem was solved with the frozen coffee balls.

"I've been playing with a new drink with the round ice. Here. Try this." She poured the iced drink into the smaller cups, carefully avoiding all of Dad's junk. If his stuff annoyed her, she didn't show it, instead shooting him a little grin.

She and Dad had known each other for years, practically since I was a baby. Mom had talked Barbara into working at Perkatory from the beginning, saying she needed a place to showcase her art—Barbara made cute collages and cozy signs from reclaimed and recycled beach garbage.

She didn't call it "garbage," of course, but rather detritus, or found objects, or "beach remnants." I knew better, even if I did love the end result. We had several pieces on display and for sale in Perkatory, with slogans in cursive that said witty things like "Beach, please!" and "Aquaholic."

"Try it." Barbara slid the cup toward me and one to Erica.

We sipped and swallowed. It was a creamy, sweet concoction with a hint of hazelnut on the aftertaste.

"Wow. That is . . . yikes. I think I got a cavity from all the sugar. What is that?" Erica scowled into the little plastic cup. She liked her coffee bitter.

"Nutella," Barbara declared. "I think customers will love it. Nutella iced latte."

I gulped the rest of the drink. "I think you're probably right, that people will like it. It's not our preferred flavor, Erica, but the biggest feedback we get on our social media accounts is that our coffees are a touch too bitter."

"Wusses." Erica snorted aloud.

"Remember, what we like isn't necessarily what the public enjoys." Erica and I frequently had this discussion, and I had to remind her—and myself—of this often.

"Imagine if everyone had Erica's taste?" Barbara teased.

"We'd be living in a tropical goth paradise," Erica quipped, and I snickered. "Tropi-goth. I should trademark that."

"Okay, so listen up, kids." Dad was staring at his phone. "At nine this morning, Jack put up a long rant on his Facebook page about the community garden. Well, and about the problems he had with a guy who was building a new porch. Jack liked to complain. This is juicy. I'm going to read it to you."

We all scooted our chairs in closer to listen.

"'Some of you may be wondering why I'm no longer at the community garden. As a founding member of Peas on Earth, it pains me to say that I've been banned from my own plot, all for questioning the current management's decision to stop me from using a certain brand of heirloom tomato seeds . . .'"

"The horror," whispered Erica, and I giggled then shushed her.

Dad continued. "Jack goes on to talk about the seeds for several paragraphs, something about open pollination and bees, and how cultivars must be fifty years old to be deserving of the term . . ." He droned on for a couple of minutes about seeds and I saw Erica's eyes fluttering shut.

"Okay, get to the good stuff, Dad."

"Right, okay. Here we go. He wrote, 'I realize that I've also had a complaint against me from a neighbor who said I played Bob Dylan albums on the boom box too loud on Saturdays. She said it interfered with her son's naptime and snacks. Well, I'm sorry that her precious prince had to hear the master himself while slumbering and stuffing food into his piehole.' He then goes on for several paragraphs about how Dylan is as culturally important as Shakespeare. Odd, Jack didn't get any likes or comments on this post."

Dad looked up, and Erica and I couldn't contain our giggles any longer. We doubled over with laughter.

"Is that an SNL skit?" Erica asked. "Boom box! Album! Piehole!"

"Not Bob Dylan," I cried.

I wiped tears from my eyes. "I'm sorry, but that's the most Devil's Beach thing I've ever heard. The old hippie guy was playing 'Blowing in the Wind' and a woman complained about it being too loud."

Even Dad cracked a smile. "It's true that some of the newer residents resent us old-timers. Even your generation doesn't seem cool with us being free spirits."

"Yeah, you'd better watch out, Dad. Someone might complain about you protesting on behalf of monkeys or listening to your techno music too loud."

He sheepishly glanced at Barbara and pointed. "She likes my music."

Barbara bugged her eyes at me. AWFUL, she mouthed at me, and I nodded.

"Let's see what else Jack posted on Facebook recently." Dad turned back to his phone. "Here's a rant about Darla. He claimed that she was interfering with his constitutional right to free speech."

I screwed up my face. "Hunh?"

"Jack said, and I quote, 'planting my preferred brand of tomato seeds, and using the fertilizer I choose, is covered under the First Amendment, and not allowing me freedom of choice is a violation of my constitutional rights.'"

Erica and I smirked at each other. "That's a little much. Seriously, what does any of this mean? Why pry into this poor dude's life? Let the man rest in peace. Good Lord, he just wanted to pick his tomatoes."

I took a long drink of my iced coffee, which thankfully wasn't as sweet as the Nutella brew. "You know, Barbara, Erica, let's start making the Nutella coffee tomorrow. We'll put it up on the sign board outside and on the chalkboard inside. Maybe the Nutella coffee with the coffee ice balls. A winning combo."

We were chatting about the right coffee-to-Nutella ratio when I spotted a tall, dark-haired man rounding the corner. My goodness, he was gorgeous. I sat up a little straighter, and then I realized: that's my boyfriend.

Noah was walking toward us, seemingly untouched by sweat and still in his suit. His expression was no less grim than when he was in the garden a couple of hours ago.

"Hey, sweetie," I chirped. "Come sit with us."

He grabbed a chair from an empty table nearby and plunked it next to mine. Stanley, realizing his favorite human was near, woke from his slumber and barked once, then stood on his back paws while clawing at Noah's knee.

"Down." I pointed to the ground.

"It's okay. C'mere, buddy." Noah scooped my dog up in his arms and kissed the top of his tawny head. A swoony, melty feeling took over my body at the sight.

"How's it going? Everything finished over at the garden?" I asked.

Noah sighed. "No. The crime scene techs just arrived."

Dad's head snapped up from his phone, and Erica stopped sipping her coffee. Even Barbara leaned in.

"Crime scene techs?" I asked.

"Vern came and found some things. He doesn't think it was a natural death. We're launching a full investigation."

"Oh, really?" Dad said, in an I-told-you-so tone. "What kind of things?"

Dad made air quotes with his fingers around the word "things." This would certainly set Dad off into an interrogation spiral.

"Do you want something to drink?" I asked Noah in a low tone. "You look parched."

"That would be amazing. Thanks." Finally, he shot me a smile.

I went into Perkatory and grabbed a bottle of water and some decaffeinated peach tea. Noah wasn't a fan of caffeine of any sort, and rarely drank coffee. At first this had made me doubt whether our relationship would last, but he'd lately gotten into various iced tea flavors, thanks to me. If his only fault was that he didn't like coffee, it was one I could live with.

When I went back outside, Dad and Barbara were gaping at Noah. Even Erica looked shocked.

"What did I miss?" I set the beverages on the table.

Noah cracked open the bottle and took a long drink. I looked to Dad, then to Erica, and finally to Barbara. All of them blinked at me, as if I'd recently arrived unexpectedly from a long trip.

"What's going on?"

Noah recapped the water. "Got a call from Vern. Preliminary results show that Jack had a fatal dose of drugs in his system. Vern found a needle mark in Jack's skin, and our techs discovered a syringe underneath his body."

My jaw went slack. Now it was my turn to be shocked. "You are kidding me. He ODed right there in the garden?"

"You know I don't kid about murder, cupcake." Noah took gulp of the tea.

"Why didn't we see the syringe?" I asked. "Hang on. Murder? He didn't OD?"

"Highly unlikely. It was on his shoulder blade, back here. Not a place where one normally shoots up." Noah leaned in and touched the spot in between my shoulder and my spine, massaging briefly. "And it was a small syringe, lying underneath him, with a puncture wound. Looks like the needle pierced his clothes."

"Someone intentionally plunged a fatal dose of something into Jack's back while they were in the garden, then left him there to die!" Dad's voice was loud, and two tourists in bikinis and sarongs walking into Perkatory looked over, alarmed.

"Dad," I hissed. "Talking about murder is bad for business. Shush."

"Oh, right." Dad nodded. "So, what are we going to do about this?"

Noah's eyebrows lifted almost to his hairline. "*We* are not doing anything about it. My department is investigating. We, especially Lana, are staying away from this case. We don't know who injected Jack with the substance."

"What kind of substance? A drug?" I asked.

"There was still some liquid in the syringe. Vern's testing the liquid now, but he believes it to be fentanyl. Vern handles a lot of ODs, so he knows his fentanyl."

Weird. I also knew a lot about fentanyl—a synthetic opioid that was a hundred times stronger than morphine—because I'd written several news articles about the rising popularity of the drug on the streets. It had killed thousands in Florida over the years, overtaking heroin as the fix of choice.

"How do we know Jack didn't inject himself?"

Dad looked at me over the top of his clip-on sunglasses. "Who would inject themselves in the shoulder blade? This has to be murder."

"Maybe so," I muttered.

Noah held a hand in the air, in a stop motion. "Let's not get too caught up in the details, gang. This is a criminal investigation, not a crowdfunding sleuth session."

I pressed my hand to my breastbone, slightly peeved. "I had no intention of getting involved. Why would you think otherwise? What would lead you to believe—"

"Because you've gotten involved in the last three murders on the island."

Erica snorted. "I think she was justified in sleuthing every one of those deaths. And without her you wouldn't have solved anything, my dude."

"No. This isn't a free for all. Lana is not a private investigator. The rest of you are not detectives." Noah shook his head and stared at the ice in his tea, probably wondering how he got tangled up with the likes of us.

"She could be, though. Munchkin, you should really think about getting your PI license. How much does it cost?" Dad said. "I'll pay for it. Hey, that's an idea. Noah, you could retire from the force and you and Lana could open a PI business together. And you could still be a charter boat captain on the side."

At that, Noah almost choked on his tea. I handed him a napkin.

"Dad, that's the last thing I need. I'm all set with my first two careers and am not planning a third. Seriously, Noah, I'm not interested in this murder. Or any murder. Trying to put murder in the rearview mirror, in fact."

It wasn't entirely a lie, but it wasn't fully the truth, either. Being a former crime reporter, my curiosity was always piqued whenever I heard about an unsolved homicide. Noah probably suspected this because he stared at me with a lopsided smile.

"Honest," I said. "I don't have time. Not this week. I need to figure out the menu for next Saturday, deal with some things at Perkatory, and get Stanley groomed. He smells like a clam. So there."

The last thing I wanted was a smelly shih tzu mauling Noah's mom.

The tourists with the bikinis came out of the café, holding giant cups of iced coffee and chattering loudly.

"Can you believe someone was found dead today in a garden on this island? What kind of place is this?" one said.

"I think I heard about this island on a true crime podcast, one that's based here," exclaimed the other. "It's kind of famous for weird things."

"Oh. Em. Gee. Can you send me the link to the podcast?"

Erica snickered as the women walked by, talking loudly about crime on the island, and how it seemed like such a calm, gentle place to live. "I wonder if Perry and Jeri will do a show on Jack."

They were a couple who lived across the street from me and happened to run a popular true crime podcast. Erica and I had been bit players on one episode, when a man on the block was killed by an exploding leaf blower not too long ago.

"There's no telling what they'll do," I said.

Our group lapsed into silence, with Dad checking his phone, Erica watching people, and Noah and I stealing glances at each other. Barbara stood and said she was going inside to close, then stopped when she was about to pull open the door.

"Oh, Lana, you got a FedEx package. Let me grab it."

Dad announced he would help and loped inside.

Erica, too, climbed to her feet. "I'm headed to the Square Grouper. Want to come?"

That was her boyfriend's restaurant. I shook my head. "It's been a long day. I think I'll head home and eat leftovers."

"'Kay. See you tomorrow, early." She scratched Stanley behind his ear and sauntered off.

I was finally alone with Noah and wasn't going to miss this opportunity to privately ask him about Jack. I didn't want him to think I was too interested in the case, though.

"You know," I said in my most casual tone, "it's quite interesting how quickly Vern determined how Jack died."

"A needle puncture in the shoulder is something that stands out to a medical examiner."

"But fentanyl. Wow. That's kind of odd, isn't it? Has Vern done all the tests yet? I mean, maybe it wasn't fentanyl and Jack was taking something herbal and strange. Wouldn't be the first time supplements killed someone. Or was Jack secretly being treated for, I dunno, cancer? That would explain the fentanyl. Cancer patients use it, you know." I inspected my nails, trying to appear like I didn't care much about the answer.

"No, Vern's not finished with the tests and probably won't be until tomorrow. And Jack wasn't taking any supplements or prescription medication. Apparently, he was quite healthy, according to his primary care physician, who gave us Jack's medical records this afternoon. There were traces of fentanyl still in the syringe."

"Oh, goodness. That does seem to point to homicide, doesn't it?"

"Lana."

"What?" I fluttered my eyelashes.

"I know what you're doing." Noah pinched the bridge of his nose.

"What am I doing?"

"Trying to ferret out information about this case."

"Do I look like a ferret to you?"

Finally, Noah cracked a grin. "No. You look like my beautiful girlfriend."

And that was all I needed to drop my questions about Jack's untimely death. I was no longer a reporter, and news didn't concern me. I even texted Mike at the paper and said I wouldn't be talking about today's discovery. This was what passed for progress as a recovering news junkie.

Noah and I were discussing what to do about dinner when Barbara came out, holding the FedEx package.

"I didn't want you to forget this," she said.

I thanked her, and she returned inside. While Noah checked his email on his phone, I opened the box.

"What's this?" I muttered as I slid an expensive-looking binder out of the package. "A coffee printer? Whoa."

Noah looked up and leaned over to study the brochure with me. It was from a company called L'ARTE—all caps—which I guessed was a mashup of "latte" and "art."

"A printer for coffee drinks? I don't get it," Noah said.

Of course he wouldn't, because not only did he not drink coffee, but he wasn't up on coffee trends.

"This is a machine that prints foam art, or logos, or photos, onto a latte. See?" I flipped through the binder and showed him a few pictures. One had a gorgeous latte with a coffee shop's logo. Another showed a detailed salamander. A third was a photo of a dog. All in white and brown foam art atop a drink.

A note inside an envelope said someone from the company would swing by in two days. I read this aloud to Noah.

"Maybe this would be fun for the café. It looks like the drinks are quite Instagrammable."

I'd come to realize that cuter and more photogenic drinks were free marketing for Perkatory. Everyone felt the need to share their beautiful coffee drink on social media, and each of the baristas at the café had mastered the skills of one basic, pretty latte. My specialty was a heart, Barbara and Dad's, a rosette, and Heidi's a tulip. Erica could do them all, and several other complicated designs, because she was a true latte artist.

"The things people think of these days. When I used to drink coffee, it was about how strong I could brew it, and how fast I could suck it down so I could forget about the bitter taste." Noah sounded amused. "People will actually pay extra for latte art?"

I shut the book and smiled at him. "Don't you think I'd spend an extra three bucks to see Stanley's face on a latte? Or yours?"

"Why would you spend extra when we're both right here?"

The furrow in his brow was so adorable that I leaned over and kissed him right there.

Chapter Five

I pushed Jack's unusual and public death into the recesses of my mind all the next morning. Thoughts of anything other than the immediate needs of the café were impossible. Erica and I were slammed with customers, a never-ending flow of spring breakers, surfers, and our regulars who worked downtown.

The regulars were beautiful, kind, all that is good in the world. Most were fellow retail jockeys, sleep deprived and overworked, needing their morning caffeine to make it through the daily grind. March was a bear of a month in the tourist towns of Florida.

The surfers were also pretty cool, eager for a jolt prior to their adrenaline rush. The waves near the island were small compared to those of California or Hawaii, but people still had a blast paddling around.

The spring breakers, on the other hand . . .

"When did the youths get so annoying?" Erica whispered to me, and I shook my head. Every other customer under the age of twenty, it seemed, had some detailed, picky request or comment.

"Can you comp this drink? I'm a TikTok influencer," one asked us in a whiny voice.

Erica rapped her knuckles on the counter. "You know what season it is?"

The wannabe influencer, a guy with poufy hair and a smile so white that it would blind the sun, shook his head.

"It's the season of NO." Erica glared at him, and he slunk off.

Ten minutes later, a girl, who probably wasn't over eighteen, asked if we had any whiskey to put in the coffee.

"We're not a bar," I said in a sour tone. "We're a coffee shop. The tiki hut on the beach will probably pour you a shot. Or next time, bring your own booze."

Then the kicker, shortly before ten. A woman in a neon yellow bikini—nothing else, just a bikini, and the kind that looks like butt floss—came in smelling like an overripe coconut. She ordered a double chocolate muffin, no drink. It was the last muffin in the case near the register, and I'd secretly hoped to eat it myself, since the chocolatey, cake-like goodness was too tempting to resist. Still, they were there for the customers, not me.

I helpfully pointed out, as I always did, that the muffins were made by a local artisan baker who appreciated the support for her small-batch pastries. I was about to hand her one of the baker's business cards when the woman dove into the muffin, tearing the wrapper and leaving little frayed bits of muffin cup everywhere.

The woman bit into the treat, and some crumbs fell into her cleavage. Then she spat the mouthful out on the counter. Erica and I took a step back, horrified.

"It's too chocolatey. Yuck." She discarded the half-munched muffin on the counter with a disgusted grunt. She turned and sashayed out in her matching yellow flip-flops.

"Mondays. What the fluff?" I hissed, reaching for a towel and the bleach so I could disinfect the counter.

"It's gotta be a full moon," Erica replied, shaking her head.

It was so busy that we didn't even get the chance to redraw our chalkboard to reflect the iced Nutella espresso drink. By the time eleven AM rolled around, we were able to breathe, and Erica and I leaned against the counter.

"I think we're going to have to hire another person if this keeps up. Man, today's been wild," I sighed.

"How can a double chocolate muffin be too chocolatey? I'm still fuming about that. Who spits out a mouthful of muffin in public? Raised by wolves."

"Who wastes a perfectly delicious muffin? That was going to be my midmorning snack. Now I'm starving and we have no baked goods left." I rubbed my stomach and affected a whiny expression.

"If you think you can handle being alone, I'll run out to get food."

"That sounds good. But first I wanted to show you something. Needed to wait until things died down, though. Hang on."

I went into the back room and retrieved the binder I'd received yesterday from L'ARTE, the coffee contraption company. When I returned to the counter, I plunked it down and opened the cover.

"This company makes machines that imprint images on drinks. Check this out."

I tapped on a photo of a latte emblazoned with the words "IT'S MUSTACHE SEASON."

"See, you can get their templates, or people can upload their own photos in an app. Look how cute this penguin design is."

Erica scrunched up her face as if a foul odor was in the air. She reached over and flipped back a few pages. She tapped on the picture. "Why would anyone want an image of Mick Jagger on their latte?"

"Maybe we don't do Mick Jagger, but we could do the Perkatory logo. Or . . ." I thought for a second. "Stanley! Or even a funny image of Dad! Perhaps a photo of him making a peace sign. Like Cheech and Chong, but with coffee instead of marijuana."

Erica scratched her neck. "What's wrong with our latte art? It's not good enough?"

"No," I cried, mindful of my bestie's feelings. "It's perfect. Your latte art, especially! I was thinking this could be another marketing tool. For a couple grand we get this machine, and you know dang well the customers who would buy these drinks will also put photos all over social media. It's like free advertising."

Her cheeks puffed out as she sighed. "I know. You're right. This machine could be really cool."

"Then what's wrong?" I shut the book, needing to hear Erica's take. Since she was the best barista I'd ever met, and my trusted friend, I valued her opinion more than anyone's.

"Technology, man. It's taking over. It's ruining all the good stuff."

"You're not wrong. And I think people still will want handmade lattes. Let's meet with the rep from this company. Apparently, they're sending a guy here tomorrow."

"I'll try. I'll be on my best behavior. Promise." She held up crossed fingers. "Now. About lunch."

"Ooh. What about the grouper chowder over at Bay Bay's? I'm craving it. Can you get me a bowl of that? With those little, tasty Cuban crackers?" Bay Bay's, a casual seafood restaurant and bar, was nearby.

"Oh, good idea. Love that chowder. Okay, later, alligator." Erica pulled off her apron, hung it on a rack, and left.

I gave the counter a fourth wipe-down, still salty from the woman spitting her mouthful of muffin. As I put a little elbow grease into it, I swept a glance over the shop. Despite the busy, sometimes contentious morning, Perkatory right now was at its best. Every table was taken, mostly with people chatting, while a couple of others tapped away on laptops.

On the sofa, a couple in their sixties sat close, laughing and flirting. The man leaned over to kiss the woman's cheek. Aww! In the background, my special yacht rock mix played, with Pablo Cruise's "Love Will Find a Way" making at least two people boogie in their chairs.

Most of all, everyone looked happy. This was a huge change from when I was a journalist, where my news articles made people angry, despondent, and terribly sad—but never joyful. My job, and the life I used to live, made me feel much the same way, and as much as I'd fought the change in coming to Devil's Beach, I'd finally accepted that I'd moved on.

And I was happy here.

The bells on the front door jangled, signaling a new customer. I looked over, and there was Darla Ippolito, barreling in like a bull in a china shop. Her brown hair was pulled back into a messy ponytail, and she wore jeans and a tank top that made her broad shoulders look even wider. Her lips were turned down, giving her a decidedly frosty expression. Eep. She even knocked someone's newspaper off a table, then apologized profusely.

For a moment, I thought perhaps I'd done something wrong at the garden. Or she found out that I actually hated her taffy. Then I remembered Jack and braced myself.

I greeted her with a small yet sympathetic smile. She must be overwhelmed with all sorts of unsavory details and tasks since Jack was discovered dead in her garden.

"I'm so sorry about what happened. I should've called you last night, but figured you were busy, or grieving." I bit my lip. My gaze immediately went to her earlobes, and for the first time, I noticed that she had multiple piercings in each ear, all the way around the upper part of the cartilage. Every hole was filled with small, dainty star earrings, which looked pretty cool. But there was no way she could fit the gold watering can earring on her lobe.

"Lana, we need to talk," she said brusquely.

"How about a coffee first?"

Her gaze shifted to the La Marzocco, our gleaming, stainless-steel espresso maker. "Yeah, I could use an Americano."

Her usual. "Excellent choice." I tried to keep my tone even and soothing, but something about her nervous energy left me feeling unsettled.

I started with a mug of hot water, then pulled two espresso shots. Some baristas in other shops—like at Island Brewnette, Perkatory's main competition here on the island—pull the shots first then dump the water into the coffee.

Not here.

I was of the belief that shots into water first breaks apart the espresso, creating an inferior drink.

Once the shots finished, I poured the espresso slowly into the larger mug. It's a subtle difference, but an important one. Knowing that Darla liked one packet of pink sweetener, I added that into the cup and stirred.

"There you go." I set the mug down on the counter and looked around the shop. There were no customers in line, and the people sitting around the café were largely regulars at this point in the day. "Want to chat over by the window?"

That was my unofficial office when I wasn't behind the counter. Upstairs was my official office, but I couldn't leave the floor unattended.

Darla picked up the coffee and nodded. I couldn't help but notice how her breath shuddered a bit whenever she inhaled. Poor thing. I was all too familiar with a workplace death.

We went over to the barstool seats pulled up to a long wooden counter near the window. It overlooked downtown Devil's Beach if you stared straight ahead, and if you turned to the right, the beach was across the street.

The best location in town, Dad always said. His great-great-grandfather had built the place when Devil's Beach was first founded.

Darla and I hopped up on the stools and stared at each other.

"So." I massaged my arm nervously. "I'm sorry about everything that happened at the garden. You must be broken up."

She took a sip of her coffee and briefly shut her eyes. "My goodness, that's delicious. You have a way of making the best coffee, Lana."

I smiled tightly. Why did it seem like she was buttering me up? "Thanks. I'm a fan of Americano coffee. Nice and simple."

"Look, I'm not going to beat around the bush. I need your help."

"My help? With what?"

She shook her head, and I could've sworn that I spotted tears in her eyes. This was shocking because Darla always seemed like a tough and resilient woman. But what did I actually know about her, beyond the fact that she adored saltwater taffy, dressed strangely in cold weather, and harbored a love of exotic mushrooms?

"I'm a suspect in Jack's death."

"Oh! Oh. Yikes." That escalated quickly. "Are you sure?"

"Even in death that guy's yanking my chain."

I couldn't help but notice that her face had become flushed.

"Oh dear." The magnitude of her words sank in.

"It all started shortly after I was elected president in November. He gave me a hard time about every. Single. Thing. Every decision I made, he'd write a ten-page email rebutting it. Every time I asked him to not use certain fertilizers, he'd argue like he was going before the Supreme Court. And his stupid boom box with Bob Dylan? If I never hear another Bob Dylan song again, I'll be happy."

Spittle had formed at the corners of her mouth, and she took a sip. I looked around helplessly for a napkin and came up short.

"Yikes," was all I could muster.

She swallowed her coffee. "Lana, you have to prove my innocence."

"Um." I cleared my throat. Ordering me around was the worst way to get my attention. "I think this is above my pay grade, Darla. Why me?"

She licked her lips. "You solved, or helped solve, three homicides here on Devil's Beach. There was your barista, Fabrizio."

"I was a suspect in that, so I had a vested interest."

She held up two fingers. "Then there was the murder of Raina, the yoga teacher next door."

"I stumbled into that because I was asked to freelance a couple of newspaper articles."

"And then there was Gus, your next-door neighbor. You figured out the killer within days. It's wild, I still can't get over that one. It was such a shock when that person was arrested." She shook her head. "You never know about other humans. Animals and plants, those are the only things you can rely on."

I couldn't argue with her logic. "All of those cases were lucky breaks," I tried to hedge.

"Please? I'll give you as much taffy as you want. Hey, I just made a huge batch of strawberry. Should've brought you a bag."

I fought back a wave of nausea at the thought of strawberry taffy. I don't know why, but I hated the stuff. Adding strawberry flavor made it extra nauseating, because I deeply disliked the fruit. "Technically I had a special interest in that last case too, because Erica was the main suspect."

Darla flopped her hand in the air. "Irregardless. You solved all those cases. Now I want you to solve this case and prove I'm innocent."

I inhaled deeply. Darla's use of the word "irregardless" aside, I felt her pain. She stared at me pleadingly, then whispered the word, "Please?"

Air leaked out of my lungs, and I glanced out the window. A group of tourists in matching hot pink shirts that said "NO PLOT ONLY VIBES" were headed to the beach.

I was not feeling the vibes, or the plot.

"It's not that easy. I'm not a private investigator. Not a detective." I was practically parroting Noah at this point.

Darla leaned in. "That's a good thing. You're an outsider. You're not part of the local cop corruption scene."

I tilted my head. "I'm not pro-cop, Darla. When I was a reporter in Miami I didn't hesitate to write about bad cops. But you are aware I'm dating the town's police chief, right?"

She pointed in my direction. "Another reason you're the perfect person to help me. You can get inside information. You know. Pillow talk."

I glanced around, as if looking for answers. Darla was seriously misinformed if that's what she thought it was like to date a cop. Our pillow talk involved our favorite TV shows and what we were going to make for breakfast. "I don't think Noah would appreciate me poking around."

She rolled her eyes. "Are you going to let some man dictate your life?"

I tugged on my ear, hoping that Erica would be back soon. Maybe she could talk Darla away from this tangent. Then again, Erica might be thrilled at the prospect of sleuthing another murder. I know Dad would. Lord, I hoped Darla hadn't hit him up with this request.

"Geez, Darla, I don't know. What about a good attorney? I could help you find one. Lawyers often hire private investigators, and I think they'll be better equipped than me."

She shook her head mournfully. "I don't have the cash. I had to buy a new, used car a couple of months ago, and I'm still digging out of that hole. Plus I went on vacation with my new boyfriend. Probably not the wisest financial decision, but you know how it goes. Oh, and my rent went up to $1,500 a month. For a small one bedroom, can you believe that? It's expensive to live here on Devil's Beach, and retail doesn't pay that much, even a manager job."

I nodded sympathetically. Here on the island, I was one of the lucky locals, because I lived in the home I grew up in, mortgage and rent free. Dad and Mom had built a home by the beach before Mom died but had never sold their old bungalow. "The cost of living here is out of control."

"No working-class person can afford it. I was even thinking about getting a second job, but now with this scandal, who's going to hire me? As it is, I worry the owners of the taffy shop will find out about Jack and I'll be out of that job. Thankfully they're traveling in Europe now, but it's only a matter of time before they hear about his death."

I reached over to touch her hand. "I'm sure Noah will get to the bottom of Jack's death soon. He's not corrupt. He's the most honest man I've ever met."

A single tear rolled down Darla's face. "I don't have an issue with him personally. I'm sure he's a great guy, and from what I've seen, he's not awful like other cops. But, Lana, when he finds out about my past, he and his officers will train their sights on me like a laser on a rifle."

"Really? Why is that?"

"Because I've done some things. Been around the block. Haven't told anyone here much about it." She brushed away the tear on her cheek, and I recalled how Erica mentioned something about Darla's arrest record. "I used to have a drinking problem when I lived up north. Got into a lot of fights. Even was arrested for assault one time but was able to plead it down to a misdemeanor. Spent a month in jail. That's what set me straight. I stopped drinking and moved down here so I could put all that behind me. Been sober and trouble free for three years. Until now. Still sober, but I'm obviously in trouble."

I nodded, but inside wondered why someone with an alcohol problem would come to a Florida vacation spot where the number one pastime was drinking. It wasn't much of a surprise that Darla had a colorful past—so many people who flock to Florida do, and that's why they come here.

To forget. To run. To start fresh.

Darla had done all three, but now her past was colliding with a murder. I could understand why she was so nervous.

"I'm sorry. That's really difficult, and I totally get why you'd be wary of police. But please don't worry."

Her eyes widened. "Does that mean you'll help me?"

My natural instinct to people please was at war with my running to-do list. If I was going to help Darla, I'd have to dive in and start researching Jack's background and life. Sure, Dad and Erica would help, but sometimes they weren't the most useful.

Noah wouldn't be happy if I poked around. And then there was Saturday night . . .

"I'm going to have to think about it for a day or two, okay?"

She winced. "That long? I could be locked up in a day or two."

I opened my mouth, but nothing came out. Why was she pressuring me? "Ah, yeah, it's going to take me a little while to decide. I've got a lot going on in my life right now, and . . ."

The bells on the front door jangled, and I spotted Erica strolling in with a paper bag with twine handles. ". . . And I'm going to have to chat about this with Erica. She helped me with all those previous murder cases. Would you mind if I shared this information with her?"

"No, of course not! I love Erica." Darla looked over my shoulder and waved. "Erica! Over here."

Erica walked over. "We got the last two bowls of grouper chowder. Hey, Darla, what's the word, hummingbird?"

Darla rubbed her hands together. "I'm a suspect in a crime."

Erica nodded thoughtfully. "No way! Are you innocent?"

I swear, nothing fazed that woman. My gaze slid to Darla, anticipating her answer.

"Innocent as a lamb. And I'm trying to convince Lana to use her investigative reporter sleuthing skills to prove that I didn't kill Jack. She's reluctant, though, and I was hoping you'd talk her into it."

Erica beamed, and I could tell that the prospect of once again being an amateur gumshoe excited her. "Leave that to me. I'll work on her."

Chapter Six

For the rest of the shift, I didn't bring up Darla's request or Jack's death, and neither did Erica.

As much as I would've liked to help Darla, I had to be mindful of other obligations. I listed all the things in my mind as I tidied up the café.

Thing one: my promise to Noah that I wouldn't poke around.

Thing two: meet with the latte art machine representative.

Thing three: the dinner that I was hosting in a few short days.

Thing four: the fact that I'd investigated three other untimely deaths on the island and put myself in danger in each scenario.

There were no winners in this latest case, I determined. Not Darla, not me, and definitely not Jack. This nagged at me because I always prefer to see justice prevail. What if I could keep Darla from being unfairly accused?

Barbara came in for her shift, eager to hear the latest on Jack. While denying I knew anything, I said goodbye to her and told Erica that I'd be over to her place later to drop off some books I'd been wanting to give her. We'd been on a domestic thriller kick lately. Erica wouldn't be leaving Perkatory for another couple of hours, which meant I had time to hang out with Stanley and make one large to-do list.

On Mondays, I opened the café by myself, and Erica came in a couple of hours later and left after I did. That way, we covered most of the café's busy periods.

As I walked home, I thought about all I had to do, from making a shopping list to buying flowers for the dinner to getting Stanley groomed. But my mind kept returning to Darla and her sad expression.

Covering crime in Miami, I knew how difficult it was for people with criminal records to obtain meaningful employment. That Darla had knocked around the criminal justice system and had started her life over as the manager of a saltwater taffy joint—a job she adored—was nothing short of a miracle.

Being wrongfully accused of Jack's death would derail all her hard-earned progress. Maybe I could help her avoid all that.

By the time I opened my front door I was still conflicted. Stanley greeted me with sharp, excited yips, and I bent down to scoop him up. I planted a big kiss on the top of his head.

"You smell more like a clam today, buddy. We're going to call the groomer right now."

I'd only had Stanley for less than a year, and he was a puppy when I informally adopted him. His previous owner, my barista Fabrizio, had met an untimely death after plunging off the roof of the Perkatory building.

After all these months I'd never gotten the dog groomed, mostly because he looked so adorable with his long fur. Rather, hair. Shih tzu had hair that grew and grew, and right now, he looked like a cross between a mop and a Wookie.

I'd taken to brushing his hair out of his face into a topknot, which made him look adorable. Still, I knew he hated the elastic atop his head because he kept trying to paw it off. Today his hair flopped over his face, and I suspected he could barely see.

"Yeah, it's time for a spa day." I set him down and walked to the yard. The pupper followed me and darted into my fenced-in yard, excited to find a tennis ball that he'd been playing with the other day.

While he amused himself with that, I dialed the local groomer, Pooch to Perfection. The owner, Kevin de la Cruz, was a former high school classmate and a customer at Perkatory. He answered on the second ring.

"Lana!" he cried. "Oh Em Gee, I was just talking about you!"

"Really? Were you telling someone about our exploits in marching band in seventh grade?" Kevin and I had been band geeks together, and we'd both been quiet and shy. Being gay and Filipino wasn't an issue on progressive Devil's Beach, and after graduating, Kevin had stayed on-island and became a pillar of the business community. He was active in the town's Chamber of Commerce and tried to get me involved when I took over Perkatory.

"No, I was gossiping with my boyfriend about Jack Daggitt. I speculated that since you found the body, you'd surely be investigating the murder too. You've gotten quite a reputation around town as a sleuth."

"Great," I muttered.

"So, are you looking into the death?"

I ran my tongue over my teeth, unsure of what to say. "Probably not," I hedged.

"Ohh, well, too bad, because my boyfriend knew Jack and has a lot of dirt. Like an entire bagful of dirt. Dirty dirt."

His declaration didn't shock me. Everyone on Devil's Beach thought they had the goods on everyone else. "That's super interesting, but I'm calling about something else. I know this is really late notice, but I need Stanley groomed before Saturday. I'm hosting an important dinner party."

"Oh, really?"

"Yeah, I'm meeting Noah's mom for the first time, and I don't want Stanley to smell like he dove into a bucket of fish."

"Girl, you should've brought that little cutie pie into the shop earlier to get him used to being groomed. You need to impress Mrs. Garcia. Because God knows, you don't want to lose that hunk of a man."

Noah was widely considered one of the most handsome guys on the island. Next to Dad, of course. Those two facts didn't square in my mind, and I tried not to dwell on them.

"I know. I know. But I love him with his long fur. Usually, I can keep up with bathing him, but not this week. Maybe a trim or something."

"We'll fix him up with the cutest cut. Let's see. I have a cancellation today at four thirty. Can you come then?"

"Perfect." I let out a sigh of relief. One crisis averted. "See you then."

I hung up and looked at Stanley, who was sitting in the grass like a loaf of fluffy bread. I could only hope that he remained that chill on Kevin's grooming table.

* * *

After dropping Stanley off with an enthusiastic Kevin—who had decided that instead of a "puppy cut" he wanted to do a "lion cub cut" on my dog, whatever that was—I headed to the marina where Erica lived, with the stack of books in my bag.

The sky was a bright blue without a single cloud. The sun shone down brightly on the bone-white boats that rocked gently in their berths. The air here was pungent with the aroma of salty sea and wet sand—unlike the beachfront, it wasn't laced with the scent of coconut oil and suntan lotion.

My friend and fellow barista had sailed her boat to this marina on Devil's Beach less than a year ago, something of a goth hurricane hitting a bright, sunny beach. Physically, she stuck out like a hot dog at a hamburger party. But she and the island community had embraced one another, and she put down roots here, renting a slip at the marina and even dating Joey Rizzo, another local guy I'd gone to school with.

The marina was one of three on the island. It was a prime spot for service workers, hippies, and other counterculture types, all of whom lived on boats of varying sizes at an economical monthly docking fee. Most of the vessels were modest, perfect for one person. A few boats were large and luxurious, and everyone in town assumed their owners had done something illegal to afford them.

I walked along the dock toward Erica's boat. The sound of water gently slapping against the hulls, along with the cries of the seagulls, was soothing.

Erica was in a black tank top and black shorts, spraying water on the side of her sailboat, when I rolled up. Her vessel was called *The Mutiny*, and she'd painted a flamboyant lady pirate holding a dagger in her teeth on the hull.

"Greetings and salutations," she called out, shutting off the hose. "Want an iced coffee?"

I checked my watch. I'd been up since five and started work at six. "It's four thirty in the afternoon. But I can sleep when I'm dead, I guess. Sure."

She went below deck to her living area, where she had a small galley kitchen. A few minutes later, she emerged with two coffees. She handed me one, and we clinked. The drinks were in beer mugs, with ice, garnished with a piece of gooey caramel on the rim of the glass. I ate that first.

The java went down nice and smooth. It tasted both light and sweet, which wasn't usually Erica's preferred flavor profile. If I didn't know better, I could've sworn I was on a charter boat from the fancy look of the coffee.

"Dang, this tastes good," I said after my first sip.

"Vietnamese coffee. It's cold brew and condensed milk, with a hint of caramel syrup. I've been playing around with sweet new drinks. Oh, and the caramels are local, from that new candy shop."

"Love it."

I told her about Stanley, and for a while we speculated about what a "lion cub cut" entailed.

"Maybe it'll be really short," I said. "I hope he doesn't look weird."

She shook her head. "I think he'll look like a tiny, adorable lion. Mrs. Garcia won't know what hit her. She'll walk in, smell the baking lasagna, and then, boom! She'll spot Stanley and force Noah to propose to you right there."

I snorted. "I highly doubt that. And I'm not sure I'm ready for that big of a step. Let's get the dinner over before we move on to the proposal."

I'd already been married, and divorced, to a man in Miami. I'd always sworn that I wouldn't get hitched again, but then I'd met Noah. My relationship with him was going so incredibly well that I almost was afraid of any change.

Erica stared at me long and hard, and I braced for the inevitable question about what I wanted out of my relationship with Noah. It was a common discussion between us, mostly because she couldn't fathom being married, and I was so on the fence about the entire institution.

"So. What are you going to do about Darla?" Erica asked.

My lips stretched into a grimace. Nothing escaped my best friend. "My heart tells me to help her, but my head tells me not to mess with my police chief boyfriend the week I'm supposed to meet his mother."

She nodded. "Fair."

"Darla told me about her criminal record." I lowered my voice, although there was no reason why, since we were sitting on a sailboat at a marina and there was no one around on the other, empty boats.

"Did she talk about reading the mnemonics book in jail? Darla and I had drinks one night and she told me all about it. She never told me why she was in the can, though. Do you know?"

"Misdemeanor assault. She also said she'd had a drinking problem." Could Jack's provocations have caused her to relapse and snap?

"Interesting. We actually have a lot in common, us having questionable and shady pasts before coming here."

Erica had told me previously that she'd had "anger management issues" before she came to Florida, but I'd never probed, even though I wanted to. She had a bit of a fiery temper, but nothing I couldn't handle. As far as I was concerned, she was a loyal friend and an excellent employee. There was no need to dredge up her past.

Goodness knew I had a past of my own. Nothing that involved arrests, but my breakup with my ex in Miami was nothing short of scandalous, considering he was a semi-famous national network TV reporter who left me for a much younger woman. And getting laid off from my newspaper job. Running from one's past also included fleeing from humiliation, and that's what I'd done when I left Miami and returned to Devil's Beach.

"What do you suggest I do about Darla? What's your take on the situation?" I asked aloud.

"You mean, we?"

"Uh, yeah, I guess. We. Since we've been a sleuthing team on previous cases."

"Darla came back to Perkatory after you left and gave me the same pitch. Asked me to help her clear her name." Erica took a long pull of her coffee. "Begged me to talk you into investigating Jack's death."

"She did? Wow." That seemed excessive, but not out of character. Darla was intense.

"It's a pretty dire situation for her. Technically, she's on probation."

I gaped at my friend. "She didn't tell me that."

"She's in the final four months so she doesn't want to do anything to mess it up."

I sucked in a breath. "That seems excessive for a misdemeanor. I wonder if she wasn't telling the truth about her criminal charge. But this changes things, I guess. Or maybe it doesn't. I don't know. I'd almost rather give her money for a lawyer."

"That could work too. If we found the right lawyer. Do you know anyone?"

I sucked in a breath and shook my head. "In Miami, yes. Here? Not really, unless you count Dad's buddy who does slip and fall cases."

Erica and I drank our coffee in silence. Then my phone pinged with a text from the recesses of my purse.

"Maybe Stanley's ready," I said, taking the cell out. "Nope. It's Dad."

Hi munchkin. Do you want to go to a monkey meeting at City Hall tonight? Jack's nemesis will be there. Well, one of his nemesis. What's the plural of nemesis, anyway?

He ended the text with an emoji, and I squinted at the screen. I wasn't confused by the monkey part, because I'd heard that the City Council was going to hold a hearing about the future of the island's wild monkeys. This was the latest in the never-ending saga of the primates, and I expected it to be quite wild, given how intense emotions were surrounding the monkey colony.

"What's up?" Erica asked, and I read the text aloud.

"I can't figure out what this emoji means, though."

I passed the phone to her, and she stared as if she was trying to decipher hieroglyphics. "I think that's a pager."

"Why is there even an emoji for a pager? Does anyone use pagers anymore? And why did Dad send that?"

Erica shrugged.

"Want to go to City Hall with us tonight? We can meet Jack's sworn enemy."

Erica shook her head and returned my phone. "Can't. Joey and I are going to a succulent party."

I squinted one eye. "Excuse me?"

"We're going to that florist on Main Street to learn how to plant succulents in tiny plastic dinosaurs." Joey and Erica always did slightly unusual activities. Last month, they learned to make pickled onions. I had four jars of them in my fridge now.

"Oh. Cool." My phone pinged again while it was in my hand. "Stanley's finished. I can't wait to see him."

I stood up and downed the rest of my coffee. I'd drunk so much today that a buzzing feeling had overtaken my heartbeat.

"Text me a photo of Stanley. I want to see this lion cub cut. I imagine him looking like a stuffed animal."

"Will do. I'll also message you after Dad and I poke around at tonight's meeting. Have fun with the succulents."

Erica and I bade each other goodbye, and I walked over to Pooch to Perfection, which was located off Main Street, a few blocks from Perkatory in the opposite direction from the community garden. That was one thing I loved about living in Devil's Beach—that everything necessary was within a ten-minute walk of everything else. I could stand outside of Perkatory and look at the beach across the street, two excellent restaurants, the sign on the bookstore, and in the distance, the library. It was the perfect blend.

Whenever I thought of my old life in Miami, memories of long commutes, nerve-jangling interactions with angry motorists, and frustrating moments in the car came to mind. I was through with all that, thank goodness.

Kevin was holding a panting Stanley in his arms when I walked in. I let out a little cry when I saw him, and he wuffed with joy.

I squealed my dog's name when I saw his new look. Kevin set him down and Stanley barreled toward me, whining and wuffing the entire length of the store.

"You look like a tiny lion!" I scooped him up and kissed his head. His fur smelled like bubblegum.

It was truly an amazing cut. Stanley's face had been trimmed, and his entire body washed and blow-dried straight. The fur on top of his head and around his neck was cut into something of a halo. Just like a lion's mane. The rest of his body was closely cropped, except the end of his tail, which was shaped into a ball of fur.

His little feet were also styled to look like puffs of cotton, giving him the overall appearance of wearing small, furry moon boots. Because of his tawny-colored fur, he really did look like a mini lion.

"I might die of cuteness," I gushed to Kevin.

"He was a good boy. Only tried to nip once. For his first groom, he was excellent."

I quickly paid Kevin and complimented his artistry about a dozen more times. After leashing Stanley, I paused. "Say. About your boyfriend who knew Jack . . . do you think he'd want to chat with me?"

Kevin's eyes grew wide. "Beau? Absolutely! He's here now, blow-drying Johnny Cash."

He beckoned me behind the counter and led me to a Dutch door. "Beau? Babe? Turn off the blower for a sec."

We paused at the half-door, which came up to my belly. I peered inside the room beyond the door. A giant of a man wielded what looked like a shop vac on a floofy black dog that was perched on a stainless-steel table.

Johnny Cash was a handsome Pomeranian.

Beau flicked off a switch on the blower and unhooked the dog, giving him a kiss on the top of the head before setting him down. Aww. There was something about men who were kind to animals that made me melt inside.

The dog immediately shook himself and Beau lumbered over. He looked like a giant, friendly bear with shaggy brown hair and a matching color beard.

"What a cutie," I called out. "Er, the dog, I mean."

Beau laughed. "I know what you meant."

"You're cute, too," I said, grinning.

"This is Stanley's mom. Her name is Lana," Kevin said, putting his hand on my arm. "We were in band together. We even went to band camp one week in seventh grade."

"I had to leave early that year because I swallowed a bee," I said.

"A bunch of other stuff happened to us in high school too," Kevin added.

"Were you the one who groomed Stanley?" I asked quickly, hoping Kevin wouldn't bring up Gisela. He'd been friends with her when she disappeared.

"Nice to meet you, and yes, I shampooed him," Beau said, wiping his hand on his apron and then extending his arm for a shake. "Sorry, I've been up to my elbows in doggie bubble bath today."

"No worries." I waved him off.

"Lana's a reporter," Kevin said.

"Former reporter," I countered.

"Whatever. She's the one who found Jack dead in the garden."

Kevin's mocha-colored eyes grew wide. "No way."

"Way. I was wondering if you knew him."

Beau snorted. "I knew him quite well. Worked for him for five years, walking his dog."

My reporter antennae perked up and I leaned my elbow on the half-door like I was bellying up to a bar. "Oh, really?"

"Yep." He shook his head, and I could've sworn tears came to his eyes. "I miss Bella Pugosi something fierce."

"That's quite a name. Was that his dog?" I probed gently.

Beau nodded. "A puggle. A doll of a doggo."

"Did you like working for him? How'd you meet him?"

"He found me on one of those pet-sitting apps, back when I was starting my walking and grooming business here on the island. I adored Bella immediately, and since Jack was getting up there in age, he asked me to walk her six days a week."

"Hmm," I said, hoping Beau would continue talking.

"Jack was a bit finicky about Bella. Didn't want me to take him to the dog beach, didn't like the dog park at all. I didn't mind, though. Bella seemed to enjoy half-hour walks around the neighborhood. But what Jack did later really torqued me off."

"What happened?"

"One day, about six months ago, on a Tuesday, that's when it all went down. It was my day off and I went for a hike by myself. Usually, I never walk without a dog or Kevin, but that day I needed some quiet time, you know?"

I nodded enthusiastically. My quiet time generally revolved around my sofa, a cup of coffee, and a book, but to each their own.

"As I was walking, I was deep in the Swamp. You know, the one with the trails and the monkeys in the middle of the island?"

I nodded. I was well familiar with the Swamp because Dad was a monkey activist, trying to keep the primates on-island and contained to that park.

"Well, I saw Jack there on the trail. Not on the boardwalk, but the muddier part, well in the Swamp."

"What was wrong with that?"

Beau's eyes flashed angrily. "He was with Bella. Unleashed."

His last word hung in the air, and I reared back, stunned. No one takes their dogs unleashed into the Swamp.

"I told him that wasn't a good idea because of all the gators, but Jack laughed at me. Said the dog was smart enough to stay away from the gators. We got into a huge fight, there in the Swamp. Practically came to blows. I was ready to take the dog into my custody."

"Whoa." A wave of fear crept up my neck. Who would let their dog run loose in the Swamp? The idea of a free dog in that place, with all those gators, should send fear into any pet owner's heart.

I needed clarification. "Are you sure the pup wasn't on one of those thin retractable leashes?"

Beau's shaggy hair swayed as he shook his head. "One hundred percent unleashed. I know because Bella ran up to me, and I picked him up. Almost took him home with me. I would have, too, but I knew Jack would've sued me for everything I own. He's one of those litigious types."

"I don't blame you for being upset." I couldn't help but notice that Beau's large hands had curled into fists.

"That's when Jack fired me, and I never saw Bella again." Beau sighed. "That was the thing about Jack. If you didn't cross him, he was a sweet, if a little ornery, old guy. But if you got on his bad side he was the nastiest dude you'd ever meet."

"In-ter-est-ing," I drawled. "Who do you think killed him, anyway?"

Beau chortled. "Honey, could be anyone. Jack made so many people angry. His disposition turned like that." He snapped his fingers. "Folks at that garden, neighbors of the garden; heck, I wonder if his own daughter liked him."

"Daughter? He has a daughter?"

"Yeah, she doesn't live here. Or maybe she does now. Not sure. I think her name's Willa."

I mentally filed that information away. "Well, thanks. That's important info. And thanks for doing such a great job with Stanley. He looks super cute."

Beau beamed. "Bring him back any time!"

I bade Beau and Kevin goodbye, but not before accepting a frosted dog cookie for Stanley when we got home. We strolled outside. It almost seemed as though my dog was proud of his new look, because he strutted as he walked, his head high.

Beau's words echoed in my brain. *Jack made so many people angry.* I wonder if Noah knew this.

Stanley and I passed by the stately town library, the row of tall palm trees lining Main Street, and the Blue Bottle Emporium, a bar that was half-full with a mix of tourists and locals. It was downstairs from the town newspaper. The joint had a large, open-air window in front, which allowed a row of drunks to give running commentary on anyone walking by.

Stanley and I were no exception.

"Maybe try smiling," one tourist said to me.

Does every woman hate that, or what? I shot the guy a simpering look.

"Hey, look at that toy poodle," someone else said.

Of course, I ignored that. Stanley looked nothing like a poodle. In fact, he looked so adorable that I needed to take photos of him and post them on the Perkatory Instagram account, where he was something of a cult figure. Dad would also probably snap some photos because he'd started a separate Insta for Stanley.

I couldn't resist stopping at the café to show him off, even for a few seconds. Barbara cooed over him, and so did several customers. We took a couple of quick pictures with him and an (unopened) bag of Perkatory-branded coffee beans. I quickly posted it to the café's social media.

On my way out, I almost ran smack into the chest of Lex Bradstreet, a tall, good-looking surfer. He'd been friends with Fabrizio, my former (and deceased, may his soul rest in peace) barista. They'd been surfing buddies, and knowing how handsome both were, most likely were each other's wingmen when picking up women.

"Hey, Lana dude, what's up?" Lex said, holding the door open for me as I walked out with Stanley in my arms. "What's that little creature right there?"

"This is Stanley! Don't you recognize him?"

"Fab's dog? The one you adopted?" Lex frowned.

"The same one."

"Wow, he looks a lot different. He looks like . . ."

"A lion?" I offered.

He tilted his head. "I dunno about that, exactly. He looks more like a, hmm. Poodle?"

Hush your mouth, I wanted to say, because my dog looked like a regal lion. "Nice seeing you, Lex!" I sailed through, wanting to get home. I had a monkey meeting to attend, and, possibly, a murder to investigate—or a friend to disappoint.

As we walked the few blocks home, I realized I should've asked Beau two more questions about Jack.

What had happened to Bella Pugosi, the dog, now that Jack was dead?

And where was Beau the day Jack was murdered?

Chapter Seven

I still hadn't determined if I would truly dive into the details of Jack's death or if I was going to politely decline Darla's request for help.

As much as I wanted justice to be served, I knew that getting involved with a fourth homicide would put a strain on my relationship with Noah, right at a time when we needed to be tighter than ever. As he liked to remind me, I wasn't a detective or a private investigator.

I'd been an investigative crime journalist, and a good one at that. I'd have to chat with Dad tonight and then sleep on it. I'd give Darla an official answer tomorrow since she usually came in on most mornings for her coffee when I was working.

After feeding Stanley the cookie from the grooming shop, I left my house and biked over to City Hall. I knew that parking would probably be difficult, given how many people this meeting was expected to draw.

My instincts were correct. The community room was overflowing with people, so many that I didn't immediately spot Dad. I wove my way through groups of citizens and made it to the front of the room, searching for two empty seats. Finally, I found some to the left, right up front.

The minute I plopped down, a woman leaned over. "Are you pro- or anti-monkey removal?"

I froze, taken aback by the question. "Uh, anti, I guess."

She nodded sagely. "Good. Because this"—she waved her hand in the air—"is the seating area for people who want the monkeys to stay. Those other people are over there."

She jabbed her finger at the right side of the room with a sneer.

"Good to know." I scooted down into my seat. I, personally, didn't have a monkey in this fight. I saw it from both angles, and would've preferred to sit somewhere in the middle, like I used to when I covered community meetings as a reporter.

Finally, I found Dad. He was wearing his cargo shorts and a button-down white linen guayabera shirt that I'd gotten him in Miami several years ago. Flip-flops adorned his feet, and with the silver goatee and his tan, the overall look screamed "beach bum."

I waved and he came over, greeting people with hugs and kisses along the way. I swear, Dad knew everyone in town. Sometimes I thought he should run for the council, and efforts had been made to draft him on more than one occasion.

When he reached me, I moved my purse from the empty seat next to me and he plunked down and leaned into me. "Word has it that two people who hated Jack will be here tonight."

"Ooh, great," I replied. "Oh, check this out. Stanley went to the groomer today."

I pulled out my phone and showed him the photos we took at Perkatory. Dad nodded gravely. "Did you know that shih tzu are sometimes called fu dogs? They were holy beings in Buddhist texts because of their lion-like resemblance. Well done, munchkin."

"Thanks, Dad. Hey, why aren't you wearing your monkey costume?" Not that long ago, Dad had led a pro-monkey protest downtown while dressed in a furry primate suit.

Dad wagged his finger. "The council said that anyone in costume or holding signs would be expelled. Seems like censorship to me, but we're trying to play by the rules for this meeting. Go along to get along, instead of being combative."

"Seems wise," I agreed.

There was a tapping noise on the sound system, and Dad and I shifted our gazes to the front of the room. The City Council members filed in, followed by the mayor, and all took their places on the dais. Noah also walked in and assumed a seat at a table in front, facing the council. I tried to catch his eye and give him a little wave, but he didn't see me.

"I'm surprised Noah's even here, since he must be busy with Jack's homicide," I hissed to Dad.

"Monkeys are an important issue too," he retorted, a little too loudly.

By now, there was an anxious, even hostile, current in the air. I glanced to the right side of the room, and an older woman scowled at me. Yikes.

This was probably the most contentious local issue the island had endured in a while. At least since a city parking enforcement worker was caught stealing coins from the meters and stuffing them into a specially lined jock strap.

That had made the national news about five years ago. Tonight, I was shocked that there were no reporters from big outlets. I only spotted one journalist from the local paper, a woman who looked entirely too exhausted and frazzled. I telepathically sent her a message: *I feel you, sister.*

The mayor cleared his throat as he stood. "I want to remind the citizens of Devil's Beach to kindly allow others to speak without interruption tonight. I know everyone's emotional right now over this issue, but I have to remind you that if anyone steps out of line, I'll have an officer escort you out."

At that moment, Noah turned to look at the crowd. We locked eyes, and I could tell he was fighting back a smile. He was the only one, though.

Between the dour and weary looks on the local politicians' faces, and the too-bright fluorescent light overhead, I had a flashback of my early days in journalism, covering City Hall in Aventura, a suburb of Miami.

I didn't miss those meetings one bit. Normally local hearings were as boring as the behind the scenes look at a sloth's life. But this one, I felt, would be different.

Devil's Beach. The rules are different here.

While the mayor droned on about how this meeting was subject to the state's open records laws, I studied the back of Noah's head. Tonight he wore his chief's uniform and looked entirely too formal for this crowd of beach residents. Still, I ogled his neck and that sharp, dark hairline of his. And the way his muscles strained at his shirt.

Noah looked so gorgeous that I was going to text Erica with my observation. It was kind of a running joke between us: me telling her about the hotness level of my boyfriend, and her telling me that I was the goofiest person alive and immature to boot.

All of those things could be true.

The mayor coughed nervously. "This evening, we'll hear from the Department of Wildlife, our police chief, and a primate consultant from the University of Florida. First, I'd like to give a short presentation about the history of the primates on Devil's Beach."

"Here we go," Dad said, crossing one lanky leg over another. I spied someone on the anti-primate side of the room leaning over and glaring at Dad. Hoo boy.

A giant, automated projector screen rolled down at the front of the room. It hung slightly behind, yet above, the council, and they turned in their seats to gaze up. The lights in the place dimmed, and an image flickered to life on the screen.

It was a black-and-white photo of my grandfather's roadside attraction. HOUSE OF PRIMATES it said on a hand-painted sign. On the far left of the screen was a wiry man with a floppy hat, his arms folded.

"There's Grampy," I whispered to Dad.

"That hat is somewhere in your garage," he replied.

Good luck finding it. The garage was stuffed full of my parents' junk.

The mayor stood, holding a microphone in his hands. "A lot of people don't know the history of the monkeys here on Devil's Beach. Well, it all started with Charles Lewis and a roadside zoo."

Beside me, Dad sat a little straighter. Charles was his father, and Dad had grown up next to the zoo. He had all sorts of stories about caring for monkey babies as a kid, even smuggling one into school inside his book bag when he was in third grade.

The mayor continued, and another slide flashed before us. It was of a small primate, perched on Grampy's bare shoulder.

"Why did they have to use the shirtless photo?" I hissed to Dad.

The mayor scowled in our direction. "Now, it would be politically incorrect to own a roadside zoo, but back then—"

Dad stood, cupping his hands around his mouth. "My father gave those monkeys the best care possible," he called out. Heads turned, and some in the audience snickered. A few on the anti-primate side booed.

"Dad. Dad!" I thwacked his leg with my hand. "Hush."

Now wasn't the time to try to redeem my family's complicated primate legacy.

"I'd like to remind everyone that if anyone in the audience gets out of line, we have the Devil's Beach Police standing by," the mayor warned. "I won't hesitate to expel you, Peter Lewis. Or have you detained."

Awesome. That was all I needed, Dad getting arrested (again) for his monkey activism.

Dad remained standing as the next image flashed on the screen, while a few people behind him murmured their displeasure. It was a news wire service clipping.

ANIMAL RIGHTS ACTIVISTS FREE MONKEYS FROM ROADSIDE ZOO, the headline read. It featured a photo of my grandfather, in his signature floppy fisherman's hat, smoking a cigar outside of the sanctuary. A monkey in a diaper sat on a tree stump nearby.

"That man practically built this island," Dad cried.

"Dad. Come on," I hissed.

Noah twisted in his seat, his eyes wide. I shot him a pleading look, as if to say, *take me away*. He fought back a grin, shook his head, and turned around.

"Peter Lewis, you're on thin ice," the mayor said, pointing at Dad.

Finally, Dad sat down.

"Keep it together," I murmured. "There will be plenty of time at public comment to share your opinion."

"That guy doesn't know what he's talking about," Dad retorted.

"Can you two keep it down? I'm trying to listen here," the woman in front of us complained.

I gave Dad a stern, warning look and swiped my hand across my neck. If it weren't for him and this whole Darla–Jack situation, I'd be home with Stanley, snug on the sofa with a book and a glass of wine.

Dad managed to contain himself while the mayor hit the high points of the monkeys' history. He detailed, with two video clips and dozens of photos, how the animal rights activists opened the cages back in the 1970s, and how they transported some of the animals to Angelwing Park—aka the Swamp. The mayor showed several photos of monkeys living their best lives in the mangroves and live oaks of the park, and even an adorable photo of a momma and baby monkey that made the entire room collectively go *awwww.*

At least everyone in the room agreed that baby monkeys were cute. Maybe that was a start for community healing.

But that turned out to be the extent of the goodwill for the primates, because the photos and the mayor's presentation took an ominous turn. Monkeys charging at tourists, monkeys screaming at tourists while diving into the water, and finally, a viral video in which a large male monkey flung feces at a jogger on the boardwalk.

"We've seen enough," a man on the right side of the room cried. "Cart 'em all away! Send 'em to a research facility, even. I don't care! They're menaces to society."

"I'm calling PETA," Dad yelled. He tried to climb to his feet, but I kept him rooted by attaching myself to his arm.

"I'll stay seated. Jerks." His eyes flashed, and I knew Dad was loving every second of this, probably because it would result in days of conversation and gossip around town.

This all touched off a ripple of discussion among the crowd, drowning out the mayor's nasal tone. I crossed my arms and shut my eyes for a brief second. Conflict wasn't my thing, and I was right in the middle of a community smackdown.

I endured an hour and a half of this, tuning out the mayor's commentary and most of the state expert's report on the size of the monkey colony (approximately three hundred animals during the last census). All of these details had already been covered ad nauseam in the local paper. Hardly a day went by without a monkey article in the *Beacon*.

When my boyfriend took the microphone, I sat up and paid attention. So did everyone else, it seemed. Well, at least most of the women in the audience. I heard someone behind me whisper, "I'd like him to arrest me," and I almost laughed aloud.

Noah didn't have much to add to the conversation, and I got the impression that his address was something of a salve for the number of hot tempers in the room. He pointed out that other communities had struggled with similar issues in Florida: iguanas in Deerfield Beach, a rare bat in Ocala, and an endangered mouse that only came out at night on a small Florida key.

"All of those communities got through their debates without strife. I'm confident Devil's Beach can do the same."

I wasn't so confident, but it was cute how Noah seemed to believe his words, because he smiled genuinely at the crowd, who applauded (for the record, the only speaker of the evening to win applause). Heck, I was ready to give him a standing ovation.

When he was finished, the mayor announced a twenty-minute break before the floor was opened for comments.

Dad turned to me. "Public comment will be off the chain."

How did dad know these phrases?

"Okay, so where are these people who hated Jack? I'm only here for that, you know." I wanted to move this night along.

Dad popped his head up and looked around like a meerkat. "Let's see. I think Joanie Clarke is here somewhere. Maybe outside, smoking. And Olivia. Hm. Where is she? Ah, there. By the fundraising table. Let's go."

Dad stood and made his way out of our row of folding chairs. I followed, and we weaved through the crowd, finally stopping in line at a table selling baked goods for the local theater company.

"She's buying brownies now. The one in yellow."

Being short, I had to crane my neck around a tall person in front of me. I spotted a woman with perfectly highlighted blonde hair, wearing a bright yellow sundress.

I turned back to Dad. "What are we going to say? And who is she, anyway?"

"Let me handle it. I know her from the café."

"Really? I've never seen her."

Dad shook his head. "She had to stop drinking caffeine."

Before I could ask why, Dad's face lit up. "Olivia! Long time no see."

I watched as Dad hugged the woman. She was in her mid-thirties, with carefully applied makeup and a large, silver statement necklace with matching silver earrings that looked to be pierced. She had the glow of a rich woman who was into organic produce, alkaline water, and hot yoga.

After they stopped hugging, Dad set his hand on my shoulder and introduced us. "Lana, Olivia Jenkins owns a boutique in that shopping plaza near the bridge to the mainland. Great yoga clothes. You should check it out."

Not a ghost of a chance, since I disliked yoga. I nodded enthusiastically. Dad plowed on. "Did you hear about Jack Daggitt? That he was murdered? Or has news not traveled that fast?"

I had to admire Dad's method of making small talk. He knew heckin' well that everyone in town was aware of Jack's death. But by asking a folksy question, it set Olivia up to gab.

And gab she did.

"I did. Can't say it was a shock." She pursed her lips and stared at me. "Your father knows how I hated the man."

"Oh dear. Why?" I pretended to be surprised.

"I live right behind the community garden."

My eyes widened. Was this the woman Jack had mentioned in his Facebook post? "I see."

"He would get out there and blast his oldies music. Now, I don't have anything against Bob Dylan, but have you ever tried to get a three-year-old to take a nap while a guy who sounds like a dying whale sings at the top of his lungs?"

I coughed into my hand, not wanting to laugh. Which man sounded like a dying whale? Jack or Bob Dylan? Poor Bob. Between Olivia and Darla, he probably should cross Devil's Beach off his vacation list.

"No, I haven't," I responded.

"Well, when I asked him to turn the music down—not off, just down—he was livid. He wrote a public Facebook post that was so nasty about my precious son. Can you imagine?"

"Sounds like a real peach," I said.

Dad leaned in with a grin. "But you wouldn't kill him over that, would you, Olivia? Where were you on Sunday?"

I gaped at Dad, open-mouthed. So did Olivia. Dad needed to work on his lack of filter.

Olivia burst out laughing. "Of course not, Peter. Oh, you. He's such a jokester. Lana, I can't imagine what it was like to grow up as his daughter."

"It was an adventure," I murmured.

"I didn't kill Jack. My family and I were in the Keys on the day Jack's body was found. We got back yesterday. Now if you don't mind, I'm going to return to my seat to eat this brownie before public comment starts. Nice meeting you!" She waggled her fingers at me and sashayed away, all that silver jewelry sending tinkle sounds into the air.

Dad tilted his head to look at me. "Well, that's that. Let's go find Joanie Clarke. Uh, first I want to grab a brownie, though."

We were next in line, so it didn't take us long to donate ten bucks to the theater company and come away with two delicious-looking brownies. After finding an open spot on the side of the room, we surveyed the crowd while snacking.

"Ah. There she is. Talking with the mayor by the stairs to the stage."

"What do you know about her?" I asked.

Dad popped the last of his brownie into his mouth, leaving a small crumb behind in his silver goatee. He munched thoughtfully while tapping his finger on his lips. I figured the crumb would fall away, but instead it clung to his whiskered chin and I couldn't stop looking at it.

"She's probably one of the richest people on the island. Owns a development company. You know those generic apartments on the mainland, the ones that look like brown boxes with the faux-rock trim?"

"I do. Remember I almost lived in one like that in Miami until I scored the art deco place on the beach?" I smiled, thinking of my first post-graduation studio apartment.

"Those are the ones. Her company pioneered that design. Rumor in the real estate world is that she cuts corners, possibly pays off county zoning officials, likely ignores regulations. Uses subpar materials. Typical shady development stuff."

I sized up Joanie Clarke, who was tipping her head back and laughing at something the mayor said. I knew the guy, and he wasn't *that* funny. "That's interesting. How did she cross paths with Jack? He didn't seem like kind of guy to move in developer and real estate social circles."

Dad turned to me, his eyes glittering. Gossip always did this to him—got him all worked up. "About six months before you moved back to Devil's Beach, Joanie and her company submitted plans to City Hall and the county to raze the strip mall on the south side."

"The one with the hardware store, and the barber shop, and the cigar place?" I screwed up my face. That shopping center had been there since before I was born and was the only hardware store on the island.

"Yep. Joanie owns that property. She wanted to tear it down and build the apartments. Claimed they would be affordable housing."

"That's not a bad thing, though. Hardly anyone who is working class can afford a place to live here."

"True. But this is where Jack comes in. He opposed the plans because, apparently, behind the hardware store in that little wetland, there's an endangered lizard."

"Don't tell Erica."

"It's called a mole skink. It looks like a snake that sprouted tiny legs." Dad pantomimed the reptile, holding his hands at chest height and looking more like a T-rex. "Because of Jack and the skink, the development wasn't approved. Joanie never forgave Jack. She hates his guts."

"Hmm. But would she murder him for that?"

Dad and I stood shoulder to shoulder, watching the crowd.

"There's only one way to find out. Let's go chat her up. Wait, you've got some chocolate on your face. Right side." I wiped, and he balled up his paper napkin. Finally, the crumb had worked its way out of his goatee. "Remember when you were little, and I used to clean your face with napkins?"

I grimaced. "I remember you used to lick the napkin and wipe my face, which is the grossest thing ever. Here. Throw mine away too."

He did, and we threaded our way through groups of people deep into heated conversations about the monkeys. I knew Dad yearned to be a part of each discussion. He was that passionate about the monkeys. But I also knew that he couldn't let go of a mystery.

Neither could I, truth be told.

I kept my eye on Noah as we approached Joanie. He was chatting with two City Council members, and his back was to me. He was smart enough to know when I was sleuthing, and I wanted to conceal my investigation.

Chapter Eight

"Peter Lewis, you big smooch of a man."

Joanie Clarke spotted my dad and her eyes lit up. Her demeanor was either entirely fake, or she had an enormous crush on my father. Either way, I felt a visceral discomfort. I knew that Dad was a desirable prospect in the over-fifty demographic here on the island, but I preferred not to be reminded of that fact.

Joanie pulled Dad into a hug while never taking her eyes off me. "This must be your daughter, Lana. I've heard so much about you over the years, dear. You're practically a local celebrity."

What did that mean? Because I'd been a journalist in Miami? Because I ran Perkatory? Or because I'd now been involved in four untimely deaths?

"Nice to meet you." I smiled.

She turned back to Dad and playfully swatted his arm. Her voice had the va-va-voom tone of an old screen siren. "You rabble rouser, you. Standing up and speaking out of turn when the mayor was trying to make his presentation."

Dad and Joanie chatted about the monkeys for a few minutes, which gave me time to size her up.

She wore a dark blue pantsuit that hugged her thin frame, and her hair was pulled into a neat bun. As she spoke, the light bounced off the colorful, beaded necklace she wore, drawing attention to her perfectly unlined face. Her age could have been anywhere between forty and sixty.

Her hair was a bright red, coiffed to perfection yet oddly out of place, like a bright flame amid the ashes.

That's when I zoned in on one detail: she didn't have pierced ears. Her lobes were unmarred by holes, unusual for a woman these days. I flashed back to the earring in the dirt at the garden.

Could she have murdered Jack? She didn't seem like the type to set foot in a garden, much less wear twee-looking earrings in the shape of watering cans. Plus, from the look of her jewelry—the colorful necklace, along with a stack of matching bracelets and many silver rings—something told me she wasn't partial to gold.

"Can you believe the news about Jack Daggitt?" Dad said this with the casual tone of someone remarking about the weather.

Joanie pressed a well-tended hand—French manicure, square-shaped nails—against her chest. "Tragic. He was such a good man, always fought on the right side of every issue."

When she saw the looks of confusion on our faces, she followed up quickly with, "Well, most issues. We certainly had our disagreements. But I admired him deeply. And between the three of us . . ."

Her eyes twinkled and Dad and I leaned in.

"Jack and I had a little fling some years back, when I was single. Is that too much TMI?"

Dad shook his head enthusiastically. He lived for this sort of stuff. "There's never too much TMI, that's my motto."

It wasn't mine, however, and I braced myself for more cringey revelations.

"He was a great lover," she whispered, loud enough for others nearby to hear and laugh.

I gasped, not because I was scandalized that a middle-aged woman was discussing her sex life. I had startled myself with a memory.

Joanie had a fling with Fabrizio, my late barista. Well, at least according to Dad. Somehow, I'd forgotten that salacious detail. Then again, Fab had flings with half the island's female population, except for me. Still, the cross-pollination of the two deaths, with Joanie in the mix of both, was intriguing.

And way creepy, because I didn't want, or need, to know about anyone's sex life. If I desired that, I could read a romance novel.

"Wow" was all I could muster saying. "Well, then."

Joanie winked at me. "You're dating the chief. He's a smoke show. You know exactly what I mean."

I opened and closed my mouth, then opened it again. "I guess so?"

"And speak of the devil! Look who's here, the handsome Chief Garcia himself," Dad boomed.

I breathed out a sigh of relief that Noah was interrupting this strange conversation, but then I stilled. Surely, he'd know that I was poking around about Jack.

Noah's mirthful eyes looked from me, to Dad, to Joanie, and back to me. "What are y'all talking about?"

"Oh, nothing." I latched onto his arm.

"We're discussing you opening a charter boat business," Dad said, and Joanie's eyes widened.

"Are you opening one? I could give you lots of business," she gushed.

Noah shook his head. "Not yet, folks. Don't get your hopes up of getting me off the force."

Sensing more conversation about Noah's personal life was ahead, I tugged on his arm. "Noah, babe, I need to ask you a question about Saturday. Do you have a minute alone before the meeting starts again?"

"Of course." He grinned. "Let's step over here and let Mrs. Clarke and your dad chitchat."

We booked it over to the side of the room. Hopefully no one would interrupt us. Hopefully Joanie Clarke wouldn't eat my dad alive, like a praying mantis. I let out a huge sigh. "Thanks for saving me. That was super weird. I don't even have anything to ask you. Sorry my dad keeps trying to get you to leave the force."

"Why was it weird?" His brows knit together.

"Joanie was talking about her sex life."

He grimaced. "People reveal the wildest and most inappropriate things to you."

"You don't even know." We both chuckled.

"Cupcake, I do have something to tell you about Saturday. My mom's not going to be alone."

"Oh?"

"She's bringing my sister. Will it be a problem to set another place at the table?"

I pasted on a smile as a weak current of fear ran through me. I clapped my hands together as if I loved the idea of feeding more people. "Of course not. I've bought plenty of food, I'll make an extra lasagna so we're sure to have enough."

I hadn't bought squat yet.

"You're a doll. I'd kiss you if we weren't in public."

"Tease." I winked at him. "Well, I'm going to get going."

"You're not going to stay for the fireworks during public comment?"

"Uh." Usually, public comment was the entire reason people attended these meetings. I didn't want Noah to know I'd come here specifically to snoop around, and I wanted to get home to freak out in private about the upcoming dinner. "I was only stopping by to say hi to Dad, actually. I didn't intend on staying long."

Not exactly a lie.

"Oh, gotcha. Well, I'll see you tomorrow. I expect this will go late."

We squeezed each other's hands and parted. I found Dad still chatting with Joanie about the monkeys.

"Hey, I'm going to take off. Text me when you get home, so I know you're safe," I told Dad.

"What a good daughter," Joanie gushed.

I smiled. Little did she know that Dad was pumping her for information, and he'd give me a full debrief later. "Nice meeting you."

I walked out and biked home. It was becoming clearer that Jack's death wasn't something I should delve into. Not only was I not in the right headspace, but two of the suspects had possible alibis. I also wasn't entirely convinced of Darla's innocence. Her visible agitation earlier in the day combined with her past had left an impression on me, and I wasn't eager to cross her.

And if Darla wasn't the culprit, there was no shortage of other suspects who had complicated feelings about Jack.

* * *

Two hours later, I was snuggling with Stanley on the sofa. A Lifetime movie, something about a mother who didn't want her son to marry a woman, so she turned to murder (naturally), played softly in the background.

I had a notebook on my lap and my favorite pen and had finished my shopping list. It was nine at night, and I pondered whether to drive to the all-night Walmart on the mainland.

It was a bit of a haul. I groaned aloud. "What should I do, Stanley?"

He responded by rolling onto his back and snoring.

"You don't care about any of it. Your belly's full, you're warm, you're with your dog momma. Little muppet." I smoothed the front of his lion mane with my hand. Stanley was my first dog, and I wasn't sure if I'd ever laid eyes on such an adorable creature. Sometimes I couldn't believe I shared my home with that much cuteness.

A sharp knock on the door startled both of us. Stanley flipped over to standing on his four paws, and I jumped up.

It must be Noah. No one else comes over this late.

Stanley launched himself off the sofa, barking. His lion mane had gotten flattened from all the sleeping, and at the moment he looked as though he had a cross between a bowl cut and a mullet. I made a mental note to fluff up his fur before Saturday's dinner so he wouldn't look like a weird dog version of George Washington.

I made my way to the front of the house and peered out a side window. Living in Miami for years meant I always locked all windows and doors, and never opened without checking first.

It was Dad.

I opened the door with a relieved exhale, and Stanley accosted his leg. Dad swept the dog into his arms and walked inside.

"I found out some wild information," he said. "Better get out that whiteboard."

"Oh, no. Not the whiteboard. Not at this hour, Dad." During the last murder on the island, Dad had dragged out Mom's old whiteboard from the detritus in the garage so we could easily keep track of suspects.

"It's essential. Come on, don't you want to solve this case? I heard Darla asked you to clear her name."

"Who told you that?"

He mumbled something about his "sources," which could only have been Erica. My phone chimed from the sofa. "Hang on. It's like Grand Central in here tonight. I never do anything on a Monday night. Jeez."

It was a text from Erica, a photo of a succulent planted in the hollow back of a plastic toy stegosaurus.

What are you up to?

Dad came here after the meeting. He wants to get out the white-board, I texted.

Be right over with Joey. Put on some coffee.

There was no stopping this train now. I looked at Dad, who'd made himself comfy on the sofa. Stanley was in his lap, grooming his goatee.

"Erica and Joey are on their way over. I'm going to put on coffee while you . . ."—I shook my head, knowing this would unleash more weirdness on a night when I should be focused on buying groceries—"get the whiteboard from the garage or the spare room or wherever you left it."

"That's the spirit, munchkin," he cried.

"How was the rest of the monkey meeting?" I fluffed up a pillow on the sofa.

Dad pulled the corners of his mouth into a grimace. "The mayor asked Noah to escort a pro-primate woman out of the meeting. She tried to handcuff herself to the railing on the side of the stage as a protest."

"That's kinda weird." Probably it was best if I didn't get Dad too far into the monkey vortex, so I went into the kitchen, saying that I was getting snacks ready for everyone.

The next twenty minutes were a flurry of activity. Dad unearthed the whiteboard, which still had notes from the last untimely death.

We'd collectively investigated the demise of Gus Bailey, my next-door neighbor, because Erica had been a prime suspect.

While Dad erased the board, I brewed a pot of Perkatory house blend and set out a batch of chocolate cake pops that I'd made yesterday. I liked to always have them around in case I needed a backup snack for the café.

Erica and Joey arrived, toting their succulent dinosaurs. It hadn't taken them long to get here from their class, since Devil's Beach was so small.

Stanley did his duty by barking, excitedly spinning in circles, and begging for treats. I'd recently bought him a bag of turkey meatballs specially formulated for dogs, and to keep him calm while we talked, I cut two up and put them in his bowl.

Everyone was assembled in the living room in front of the whiteboard when I brought in mugs of coffee and the cake pops on a tray. I'd added a bottle of Kahlua for good measure, since we might need the brace of alcohol.

"Look at this," Joey said. "Exactly what we need after all that Scotch."

"You drank Scotch at the succulent class?" I asked.

"Yeah, Scotch, succulents, and stegosauruses." He stated this like the three things went together seamlessly.

Joey was the perfect match for Erica. He had flaming red hair, freckles, tattoos, and piercings in his eyebrows. Tonight he wore skinny black jeans and a gray T-shirt with a bicycle on the front.

He and Erica each took mugs, and she poured slugs of liqueur into the coffee. Dad did the same. I had a mug, but it only contained Kahlua.

It was shaping up to be that kind of evening. The possibility of going to shop on the mainland was a distant memory.

Dad inhaled a cake pop and stood up, brandishing his empty wooden stick in the air. "So, we've convened to discuss the death of Jack Daggitt, may his soul rest in peace."

"Why are we being so formal?" I asked.

"Shh," Joey said, leaning forward. "Go on, Peter."

Dad gave us a recap about Jack, probably for Joey's benefit since he was the most engaged listener and the least informed.

"Who would kill an eighty-year-old man in a tomato patch?" Dad asked dramatically.

"Who, indeed," I intoned.

Dad used the red marker to write the word SUSPECTS on the board, then underlined it twice.

"Darla," I called out, and Dad wrote her name at the top. "Also, Joanie Clarke."

"The one who did the nasty with Fabrizio?" Erica piped up.

I turned to her. "How did you know about that?"

"He told me." She gestured toward Dad, who shrugged and paused.

"After Lana left the meeting tonight, Joanie told me she has an alibi for the day of Jack's murder. She and her husband were in Miami at a real estate conference. She claims there are live videos of her on Facebook at the event."

"Let's make a second list, then, for suspects with alibis. Let's put Olivia on that list too. She has an alibi, but she definitely didn't like Jack at all."

I quickly filled Erica in on Olivia and Joanie, while Dad wrote a few more things on the board.

"I think we need to consider his daughter. Does anyone know her name?" Dad tapped on the board.

Erica shook her head, but I recalled someone had mentioned the daughter's name. I racked my brain, trying to remember who. I glanced at Joey, whose eyes were shut. Stanley was wedged between Joey's leg and the sofa arm, and he was also in slumber mode.

"Is Joey asleep?" I asked Erica.

"Yeah, he's had a long day. The succulents took a lot out of us."

"What? How?" I let out a laugh.

"It's stressful deciding which succulent to choose for your planter."

"Fair enough."

We turned back to Dad.

"Okay, so we have four suspects so far. Darla, Olivia, Joanie, and the unnamed daughter," Dad said.

I raised my hand, and Dad pointed the marker at me, like we were in class. "Five. Five suspects. Beau from the dog grooming salon. Jack fired him from walking his dog. And we need to find out what happened to Jack's pug, Bella Pugosi, after Jack died. And Beau told me the daughter's name. Willa."

Dad nodded gravely and added Willa and Beau's names to the list of suspects. Then he wrote "B. Pugosi" and circled it.

Erica took a gulp of her coffee. "This is great and all, but I doubt if these are all the people who wanted Jack dead. In my experience, if a person is mean or terrible, more than two or three or four people want to unalive them."

I nodded in agreement. "We need to find out who else knew Jack. So—"

"No," Dad interjected. "We need to piece together Jack's final days, find out who he had contact with."

"That's what I was about to say. The method of death—fentanyl in a syringe, injected in the back—strikes me as a premeditated murder. But the location—in public, in the community garden—appears to be spontaneous. Like the killer couldn't handle seeing Jack walk the earth anymore."

Everyone nodded at my assessment. Well, everyone but Joey and Stanley, who were snoring by now.

"What's our plan?" Erica said.

I tipped my head back and groaned. My shopping list and Saturday night dinner loomed large in my mind. "Should we even have a plan? Why are we doing this?"

"Because Darla needs us." Erica elbowed my side.

"Because we're curious," Dad said.

I stood up. "Are those good enough reasons, though?"

Both Dad and Erica looked at me like I'd sprouted a third arm. A snore ripped through the air, and for a moment I thought it was Stanley—his brachycephalic shih tzu snout meant that he sometimes sounded like a lawn mower when he slept.

"Joey's always this loud," Erica explained.

"Here's my concern." I began to pace the living room. "I'm worried that Darla did kill Jack. She has the violent past. She's friendly, but also very private. I've known her for almost a year, she comes in to Perkatory nearly every day, and yet I don't know anything about her personal life. I didn't know she had a boyfriend until our conversation today. What if she's asking me—well, us—for help to deflect from her guilt?"

Dad nodded slowly while stroking his goatee. "That's a distinct possibility. Sometimes the guiltiest people are the loudest. The squeaky wheel syndrome."

"Is that really a syndrome, or are you making that up?" Erica asked.

"He's making it up. I, for one, don't want to aid a guilty person," I said, going to the board and circling Darla's name in yellow marker.

Erica piped up. "Then we have to investigate Darla first. If she's innocent, she'll be forthcoming with us. Once we clear her name, we can proceed on to others."

I sighed and looked at her. There was no way I had time for any of this, but I was already up to my knees in curiosity, and I loathed unanswered questions. "Then I guess that's where we begin. With Darla."

Chapter Nine

Tuesday dawned, bringing an increase in both the humidity and the heat. Inside Perkatory, Erica and I were cool and composed as we waited for Darla to arrive at her usual hour.

She sauntered in, like every other day, wearing her all-white uniform from the saltwater taffy store. She looked a bit like a nurse, especially considering she also wore a jaunty white cap to complete the ensemble, and seemingly had no shame or discomfort in walking around in that getup.

Then again, it was Devil's Beach, and anywhere there were locals, there was a possibility of people looking rather odd. There were the people like Darla, who worked various service jobs and had to wear themed uniforms. Then you had the locals who dressed like pirates for fun.

Nobody batted an eye when she walked in.

"Hey, all you crazy cats and kittens," she said to Erica and me.

"Hey, hey, hey," Erica said, and I gave a little wave.

"Your usual?" I pointed to the espresso machine.

She nodded. I busied myself with her Americano, then handed it to her. Because she had a backpack slung over one shoulder and was carrying two smaller tote bags, she had to shift those into one hand to accept the coffee.

"I've been thinking about what we discussed yesterday. Can we all chat?" I looked from Darla to Erica.

Dad was also here as part of the plan, to take over the counter while Erica and I met with Darla.

"Sure, sure!" Her eyes widened with excitement.

I wiped my hands on my apron, and went to the table where Dad was sitting, reading the *Devil's Beach Beacon*. "Hey, could you take over for a while?" I asked.

He nodded and made a beeline for the register.

I stood next to Darla and put my hand on her arm. "Let's go into my office, upstairs. That way we don't be interrupted."

"Good call," she said.

The three of us left the café through the back door and trooped up the steep, old wooden stairs in silence. Perkatory's office was on the second floor of the building that my great-grandfather had constructed decades ago. It was once a hotel, but now the upper three floors were empty, save for the office and a room I used for café storage.

"Kinda spooky up here," Darla commented as I fiddled with the ancient sticky lock on the office door. Fixing it and cleaning up the second floor were on my agenda. When I moved back, Dad and I had discussed renting studios to artists up here but had tabled the issue while we got Perkatory on solid ground.

I finally unlocked the door. "I used to think this building was haunted when I was little. One entire year I refused to come upstairs with my parents because I was convinced ghosts lived here."

Erica snapped her fingers. "We should do a haunted tour of this building at Halloween."

"You might be onto something there." It was an excellent idea. For now, though, we needed to focus on something even creepier—whether the woman sitting on the sofa in my office was a murderer.

"So," Erica said, slapping her knees. She was next to Darla, who was arranging her three bags on the floor near her feet.

"So," Darla added.

"We've taken your case under consideration," Erica began, making our sleuthing operation sound far more organized than it actually was.

I piped up. "We need to know some details before we make a final decision on whether to help you." I said this in my most even, matter-of-fact tone, the one I used to use as a reporter when I told a source bad news. "We must know exactly what you were doing the week before Jack died, and where you were the day he died."

Darla looked at Erica, who nodded. Then she glanced to me. She swallowed, hard. "Wow. Well. Where should we start?"

"At the beginning," Erica said softly.

"Mind if I take notes?" I pointed to a yellow legal pad.

"I guess not." Darla shook her head, then swore aloud. "I can't believe this is happening to me again."

"What do you mean by 'again'?" Erica probed.

Darla huffed out a breath. "Another brush with the law. The first time, well, the second time too, I wasn't entirely innocent. But now is a different story."

"I'm sure this is all a misunderstanding." I tapped on the pad, wanting to get this over with, mostly because I didn't want Dad to be alone downstairs during a crush of customers. "Tell us everything from the start."

"Well, I was born into a poor family in Ohio, the last of four children," Darla began.

Erica and I looked at each other, helplessly.

"Not the very beginning. Maybe kick it off when you met Jack," I said gently.

She nodded and hauled in a shaky breath. "Right. Okay. I managed to snag a plot at Peas on Earth right when I moved here three years ago and was growing my mushrooms there. I met Jack at the garden. We were both on the water committee one year, and we got along pretty well. I knew he could be opinionated, but he seemed to like me. At least until I became president not too long ago."

"Who was president before you?" I asked. "And when were you elected?"

"November. And the previous president was Chuck McDaniel. Did you know him?"

I tapped the pen on my chin. "Clerk at the post office?"

Darla nodded. "He retired and moved up north. That's why the job was open. I was elected unanimously, even Jack voted for me!"

"Really? What happened?" Erica swung one leg over the other and leaned in. "Did Jack want to be president?"

"No, he'd been president, years ago, and said he didn't have time for that garbage. That's exactly what he said. Didn't have time for that garbage. He was real ornery. That first month, everything was fine. Normal. Then I rewrote the rulebook and a couple of people revolted. Jack and a woman named Rouba. They had problems with some of the new regulations. And looking back, I might have been a little heavy-handed. I tend to fixate on rules and order."

Erica's brow furrowed, as if she couldn't understand the last sentence. No surprise, since Erica was something of a chaos muppet.

Darla continued. "Rouba eventually came around and agreed that we needed more rules. We were having problems with stolen fruit, and people were taking clippings of others' plants, which is a big no-no. Rouba was worried mostly about the seeds she gets from a place in Maine, but after looking into it, I decided they were organic. So we worked it out. But Jack? We really started to have our issues around the new year. Honestly? He seemed to have a problem with a woman in charge. Especially a younger woman. He was fine with me until I started running things."

"That does happen," I said with a sigh.

"I think we've all been in that situation," Erica added.

"Yeah, Jack morphed into a big jerk. He started blasting his vintage boom box, he left hoses out, he ignored me. I tried talking to him, because I was hurt. I thought we were friends, but something snapped in him. I gave him two warnings about the hoses, and then when he left a hose out the third time, that was when I lost it and banned him. I thought it would be the end of the problems, but he was on a mission to destroy me. He posted numerous things on various Facebook forums about me, everywhere from the Devil's Beach page to a community gardening page. Stuff that was totally untrue, like that I participated in age discrimination by banning him. How could that be possible? More than half of the gardeners at Peas on Earth are over sixty!"

These seemed like pretty small potatoes–level issues to me. "Did he ever actually threaten you?"

"Yes. I mean, maybe. One day in late January I found manure in my mailbox. That was a pain in the butt to clean out. I knew it was him."

"Did you report that to police?" I asked.

She shook her head. "Because of my past, I don't like having any contact with the cops."

That was understandable, if not unfortunate for her in this instance. "Anything else with Jack?"

"Someone vandalized a couple of my mushroom logs at the garden. Chopped it up as if it were firewood, then arranged the splinters to look like a middle finger in my plot."

"Back up," I said. "What's a mushroom log?"

Darla held up her hands about a foot apart, like she was holding something. "It's a log that's been injected with mushroom spawn."

"Spawn," Erica repeated.

"Fungal tissue in a carrier medium, usually sawdust. You drill holes in the logs, fill them with the spawn, seal the holes with wax, and wait for the spawn to colonize the log. You can get quite a nice crop going on one log here in Florida, because it's so humid."

I licked my lips. Never had I thought of mushrooms as spawn, and now that I considered it, the whole concept seemed a little creepy and paranormal.

"Here's a photo of what I found. I went to the garden one day about a month ago and this was in the dirt of my sweet potato patch. Whoever did it ripped out several plants, too."

She flashed her cell screen at me, and indeed, wooden splinters were artfully arranged in the shape of a hand giving a middle finger. Assorted full-grown mushrooms were in a little pile, and it was obvious that someone had gone to great lengths to display the foul gesture.

"That's definitely alarming," I said while she showed the image to Erica.

"I did go to the cops about that. I thought I'd have a difficult time getting a restraining order against Jack, but considering all his Facebook posts about me, I didn't. There were dozens of nasty posts, every single one mentioning me. So there was a trail of evidence."

Now I didn't know what to believe. Darla seemed agitated talking about Jack. Her face had grown red, and she repeatedly cleared her throat. There was one thing I hated to ask, but had to. "Where were you on the day his body was found?"

"That's the problem." She swallowed hard, like she was trying to force a lump of tears down her throat. "I was alone, at home. Sunday's my day off from the saltwater taffy shop. I work six days since I'm the manager, but Sunday's my free day, so I slept in and then messed around with my mushrooms, trying to get a new log going."

"You have no alibi? Didn't meet anyone for coffee? Didn't send any emails, didn't make any calls? Didn't post what you had to eat on Instagram?" Erica asked.

Darla dipped her head and shoved her fingers in her short, dirty blonde hair. "I sent Jack a text."

"Why?" I cried. "You had a restraining order against him."

"When I woke up that day, I saw that Jack had posted yet another screed about me, this time on the FAFF Facebook page."

"Faff?" I interrupted.

"Florida Association of Fungi Friends. Jack had practically written a book, saying that I should be kicked out of the group. It's a community that I love, and to imagine the people would think poorly of me because of Jack . . ." She practically spat his name. "I lost it. He knew how to push my buttons."

"What did the text say?"

"I'll read it to you." She tapped on her phone. "'Stand down, old man. You'd better be careful if you write one more word about me.'"

"Mmm." I rubbed my lips together. Her words could be perceived as a threat. A weak one, but a threat nonetheless. Between that and her lack of an alibi, I could understand why police thought she was a suspect. "You have no alibi *and* you sent Jack a vaguely threatening message."

Darla's eyes filled to the brim with tears, and I found a box of tissues on the desk and handed it to her. She took one and dabbed at her face. "Do you understand my problem now?"

Erica and I sighed and nodded in tandem. This was a quandary. Something told me that Darla was innocent, but as a former reporter, I knew to temper my initial reaction.

Killers were often great manipulators.

"Okay, let's get down to brass tacks." Erica slapped her thigh. "Who do you think killed Jack?"

Darla sat up a bit straighter, seemingly bolstered by the question. "There was a guy who had an altercation with him recently."

I perked up. "Oh yeah?"

"A guy named Clay. He's a surfer and Jack saw him littering. They had a big blowup on the beach recently."

"How do you know about this guy?" Darla seemed to be intimately familiar with Jack's altercation, which I found a bit odd.

"Rose Ryan, who has a plot at the garden, was friends with Jack. She's about his age and knew him for decades. She even tried to be a peacemaker between the two of us. You should talk with her for more information. She and Jack met a couple of times a week for tea at her house. She also has an incredible bromeliad crop. She told me about Clay one day when we were both at the garden."

I wrote her name down, and jotted notes about Clay. Probably Dad knew how to contact Rose, where she lived even. Heck, he might even know Clay.

"This is a good start." I clicked my pen.

"Does that mean you're going to look into it?" Darla's eyes widened with hope.

"Ye—" Erica started to say.

I interrupted her. "We need to chat with Rose and some others before we definitively say yes." My voice was firm. I needed to hear from another neutral party about Darla before I gave my final answer.

Darla nodded. "Well, that's something, I guess."

"One more question. Have you ever taken fentanyl?" I asked.

"Isn't that like heroin or morphine?"

I nodded.

"No, never been into drugs. Vodka, yes. Drugs, no." She shrugged.

So Darla and Jack's relationship had only recently gone sour. Now I was more confused than ever. I wondered if her criminal background was as benign as she claimed. Perhaps she was more violent than she was letting on, and had killed Jack. Or she could be totally innocent and telling the truth.

I stood up to signal that this meeting was over. As much as my reporter's soul wanted to dig into this, I had a café to run. Dad was downstairs, alone, and the lunch rush loomed.

"We'll be in touch. Until then, please don't tell anyone we're poking around, okay?"

Darla pantomimed zipping her lips, then gathered her bags.

When we all trooped downstairs, Erica peeled off to use the bathroom. With a sad goodbye and a wave, Darla left. Dad came rushing up to me. "Your eleven o'clock is here."

"My eleven o'clock what?" My mind was filled with thoughts of murder, not Perkatory. It was essential that I got my head back into the game before lunchtime.

Dad touched my shoulder and pointed across the room to the seats next to the window. "A guy who claims he can print photos in foam. On lattes. Sounds like hogwash to me. Want me to send him away?"

I pressed my hand to my forehead. "Oh, crud. I forgot all about that."

"Munchkin," Dad whispered. "A machine that prints photos in foam? Think about it. That must be a scam. That's not possible."

"Dad, it's not. It's a real thing. It's a machine that does the printing."

"You mean like a 3D printer? Why would you want microplastics in coffee?"

I stared at him for a second, wondering how my father's mind worked. "I'll explain later. Let me go meet with him. And when Erica comes out of the bathroom, send her over, because I want her to hear about this."

"Okay, but give me the high sign if the guy's part of a pyramid scheme. Do we need a code word?"

"A code word?"

"Yeah, like if you're in trouble." Dad nodded sagely.

"No. I'm not getting in trouble. I'm talking with a sales rep, in public, in our coffee shop." I swear, Dad was so weird sometimes.

I walked over to the only man at the counter near the window. He was standing in front of an open laptop, with sales brochures, binders, and business cards spread out on the tall wooden surface near the glass.

"Hi, I'm Lana, the co-owner of Perkatory. Thanks for visiting."

The guy turned around. His blue eyes were the first thing I saw. They were the color of ice. The second thing was his mustache. It was deep brown and handlebar-hipster style, curled up at the ends into sharp points. The rest of him looked like a twenty-something dude who listened to obscure, experimental, acoustic music.

"Lana? A pleasure. My name's Fred Pistol, and I'm the head sales rep for L'ARTE."

I dragged a stool over and hopped up. "I'm quite interested in your machine. But I'd like our chief barista to see this too, because her opinion's important to me. She should be over in a couple of minutes."

This was the first time I'd identified Erica as our "chief barista," but I liked it. Maybe I'd order her business cards—she'd almost certainly get a kick out of that.

"While we're waiting, I wanted to show you our new fact sheet. And later, we can fire up the machine and make a few lattes, if you'd like." He pointed to a medium-sized, black, hard-sided carrying case that looked like luggage stashed underneath the counter.

"That's it? I expected it to be larger."

"It's a little bigger than most Keurig home machines. From the looks of your shop setup, you'll have no problem fitting it in."

He handed me a paper and I scanned the words. Most of it was details I already knew, information gleaned from the website. I peeked around for Erica, and found her behind the counter, staring at me.

I waved her over. In response, she waved back at me, and pointed toward the back room.

I lifted my hands, not understanding what she was trying to tell me. She mouthed something unintelligible, then gestured wildly at the back and walked in that direction.

My gaze slid to Fred, who was tapping away on his laptop. Something was up with Erica. "Excuse me, I need to check on something behind the counter. I'm so sorry to do this, but can you give me a couple of minutes?"

"Oh, of course, take your time. The nice gentleman with the goatee behind the counter made me an excellent iced mint mocha, so I'm content." He held up his drink.

"Be right back." I set the paper on the counter and slid off the stool. Then I power-walked into the back room, ignoring Dad, who muttered something about pyramid schemes while I passed him.

I found Erica in the back room, pacing.

"What's going on?" I asked.

"That's Fred Pistol," she said, her eyes flashing.

"That's right. How do you know his name?"

"Know him? I used to date him when I was a barista in Seattle."

By the look on her face, I knew that their relationship hadn't ended well, and that I had a potentially bitter situation on my hands.

Chapter Ten

I took a deep breath and let it out slowly. "Are you sure? His company's from Atlanta."

"One hundred percent. I'd know that stupid mustache anywhere. And how many men are named Fred Pistol?"

"You have a point," I mumbled, marveling that Fred had sported that handlebar mustache for years.

Erica cupped her neck with both hands, a sure sign she was nervous. I hadn't seen her do that since we spotted a snake in a tank, which had triggered her fear of danger noodles.

"I'm missing some key information here. What's the problem? Did you have a bad breakup?"

"Yeah. Very bad. Rotten. It was complicated."

"Okay, but how long ago were you together?"

She lifted a shoulder. "We dated for six months, eight years ago."

"That's a hella long time ago. You're practically a different person, and so is he. I'm sure he'll be delighted to see you. Maybe you two can be friends? Water under the bridge, and all that."

"What if your ex walked in?" She crossed her arms over her chest.

"Well, he did, a few months ago. You met him. You saw how sleazy he was." My ex-husband, a national TV correspondent for a network, had oozed in one day when my barista Fabrizio had been found dead. My ex had been doing a story on the murder, and seeing him on my turf had been as unwelcome as sand fleas on a nudist beach.

She let out a groan.

"Look, we don't have to meet with him. I can ask him to leave. Or I can meet with him alone."

"No, let's do this. I'm a professional, he's a professional, and we're here to evaluate a project."

She nodded once. I nodded right back. "That's the spirit. We'll do this quick and get back to the real issue: how we're going to poke around on Jack's death."

That seemed to make her feel better because she met my gaze with a grin. "Let's hustle."

I reached for her arm. "Wait. I have one question. Is his name really Fred Pistol?"

"Frederick Pistol the Third, to be exact. His family's from old shipping money in Seattle. He never needed to work but slummed it as a barista." She puckered her mouth as if she'd bitten into a lemon rind.

"Good to know. C'mon."

We walked out of the back room and from behind the counter together, with determined expressions. I imagined us looking badass, like crime-fighting partners in a movie, at least until Dad stopped us with a wild look in his eyes.

"Guess what? Just heard from my ranger buddy at the Swamp. One of the female monkeys had a baby!"

"That's great, Dad. We'll talk about it in a little while." I squeezed his shoulder and kept walking. Lately he'd taken to blurting out random facts, often about primates or space exploration.

Erica and I moved toward Fred Pistol III.

"Okay," I said heartily. "Sorry for the interruption. This is my head barista, Erica—"

Fred turned. His gaze immediately went to her face. I could tell she was trying to keep a scowl from marring her expression, but instead it looked as though she was horribly constipated.

"Erica Penmark? Is that you?" he whispered.

"Never thought you'd see me again, did you?"

Fred stammered and grunted for a few awkward sentences, and I almost felt bad for him. The weight of Erica's glare was heavy.

"Perhaps now is a good time for a live demo of your machine," I said gently.

"Yeah, let's do that." By now, Fred was shaking.

"When did you stop being a barista, Frederick?" The way Erica said his name, like she was spitting bullets, put me on edge. Erica had a temper.

He picked up the hard-sided case from the floor, then placed it back down. "I stayed on at the café in Seattle for a couple of years after you left. Then I started working for a wholesaler. Last month I got a job with L'ARTE and they gave me the southeast territory. I live in Atlanta now."

"Hmph," was all Erica could muster.

"What do you need from us for your machine? Milk? Espresso? Water?" I wanted to steer this situation back to neutral territory.

"Uh. Yeah. Can you make a plain latte for me?" His eyes skittered to Erica. "Please? With lots of foam?"

"I've got this." She stomped off. Maybe if I could keep her busy making coffee, this tension might be defused some. I think I heard her mutter "I'll give you foam" under her breath, but I decided to ignore it.

I clapped my hands. "Let's find a place to put that machine. Follow me."

I led him behind the counter, where Erica gave him the stink eye and Dad appraised him warily. Well, this was going well.

"Here's a perfect spot." I gathered four bottles of syrup into my arms and shoved them on a shelf. "You'll need power, right?"

Fred nodded and set the case on the counter. He flicked open the latches, and inside was a machine that resembled a home coffee maker in size and shape. Gingerly, he took it out and plugged it in.

While Erica and Dad watched from afar, Fred showed me the basics. "In under a minute, the L'ARTE will customize coffees. The image is actually made of tiny coffee bean drops. They preserve the natural flavor and quality of the coffee."

"Excuse me," Dad said loudly.

I shut my eyes for a millisecond. Oh dear.

"Yes, sir?" Fred said, seemingly relieved to talk to someone other than Erica.

"This is my father, Peter Lewis. He's the co-owner of Perkatory."

They shook hands. "Nice café you've got here," Fred said.

"Is this . . ."—Dad waved his hand at the machine—"a pyramid scheme?"

"Excuse me?"

"A pyramid scheme. A scam. Are you going to try to make us part of your multilevel marketing downline? I saw a program about stuff like this. *American Greed*, it's called. Lots of these companies are in Florida, you know."

Fred looked at me, helpless. "No, I'm selling the machines outright. No scam. If you do buy one, you get a year's free customer support and fifty image templates."

Dad made a noise that sounded like a low growl and stepped back.

"So, show me how we get these images onto the drink." It was hard to remain peppy, but I tried.

"Here's your latte, extra foam." Erica plunked a drink in one of our large, robin's-egg blue cups in front of Fred. "Nice and bitter. No sugar."

"Ooookay. First, we need the app." He took the phone out of his pocket. "I hope you don't mind but I downloaded your café's logo."

Dad and Erica stood shoulder to shoulder, united in their skepticism, but for different reasons.

"Perfect," I chirped.

He swiped and tapped on his cell, then flashed the screen at me. "You can customize the themes and images."

Taking the mug, he set it on the tray in the bottom of the contraption, then pressed a button. The tray lifted the mug up a few inches and the machine whirred and whistled. A minute later, the beeps and bloops stopped, and the tray lowered.

Left behind was a mug of coffee with a perfect replica of our logo—a coffee cup, a palm tree, and our café's name. It was surprisingly cute.

"Whoa," I said. "That looks adorable. Didn't think it would be that sharp."

Dad stared, open-mouthed. "No way, man."

Erica rolled her eyes and went to the register, where a customer was waiting. That was Fred's cue to speak more freely, and in a more relaxed tone. He explained to Dad and me how the entire drink flow worked, from the pod of tiny coffee drops that created the image, to the app, to the ability for customers to upload their own pictures.

"Customers of other cafés share pictures on social media like you wouldn't believe," he said. "And let me tell you one more thing: if you get this, you'll be the first coffee shop in Florida to have one. Given Perkatory's location, I suspect tourists will come from all over to buy a printed latte."

Dad looked at me and raised his brows. I could tell he was interested.

"Let me ask you something," Dad said.

"Of course, sir."

"What if someone wants us to print an obscene message, something rude, or something offensive?"

"You can set guidelines for your customers," Fred replied. "I have one shop in New Orleans that doesn't allow anything racist, sexist, religious, or political."

"How about anything to do with a cheating boyfriend? Should we ban that kind of thing, too?" Erica called out.

The uncomfortable looks on everyone's faces told me that I needed to wrap up this meeting. "This is an interesting idea. Is there any way we could test drive the machine for a week?"

Fred nodded. "Absolutely. This one is yours for a full fourteen days."

"Does that mean you'll be back? Oh goody." Erica spat while frothing milk. "Aren't we lucky?"

"Uh, you could always send it to me in the mail. Postage paid by us, of course." I sensed that wasn't the typical protocol for L'ARTE, but his offer had more to do with Erica's frostiness.

"Lana, perhaps you and I can have dinner and I can give you a tutorial with the instruction manual," Fred said.

I was about to agree when Erica came over. She gestured with our stainless-steel barista spoon. Normally it was used for evenly mixing drinks, but the way she was brandishing it made me wonder if she was going to thwack him across the face with it.

The last thing we needed was an assault at Perkatory.

"No. Lana and I will read the manual and figure it out ourselves." She smacked the spoon part of the tool in her palm.

Her tone was so sharp that I didn't dare cross her. "Fred, we're great with technology. I'm sure your instructions are detailed and we can sort it out."

Fred's eyes went to the spoon, then to Erica's face. He nodded. "Absolutely. But feel free to email me with any questions."

While Erica and Fred were having a stare-down contest, Dad was hovering over the logo-emblazoned coffee. He bent over to sniff it, then waved his hand over it as if he were casting a spell.

"It's like magic," he whispered.

"I think we're done here," Erica announced. She still hadn't blinked while staring at Fred.

"Oh. Yes. Yes! I should be going." Fred grabbed his phone and jammed it in his pocket. "Nice to meet you all, and to, ah, see you again, Erica."

"Can't say the same for you." She set the spoon down and folded her arms.

Fred disappeared from the café quicker than a Pabst Blue Ribbon at a NASCAR race. While Dad continued to inspect the machine, touching it hesitantly as if it might explode, I turned to Erica.

"What happened between you two? That was really weird. I've never seen you act like that with anyone, not even the customer who spit the cupcake on the counter."

Her nostrils flared. "After we'd dated for six months, Fred slept with my best friend."

My hand flew to my mouth. "Erica, why didn't you say that? I'd have sent him away without even saying hello. He's trash for doing that to you."

"I think the machine's pretty cool, honestly. And I'm over him. Let's face it, he's no Joey."

Now I understood her visceral reaction when Fred mentioned going to dinner with me. "What a jerk. You should've told me. Now I want to throat punch him. I'll always take your side, you know that, right? Ovaries before brovaries. Uteruses before duderuses."

She finally smiled, and I folded her into a hug. "No man's going to come between us."

A few minutes later, we decided that the machine was too much to deal with this afternoon, what with the business of Jack's murder, and moved the contraption to the back room, vowing to spend a few hours later in the week figuring it out.

"After Saturday night, we'll become masters of the printed latte," I said, while watching Dad carefully tote the machine in the hard-sided case into the back room. "I've got way too much on my plate now."

While Dad was in the back, I leaned into Erica. "Let's make sure Dad doesn't use that machine by himself. I think he's still a little confused by it."

"Yeah, I heard him use the word 'alchemy,' so I don't know if he understands how it really works."

When Dad emerged from the back, I gathered the two of them into a huddle. It was a slow part of the early afternoon, and now I could talk freely about Jack.

But Dad was still on the topic of the machine. "I think we should have our own slogans for the foam art. Like "every silver lining's got a touch of gray."

"Isn't that a Grateful Dead lyric?" Erica asked, laughing. I was glad she wasn't still angry about Fred Pistol.

"Or, how about this? From my favorite EDM DJ: Drum and bass will save the world." He swept his hand in an arc in the air.

"What? No. We will not print anything about drums and bass. Let me tell you what Darla said to me and Erica."

I gave him the Cliff Notes version of our conversation, with Erica interjecting important details.

"So, do you know this Rose Ryan lady?" I asked Dad.

"Of course. She grows the most beautiful orchids in Florida. Rumor has it she stole some orchids from the Everglades, but the federal charges were dropped."

"Does anyone on this island not have a criminal record?" Erica asked, cracking up.

I snickered. "Give us her address. Erica and I are going to pay her a visit today."

Chapter Eleven

When we finished our shift and were relieved by Barbara and Heidi, the other baristas, Erica and I stopped in to give Stanley some love and a bathroom break, then moved on to Rose Ryan's place in my car.

Like everything else on Devil's Beach, Rose's home wasn't far—but it was a world away from my working-class downtown street of older bungalows.

"Whoa, I didn't know this even existed," Erica remarked as we drove up Gulf Way. Unlike the rest of the island, the homes here were on a small hill. Well, a hill by Florida standards, which meant about twenty feet above sea level. For the people who lived on this street, that elevation meant the difference between catastrophic flooding during a hurricane and no water at all.

These were the luckiest of the lucky, the richest of the rich. This was what people up north dreamed of when they fantasized about moving here.

Even the Florida sun seemed to shine a little brighter on this side of the island. The homes were all newer mansions, mostly blocky modernist buildings full of angles and wide expanses of glass overlooking the glittering Gulf of Mexico. Some properties had sloping stairs to the beach.

I wasn't a fan of the architecture, but the view sure was pretty.

We pulled into Rose's driveway, which was impenetrable with a massive iron gate.

"Crud. What are we going to do now?" Erica asked.

I pulled up to a speaker-slash-intercom and rolled down my window while summoning my former reporter bravado. "We're going to ask politely to go inside. Sometimes the simplest method works the best."

My finger found the buzzer, and the intercom crackled to life. "The orchids are gone. Go away."

The voice was obviously that of an older woman. Erica and I glanced at each other. "Hi, I'm Lana Lewis, Peter Lewis's daughter. I'm here with a friend and wanted to chat with Ms. Ryan about Jack Daggitt. Peter suggested we stop by."

"You're not here about the orchids?"

"No. Definitely not."

She sighed. "Okay, then I guess you can come in."

"Not the most welcome of greetings," Erica observed under her breath.

I didn't waste any time driving into the property when the gate swung open. To say that Erica and I were shocked by what was inside was an understatement.

"This is wild," she said as we gawked at the riot of tropical plants lining the driveway. It looked more like a rainforest than a beach home. Plants with leaves the size of sheets mingled with vines wrapped around palm trees with wide fronds. A couple of live oaks were so tall and intertwined with Spanish moss that the growth canopied the road. I slowed so we could get a better look, and thank goodness

I did, because a creature with a pointy nose casually strolled across the asphalt.

"I haven't seen an armadillo on the island in years," I said.

Erica leaned forward and held onto the dash. "Is that what that is?"

"Yeah, see his roly-poly body and long snout? Does he freak you out?" I wasn't sure if an armadillo was a reptile, but it was prehistoric-looking enough that it might trigger Erica's phobia.

She scrunched up her face. "No, he's kind of cute. I'm okay with him. We can coexist peacefully. Hey, little dude."

When we finally arrived at the house—it was a long driveway, surprisingly so for a home on the island—we were no less shocked by the building. It was a small, thatch-roofed cottage, with a stone façade, oversized chimney, and a brick pathway leading to a wooden door surrounded by a vine of some sort.

It was definitely out of character on a tropical island.

"This must be the only English cottage–style home in town," Erica said, once again impressing me with her breadth of useless, yet interesting, trivia.

We climbed out of the car, and as we walked up the brick path, we were immediately hit with the scent of jasmine, probably coming from the vine that crawled over the front door. It had hundreds of delicate white flowers, and Erica sneezed.

It was then that I noticed the plantings around the cottage were more of an English variety, in keeping with the architecture style.

I knocked on the white door, and it swung open. Standing before us was a small elderly woman who probably didn't reach five feet tall. She wore jeans rolled up to the calves, Keds sneakers, and a pink sweatshirt with a fluffy white kitten on the front. Her hair was a whitish blue.

"You must be Peter's daughter." She looked me up and down. "You have his nose."

Without thinking, I squeezed the tip of my nose. Did I have Dad's nose? I'd always thought his was on the large side. "Nice to meet you. I co-own Perkatory with my father, and this is Erica Penmark, my friend and chief barista at the café."

Erica sneezed again. "I think I'm allergic to this jasmine."

"Well, let's go inside, then, and you can tell me what you want. As long as you're not trying to get my orchids, you can come in." Ms. Ryan's tone was best described as annoyed. The skin around her eyes was crinkled from decades of laughter, but the color of her eyes was a clear, bright blue.

We followed her through the door, and the interior matched the exterior—it was as if we'd been transported to rural England. The entire vibe made me feel slightly dizzy. One minute we were in a jungle, the next, Cornwall.

She led us to a gorgeous, good-sized room with one wall made up of floor-to-ceiling bookshelves surrounding a stone fireplace. "Would you ladies like some tea?"

"That would be wonderful, Ms. Ryan." My gaze went to the exposed dark wooden beams on the ceiling.

"Call me Rose, please. I had this place built as a replica of my first home in England," she said. "I worked there for many years as a botanist, you know."

"Fascinating," Erica said, walking over to the bookshelves.

"We're here to discuss Jack Daggitt, from the community garden. We understand you were friends." Might as well come right out with it, in case she wanted to kick us out and conserve her tea stash.

Rose nodded thoughtfully, as if she'd expected someone to stop by and ask about Jack. "Fine. Make yourselves comfortable, I'll go put on the kettle." She walked out.

I joined Erica at the bookcase and scanned the titles.

"Hard to believe she was facing federal charges," Erica said out the corner of her mouth.

"No kidding."

We wandered around the room, taking in the details. Everywhere you looked there was something unique and pretty, from the stacks of coffee table books about orchids to the vintage-looking palm tree prints on the walls, to the small, silver frames containing old black and white photos on the mantel.

Whatever Rose Ryan had done during her lifetime, she'd done it with class and a hefty dose of good interior design taste. I thought I'd been doing well to hang a few pieces of art on one wall in the living room, but now that I thought about my space compared to here, my home resembled that of a recent college graduate.

One who lived like a goblin approximately half the time. Okay, most of the time.

This thought sent me into a bit of a panic spiral, and I started to wonder if I had enough days to redecorate before Noah's family arrived. I'd opened my mouth to ask Erica her opinion when Rose returned, carrying a silver tray, a tea set, and a plate stacked with cookies.

"As you can see, I'm something of an Anglophile." She set the tray on a wide coffee table facing the fireplace. It was covered in a delicate lace cloth. Everything about Rose and this place was beautiful, and I quickly checked her ears.

No earrings. No piercings.

Interesting.

"Being an Anglophile is pretty cool, especially when it comes to tea and gardens. We all have our preferences," Erica said, eyeing the cookies. "Heck, I live on a boat."

Erica and I sank into the overstuffed, blue-and-coral striped sofa, and Rose sat in a matching chair, looking poised and formal even in her casual clothes. Next to her, Erica and I likely looked like sprawling slobs, considering we were still in our work outfits.

"So." Rose poured us each a cup of tea in China that looked both antique and expensive. "You're here to discuss Jack. I was wondering when someone would come around asking about him. The cops sure haven't, but what can you expect from a force as small as Devil's Beach?"

My first inclination was to bristle—after all, I am loyal to Noah and know he's a diligent officer—but this was an opportunity.

"What can you tell us about Jack? I understand that you were close friends." I picked up my cup and saucer and eyed the liquid. I didn't hate tea, but it wasn't my favorite.

"Cream? Sugar?" she asked.

I shook my head, and Erica said yes. As Rose used tongs to pick up a cube of sugar and dropped it into Erica's tea, she said, "Jack was the most difficult man I'd ever met. More difficult than any of my four husbands."

This woman was a story herself.

"Were you two . . ." Erica raised her hands, and for a second I thought she'd pantomime the universal sign for sex, but instead she bounced the sides of her index fingers against one another.

"Oh no, no. I'd never sleep with Jack. Too old. I'm something of a cougar. My current beau is twenty years younger at sixty-two." Her chortle was infectious, and I couldn't help but grin.

"You are living my dream," Erica said, reaching for a cookie. "I wanna be you when I grow up."

Rose tittered. "Jack and I shared a love of gardening. He admired what I do with orchids—I have an entire greenhouse on my property out back—and I appreciated his knowledge of Florida growing seasons. We were members of the local garden club and were kicked out at the same time. For different reasons, though.

That club is different from the community garden. I'm not sure if you're aware."

"May I ask why you were both kicked out of the club?" This was too fascinating.

"Oh, I was given the heave-ho because of the federal indictment. Which I beat, by the way, thanks to my attorneys. Jack's dismissal was far less interesting. He got into a fight with the garden club president."

"Who was that?" The list of suspects was growing by the hour.

"Enid Buchanan. This all happened about four years ago, and Enid died a year or so later. Heart failure."

Scratch Enid off the list of suspects. "Who do you believe killed Jack?"

Rose took a sip of her tea and nodded thoughtfully. "I've been thinking about this for several days. As you can imagine, I watch many English mysteries. *Masterpiece Theatre* has been my favorite for decades."

"It was my mom's favorite, too," I said, a hint of wistfulness in my voice. I could practically hear the program's intro music in my mind.

"Love me some *Masterpiece*," Erica added.

"I've been noodling on the suspects, and here's who I've come up with." Rose set her tea down and stood. She walked to a roll-top desk overflowing with papers in the far corner of the room and returned with a little floral-covered notebook. She was so prepared it was impressive.

She flipped through the pages. "Suspect number one: Bill Walker. Jack had hired him recently to redo his porch. It pained Jack to do that since he preferred to do his projects himself, but his knees were getting weak. I think Bill is shady, personally. Jack complained about him all the time."

"What makes you say that?" Erica probed.

"He wasn't reliable, and Jack hated how he'd say he'd show up, but often never did. Also, Bill kept increasing the cost of the porch project. Jack was extremely upset at how bills kept coming in, and he wasn't the type of man to hide his emotions. I suspect Jack blew up at Bill before his death. I could never figure out if Jack didn't pay Bill because he was angry about the shoddy work, or if Bill was a scammer. So many of those contractors are, you know."

"Fair. Who else is on your list?" I hooked my finger into the cup handle.

She turned a page in her notebook. "A surfer named Clay. I don't know much about him. Jack would go to the beach to pick up trash and saw this Clay character littering. They got into it, almost coming to blows. That was two weeks ago, on Sunset Beach. At sunset."

That was one of the most popular stretches of sand on the island.

"Geez, he really had conflicts with a ton of people," I said. Now there were two people who mentioned Clay as a possible suspect.

Rose rolled her eyes. "Men."

We all nodded.

"And the third and final suspect is," she flipped a page. "His daughter."

I pressed my hand to my chest. "Oh, dear. Why would you say that?"

"Because Jack was quite wealthy from his days as a software engineer, and she stood to inherit everything. From what he told me, she recently returned to Devil's Beach after losing her job somewhere up north. Jack didn't tell me much, but from what I gathered, she left under strange circumstances. Cookie?" Rose handed me the plate and I took one.

"Do you know his daughter?" Erica asked.

"Casually. I've met her several times in passing, but I've never had a lengthy conversation with her. She doesn't strike me as the kind of person to kill. Seems rather mousy, in fact." Rose sniffed.

"We have some theories, too," I said. "There's a city councilor, Joanie Clarke. My father told me that they'd clashed over one of Joanie's apartment construction projects."

Rose tilted her head to one side. "Perhaps. Although Joanie and Jack were, as the kids say, friends with benefits at one time."

I bit into the cookie to hide my discomfort. When I was a reporter, it always made me a tad uncomfortable when people started discussing sex. Not that I didn't believe in sex-positivity, I merely felt that bedroom matters should stay in the bedroom.

But the cookie was excellent. It was shortbread style, with the flavor of sweet cream.

I munched for a few seconds, then swallowed. "But Joanie said their, ah, relationship had been over for a while."

Rose shrugged. "I guess she could be a suspect. I doubt it, though. My money's on one of the three people I mentioned. Or Darla from the garden."

"Yes, about Darla. How well do you know her?" I asked.

"Not that well, but we get along. I've never had any issues with her, but Jack sure did. Darla's a bit of a wild card. She's quite passionate about Peas on Earth and has incredible knowledge of poisonous mushrooms. It's my understanding from the story in the newspaper that Jack didn't have any trauma to his body, and I wondered whether Darla had somehow poisoned him with mushrooms."

"We have some inside information, and can tell you that Jack didn't die from a poison mushroom," Erica chimed in.

Rose's entire body relaxed. "Well, that's a relief. I imagined Jack in his final moments in agony."

I wished I could tell her that it was probably the opposite. Most likely, Jack slipped into unconsciousness and had no idea that a lethal dose of drugs had been injected into his body.

Darla certainly wielded knowledge about mushrooms, but fentanyl? An uncomfortable feeling settled in my stomach. Maybe she was the obvious suspect, and I was flirting with danger by agreeing to investigate on her behalf. Just because she was sharp about poison mushrooms didn't mean she knew anything about synthetic opioids, though. Or did it?

"Oh, there's one other person. Beau, Jack's former dog walker. Do you think he could've been involved?" I asked.

Rose shook her head. "Beau's incapable of hurting anyone or anything. I know him well, because he used to groom my Yorkie, rest his little soul."

Nodding, I murmured, "I'm sorry."

"Why haven't you told the police about Clay or Bill?" Erica piped up.

Rose straightened her spine. The sunlight caught her white-blue hair, making it seem like a halo hovered over her head. "I am not in the business of cooperating with law enforcement. Snitches get stitches, and all that."

I sensed that this octogenarian had nerves—and an attitude—forged from pure steel. If she beat a federal charge, she was either incredibly lucky, had an excellent lawyer, or both. It couldn't hurt to ask her where she was when Jack died, although it might get us thrown out.

Probably best if I eat another cookie first.

When I finished, I wiped my mouth with a napkin. "When did you last talk with Jack?"

"The night before he passed. He called me to ask if I wanted to attend a garden show in Tampa next month." For the first time, she looked genuinely bereft at the loss of her friend and dabbed at the corners of her eyes with her napkin. Her expression tugged at my heart since I was all too familiar with losing a loved one.

"I feel bad we're dredging all of this up." I kept my tone soft.

"And the day of his death, where were you?" Erica asked. She wasn't used to the rhythm of an interview and was plowing ahead with the questions. I cringed silently. There was a time and place for the tough questions, and now wasn't that moment.

"In church, on the mainland. I'm an usher, and I usually stay late for coffee hour. I stayed well into the afternoon this past Sunday because we had a building committee meeting."

That was easily verifiable, plus it didn't seem like she had a motive to kill her friend. I finished the last of my tea and set the cup on the tray. "We really appreciate this, and don't want to take up any more of your time. Thank you for the delicious cookies, and the tea, and the conversation."

I stood up. So did Erica and Rose.

"I'll walk you out."

We all strolled to the door. I was hoping she'd invite us for a tour, since her house was so beautiful.

"Gorgeous place you have here," I said.

We were at the door, and she opened it. "Thank you. Please keep me apprised of anything you might find about Jack's death. You know, I never asked you. Why are you looking into this, anyway? You're not police, and you're not private investigators. You're baristas."

I scratched my arm, unsure of what to say. Unlike some journalists, I always disclosed that I was from the paper. Going undercover never worked in real life like it did in fiction.

"We're launching a true crime podcast," Erica said without hesitation.

I nodded in agreement, although the ethical journalist in me was tearing her hair out. One should never lie to get an interview. Erica walked through the door and stood on the welcome mat and promptly sneezed. We'd used this excuse before while sleuthing, and it had made me uncomfortable then, too.

"Oh. Good luck with that. I've never listened to a podcast, but I hear they're popular. I'm confident the culprit for Jack's death will be found and justice will be served." Rose's voice took on a brave, certain tone. With all the suspects in play, and the case getting colder by the hour, I wasn't certain of anything anymore.

"I sure hope so," I said.

She smiled. "What do they say? The suspect in a murder mystery is always the most obvious."

"Who is 'they' anyway?" Erica mused.

"When you find out, let me know." She shut the door.

Erica and I were silent until we got into the car.

"Well, she didn't clarify anything."

"Nope, she muddied the proverbial waters. But we do have a source who can probably tell us where to find Clay the Surfer." I fired up the car and did a U-turn in the spacious driveway.

"Who?"

"Lex Bradstreet. And I know where he lives." Lex and Fab, my dear, departed barista, had been buddies. When I was poking around into Fab's death, I'd visited Lex a couple of times—including once when I hid in the bushes to glean information. Lex was sketchy, sexy, and not the brightest star in the sky—but he was as friendly as a golden retriever puppy.

Erica chuckled as we drove off. "Ahh, yes, our resident mafia-adjacent, too-hot-for-his-own-good, surfer bro. Let's pay him a visit."

Chapter Twelve

"Dudettes, what up?" Lex grinned as he stood aside to let us enter. Erica went first, and he fist-bumped her.

When I passed him, he pulled me into an awkward half-hug. "C'mere, you. I still think about Fab every day."

"Same. You know, I was thinking about designating a table at Perkatory, with a plaque, in his memory."

Lex pulled back. "No way, that would be rad. Folks could sit there and drink coffee in tribute to Fab."

We all nodded, and Lex slapped his thighs. "Hey, do y'all want a beer?"

It wasn't even three in the afternoon. Erica shrugged. "Why not?"

"Sure, what the heck," I added.

"Let's sit out back on my new deck."

We trooped into the kitchen, where Lex grabbed three locally brewed bottles of beer out of the fridge—Cat 1 Lager from the Devil's Beach Brewing Co.—and then led us out a back door to the porch.

"What do you think? Sweet, right?" Lex waved at the spacious wooden deck.

I was about to ask who built it for him, hoping for a bit of kismet with Bill, but Lex went on for several minutes how he'd done it all on his own.

"The deck does look excellent, Lex." Maybe I'd hire him to redo mine, which was a little tired. "I'm curious. Did you ever consider hiring anyone to do this work? I heard a guy named Bill does decks around the island. Does that ring a bell?" I asked casually.

Lex shook his head. "Nope. A lot of those dudes are fly-by-night kinda guys. I figured if I wanted something done right, I should do it myself."

"That's the way to be," Erica said.

The air smelled like ocean salt and wood stain. Here, we weren't far from the beach. He gestured to some deck chairs and we all plopped down.

"It's not often that two beautiful women drop by." Lex fluttered his long, tawny eyelashes. In the sunlight, with his fluffy blonde hair, he looked a bit like Stanley with his lion cut. I had a sneaking suspicion that ladies visited Lex often.

"We're looking into something," I started.

Lex laughed. "You two are always looking into something. I've heard the rumors. That you've solved more murders than the cops. That's wild, bro."

Erica made a clicking noise with her tongue and extended her fist for another bump. Lex laughed with the easy cadence of a man who had recently smoked a joint. Unlike with Rose, we didn't have to lie about why we were snooping around. Lex accepted our presence and our methods, unorthodox as they were.

"We're interested in the death of Jack Daggitt. Did you know him?" I sipped my beer.

Lex squinted. "Is he the dude on the marina who juggles fire?"

"I don't think so. Jack was eighty. Unless Jack had a fire-juggling hobby . . ." I bit the inside of my cheek. Devil's Beach was so quirky that if our deceased octogenarian had juggled fire, it wouldn't shock me.

"Nah, the fire guy is around twenty. His name's Jack, though. That's a coincidence, right?"

"Sure. Well, our Jack died in the community garden. Murdered with an injection of powerful drugs."

Lex's jaw dropped in horror. "Heroin?"

"No, something else." I continued. "We heard that Jack got into an altercation with a surfer named Clay on Sunset Beach. It almost was a fistfight. Do you know any Clays who surf?"

"Duuuude," he whispered. "I was out drinking with Clay last night at the Dirty Dolphin. There's only one surfer Clay on the island."

Erica and I leaned in at the same time. "Oh yeah?"

"Clay's super peaceful. Like a pacific . . . pacific . . ."

"Pacifist?" I offered.

"Yeah, that. Want me to see what he's doing? He's in between jobs now, so he might be in the waves, or maybe just chillin'. Let me call him."

I suspected Lex and his pals were chillin' all the time. It was never clear to me how Lex made his money, although I'd heard rumors that he'd been involved with organized crime in Tampa. This seemed difficult to believe because in my limited experience, gangsters thrived on edge and grit, and Lex had neither.

I murmured a thanks and took a pull from my beer while Lex winked at Erica as he tapped at the phone screen.

He held the phone in our direction and from the audible ring, I knew it was on speaker.

"Bro," Clay said.

"Dude," Lex replied.

Scintillating.

"I'm so hungover. You?" Clay's voice was raspy.

"Nah, I feel excellent. Listen, I have two chicks here right now. Do you want to come over?"

Clay groaned. "I'm in no mood, bro. Thinking about going to the Dolphin for a little hair of the dog. I'm not up for romancing any girls."

"No, no, not for that. They're looking into the death of some old guy. Jack . . ." Lex turned to me.

"Daggitt," I added helpfully.

"Jack Daggitt. They heard you got into a fight with him. I was like, there's no way Clay's involved, he's a pacifist." Lex seemed proud that he pronounced the word correctly on the first try.

Goodness, he was gorgeous but dumb.

"Bro, I gotta run. Someone's at the door. I don't want to talk to no one about a fight on the beach. That guy yelled at me for throwing orange peels into the ocean."

"You sure? They're really nice and not working with the cops. You're not working with the cops, are you, Lana?"

"Nope," I said.

"Am I on speaker? You jackass."

There was a click. "Clay? Clay?" Lex held the phone to his ear and shrugged. "Guess he hung up."

Lex's powers of observation were about as sharp as his mind, but I appreciated the effort. "Thanks for trying."

"Say, where does Clay hang out? You said he doesn't have a job." Erica asked.

Lex took a long sip of his beer. "Oh, he goes to the Dolphin a lot. He thinks one of the bartenders is cute."

I set my half-empty beer on the cluttered coffee table. There was no need to linger at Lex's much longer, and we needed to speed this up. Sometime today, I had to grocery shop for Saturday night. I had four days to prepare for the big dinner.

Erica, sensing my cue, also set her half-finished beer down. "Thanks much, Lex. You've been a big help. If you hear anything, you know where to find us."

"Totally. And listen, I'm sorry about Clay. He's much more fun when he's drinking. Maybe stop by in an hour or two. If we catch him while he's partying, he'll prolly tell us everything."

Erica and I walked out. In my car, she looked at me. "Hair of the dog at the Dirty Dolphin?"

"Heck yeah, let's do it."

As we drove to the Dolphin, my phone pinged with a text. I asked Erica to read it to me.

"It's from Darla," she said excitedly. "Oh. It's nothing interesting. She thinks she might have left one of her tote bags in the office or at Perkatory and wants you to look for it."

"Tell her I'll do that tonight or tomorrow. Does she need it right now?"

Erica tapped on the phone, but a return text from Darla never came.

* * *

The Dirty Dolphin was the largest, and most raucous, waterfront bar in town. At this hour, it was packed with elderly folks hotly anticipating the early bird dinner specials coming up—starting at four and lasting until five thirty. Diners could get half off a limited menu that included a moderately tasty grouper sandwich.

The Dolphin had its rhythm. Lunch was for tourists. Late afternoons were for the early birds. The tourists poured back in for cocktails during the sunset hours.

After dark, mayhem reigned. It wasn't unusual to find biker clubs, drug runners, and former felons rubbing elbows with state politicians and even the local priest. All claimed to come for the quality of the house band, a Jimmy Buffett cover trio, and the potency of the four-dollar well drink specials.

Erica and I had come here several times, mostly for stiff drinks and people watching—although during the first week of our friendship, we spent a night doing shots here with a man we thought had killed Fabrizio.

Today, when we walked in, the place was as staid as a briefcase. Classic rock wafted through the air, and I half expected to see Dad here. Then I remembered he'd stopped eating grouper and drinking alcohol, claiming to be "California sober," whatever that was.

Erica and I went to the bar, which was empty. We hopped up on stools, and my finger traced the carving of some patron's initial in the wood. The bar was the same as it had been for years, smooth and dark and polished to a mirror shine. It was shellacked and made up of pieces from an old, salvaged ship—local rumor claimed was a pirate ship, but that didn't quite make sense from a time line perspective, given that pirates hadn't been to Devil's Beach for hundreds of years. Our barstools' legs rested on the floor and were carved in the shape of skinny barracuda fish.

Erica flagged down the bartender and ordered a Jack and Coke.

"Soda with lime," I requested.

When I saw Erica giving me a skeptical look, I explained. "I have to go shopping tonight. Can't get all messed up. I'm even going to the organic grocery on the mainland so I can get the expensive cheese platter."

"Snazzy," she said.

We sipped and did a sweep of the room. "I don't see anyone here who looks like they're named Clay, or that uses the word bro in every sentence, or is under the age of seventy."

"Present company excluded," Erica quipped.

"Don't you find it a little odd that Clay didn't want to talk about Jack?"

"Yeah, and how he hung up like that. He's definitely sketch." Erica swiveled in her seat and flagged down the bartender, a woman who was an occasional customer at Perkatory.

"What's shakin', bacon? Tabatha, right?" Erica asked. She was amazing with names.

"Yeah, you two are from Perkatory. Hey, you should bring us some of your coffee. I'm sure the daytime customers would love it."

"I'll make a note of that. Sounds good." I took out my phone and typed an email to myself. I also checked the texts, making sure I wasn't needed at Perkatory. Running a business was entirely different from being a reporter—while working at the paper, I could disappear for a couple of hours without my editor knowing. Now, I had to be plugged in and ready for disaster at all times.

My inbox was blissfully empty, and I released a breath of relief.

"You know a guy named Clay?" Erica had this way of being simultaneously blunt and chummy.

Tabatha nodded, her full afro bouncing. "Clay. Surfer Clay? Brown hair, kind brown eyes, tan? About six feet?"

"Maybe," I said. "Sounds about right."

"Sure, I know him. He comes in here every day. In fact, he should be here any minute. It's like he works here. Well, works at drinking. You know the kind of man." She rolled her eyes and the phone rang. "Sorry. Gotta grab that."

She wandered off and Erica turned to me with a pleading look. "C'mon, you can stay for a little while, right? You don't have to go shopping right now, do you? Hang out a bit longer and maybe Clay will magically appear like a day drinking fairy."

"Yeah, I have a little time. The store's open until nine." I still had some business stuff to do, like checking on payroll and emailing the coffee wholesaler. Not to mention taking Stanley for a walk.

Sometimes sleuthing cut into the daily routine, though. You had to roll with it, or you'd miss your opportunity. It's what I loved about unofficially investigating crime: it was like reporting, but without the pesky writing part. And there were no editors involved.

A half hour ticked by. Erica nursed her drink, I ordered another soda with lime, and we watched the tourists begin to arrive for sunset on the deck. A few bikers roared up on their Harleys and swaggered in, the smell of their leather jackets mingling with the beer stench.

Still no Clay, or anyone who resembled a young surfer.

"Well, I think I'm calling it a night," I finally said.

Erica, who had been fooling around with her phone, looked up. "Totally. I'm going to hang out for a while. I'll get Joey to meet me and continue to monitor."

"You sure?" The last thing I wanted was to abandon my friend.

She waved me off. "I got this."

I told her to call or text if Clay arrived, and I went home to do real-life things, putting the budding investigation behind me.

Chapter Thirteen

I didn't hear from Erica for the rest of the night, and Stanley and I fell asleep on the sofa. Sometime during the night, I moved to the bed, taking him with me. When I woke, it was Wednesday, my day off. Normally I slept in, but then again, I usually didn't have so much going on.

I was out of bed by seven, and had showered, walked Stanley, and eaten by eight. As a strong pot of coffee brewed—I liked basic house blend in the automatic drip at home—I checked my email, texts, and social media, bracing myself for calamity.

But all was quiet. Erica and Dad had opened Perkatory without incident. There were no texts from Darla, and most importantly, there was no news about Jack. Erica hadn't unearthed any more details at the Dolphin last night, and the *Beacon* ran a brief about how Jack's death was now three days old, suspicious, and unsolved.

The only text was from Noah.

Good morning, Cupcake. Sorry I didn't call last night. Was at the station late, then went home to crash. Talked to Mom today, she's really looking forward to meeting you and eating your lasagna—it's one of her favorite meals. xo

Oh dear.

I can't wait either! Headed to the mainland to grocery shop. Hopefully we can see each other later.

After sending the text and a heart emoji, I looked at my dog.

"No more excuses, Stanley. We're going to the grocery today and buying everything we need."

Stanley looked up at me with giant, espresso-colored eyes.

"Yes, we can also work in a trip to the dog park."

He barked because he knew the word *park*. So smart, my little pup.

My plan was to make Stanley work out all his excess enthusiasm at the Devil's Beach Paw Playground, then wrangle him into a pooch-carrying pouch that Dad had bought and take the dog to the organic grocery store on the mainland. Since it was locally owned by a guy Dad knew, dogs were welcome if they were in a stroller or a carrier.

I packed a duffel with our essentials: bottles of water, snacks for Stanley, his leash, poop bags, a packet of disposable, pet-friendly wipes, my grocery list, and five reusable canvas bags. Then I poured a large mug of coffee and toted everything, including Stanley, to the car.

In my opinion, the Paw Playground was one of the gems of the island, right after the gorgeous beaches. The dog park was new and enormous, with separate small and large dog areas. Patches of grass mingled with sawdust walkways, and each area had a play tunnel and fake fire hydrants.

We entered the small dog side. A handful of people were there. Three people clustered around a bench talking, while the others followed their dogs or leaned against the chain-link fence, staring at their phones. Small dogs chased balls or dodged their owners, ricocheting off one another and their human playmates. It was a place of deep joy for all, and I immediately relaxed a bit.

I unclipped Stanley and he tore off, eager to say hello to new friends. Meanwhile, I unfurled a plastic poop bag. It never hurt to be too prepared with an excited adolescent dog.

Stanley was in his element. He fell into step with a cluster of small dogs that were racing around the perimeter of the park. The pack seemed to be set off by a large German shepherd on the big dog side of the fence, and all the owners chuckled as our little dogs raced up and down, yipping and barking.

"At least they're getting exercise," I said to a woman nearby who was also watching.

She nodded and laughed. "I'm caring for my father's dog, and I'm afraid he's been cooped up for several days now. He needs to release all that energy."

We chatted for a bit about the exercise needs of small dogs. I told her that Stanley usually ran out of gas after a twenty-minute walk.

"How about your dog?"

The woman, who was in her fifties with a sleek, black bob and thick-framed, oversized, zebra-print sunglasses. "I'm not sure. He's my father's dog. Or was. I'm caring for him now. Trying to get used to his rhythms."

I nodded, wanting to probe out of sheer curiosity, but knowing that would be rude, I didn't. It was then that Stanley and a cute, brownish-red shorthaired dog came running up.

"Did you make a friend?" I bent down to scratch Stanley's head.

He and the other dog circled the woman and me, sniffing our legs. I sensed that Stanley wanted to jump on the woman in the worst way, and possibly nip at her hip-length, black tunic.

"No jumping," I warned. "Be nice."

I bent down to say hello to the other dog, who had a sweet, friendly expression. He looked like a generic mutt, with floppy ears and skinny legs. "What's your name, little one?"

Stanley sniffed the dog's leg as I held out my hand. Maybe Stanley needed a playmate. Even though Dad, Erica, Noah, and I visited him on the regular during the daytime, I worried that he was lonely at home.

"That's Bella Pugosi, my dog," the woman said.

A wave of awareness crashed over me. No. It couldn't be. How many dogs were named Bella Pugosi? I stood up slowly, studying the woman. She was about my height, with a slimmer build. Clearly, she'd taken care of herself, and by the look of her designer purse, appeared well to do.

"This is my dog, Stanley. I'm Lana, by the way." I smiled at her, hoping to forge a connection before I dove into the hard questions.

"I'm Willa. Nice to meet you."

Jack's daughter! This was definitely her. "Your pupper is adorable. What kind of dog is Bella?"

The woman smiled. "I think he's considered a pug. Or maybe a puggle. His father was a pug, and his mother had some beagle in her. Or maybe it's the other way around. I'm not sure. My father adopted him several years ago, and now he's mine."

I paused for a moment while I considered my next move. Stanley dashed off to greet a new dog coming inside the park. Finally, I said, "I think I've seen Bella and your father around. I recognize Bella's pretty face. Er, is your father Jack Daggitt, by any chance?"

She pressed her lips together for a second, then relaxed. "Yes, in fact, it is. Was. He . . . passed recently."

I clasped both hands to my chest. "Oh, my goodness. I'm so sorry about what happened to him."

She nodded curtly. "Like everyone else on this stupid island, you must've read about his death in the paper."

A nervous cough leaked out of my mouth. "Well, actually, I'm the one who found your father in the garden. I'm so sorry."

She froze, which gave me the opportunity to check her earlobes.

Diamond studs. Pierced.

"I'm sorry. I can't talk about this now. It's too much and I can't deal with it." She swallowed hard and bent down, scooping up her dog. Then she turned on the ball of her foot—she was wearing purple sandals—and marched out without a word.

"Whoa," I whispered aloud as I watched her walk the length of the dog park toward the exit.

I needed to tell someone about this, so I quickly created a group text with Dad and Erica. While tapping out a text, I shouted in Stanley's direction to stop humping a Jack Russell. Stanley loped over, probably thinking I had a treat in my pocket.

You're not going to believe this, but I met Jack's daughter in the dog park.

Freaky deaky, Dad responded.

TELL US EVERYTHING, wrote Erica.

Stanley rose up on his back paws and began to paw at my thigh. This was his signal that he'd had enough dog park. If we stayed any longer, he'd start drooling, and I didn't like to stick around when he did, because a casual observer would think him rabid.

There was one thing I needed to do before we left, and that was make a phone call. I dialed my old friend Sheila, a former newspaper coworker of mine. She was now an editor in Jacksonville and had helped me with some information in the past in exchange for a supply of my best coffee beans.

She picked up on the third ring. "Lana! Thank you for that basket of coffee last month. It was incredible. Kept me going through several long and boring meetings."

"Glad I'm still of service to the journalism profession," I quipped. "Listen, I need you to run a background check on someone."

I'd done those checks as a journalist hundreds of times. But since leaving, I stopped having access to my old newspaper's databases—and hacking in wasn't ethical. I preferred to do it this way, which was somewhat above board.

"Give me a name. I'm waiting on a trial verdict today, so I've got nothing going on but eating a bunch of crap from the vending machine," Sheila said.

"Willa Daggitt. At least I think that's her last name, or was at one time. Her father's Jack, he was around eighty years old, and he died recently. He lived on Devil's Beach, not sure about her. She's probably in her fifties."

The sound of fingers hitting keys filled my ear. "Okay, I'm on it. What is this, another murder in your island paradise?"

"Yeah, something like that."

"You should do a podcast. I'll bet it would be a hit." She took a long slurp of something.

"I've heard that suggestion before."

"This shouldn't take long at all. I'll email you soon."

After thanking Sheila and promising to send her another basket packed with coffee, I picked up Stanley, tucked him under my arm, and decided to take a quick detour before going to the mainland.

* * *

Less than fifteen minutes later, Stanley and I were ensconced in my second-floor office above Perkatory. Erica was on one side of me, and a big cup of iced cold brew on the other. My hand reached for the computer mouse and it flickered to life. I navigated to my email and there it was.

"Willa Daggitt. Here we go, a full background report from my friend Sheila," I murmured.

Erica rubbed her hands together, like she was watching a roulette table. "Come on, come on, come on."

I clicked on the attachment. "Reports like this rarely show anything significant. They're only a piece of the puzzle."

"It's still exciting. Digging into someone's background." Erica's eyes shimmered.

Stanley was in the corner, flopped on a dog bed that I'd brought here. He had a total of six dog beds scattered around the island: two at my place, and one each at Dad's, Noah's, Erica's boat, and here, all the locations where Stanley spent his time. They were all identical, olive-hued orthopedic dog beds with Stanley's initials—SL—monogrammed on the front. Dad had bought them for Christmas.

Finally, the report downloaded, and I opened and expanded it on the screen so Erica and I could both read easily.

"Okay, Willa is fifty-three, she was born in Florida, lived in Baltimore and DC. Owned a condo worth a half million." I scanned the document. "Oh look, here. A bankruptcy. Looks like she lost her house."

Erica made a clicking noise with her tongue. "That's sad."

"Doesn't mean she was a killer, though." The bankruptcy was fairly recent, and I made note of that on my yellow legal pad.

I scrolled the rest of the report, which was short and boring. Aside from the bankruptcy, there were few scintillating details about Willa. She didn't seem to have a spouse or children.

"What's that?" Erica pointed.

I was about to tell her not to put her fingers on the glass—I loathed fingerprints on screens—when I saw the words.

PROFESSIONAL LICENSES AND DISCIPLINE

In my experience as a crime reporter, this part of the report was almost always blank. Then again, I'd mostly written about gangbangers, drug runners, and people who stayed under the radar to carry out their criminal enterprises. Few of those folks were licensed by the state for any reason.

"She's a doctor?" Erica leaned close to the screen.

"You need glasses."

"Maybe. But look. What does this mean?"

"Whoa. She was disciplined and her medical license was revoked a few months ago."

We both sat back in our seats, looking at each other and sipping from our iced coffees.

"Here's a theory," I said. "She went bankrupt, lost her doctor's license, moved back to Devil's Beach . . ."

I paused because the description of Willa's dismal life wasn't all that different than my own. I hadn't gone bankrupt, but only because I'd remained poor and didn't get into too much debt. Aside from student loans, of course. I'd be paying on those when I was in the nursing home.

"Then she found out her jerk of a father had a life insurance policy . . ." Erica nodded.

"Or he had a lot of cash stashed and she was the only beneficiary, since he was divorced and she was his only child. Wait. Was she his only child?"

Erica's brows knit together. "I'll call Rose."

"How did you get her number? I don't remember her giving it to you."

"She didn't. But that doesn't mean I didn't see one of her orchid brochures and get it from that." Erica tapped her temple. "I'm working on my recall, so I'm trying to memorize things."

"Brilliant."

By now Erica was dialing. "Rose? Hi. It's Erica. The barista from the other day. No, I don't want to buy orchids."

There was a pause, and I gulped my drink.

"Lana and I were piecing a few things together for the podcast and we wanted to ask: how many children did Jack have? Oh. Un-huh. Okay. Oh wow. That's sad. Well, thanks a bunch! Later, alligator."

Erica set her phone down. "He had two children. Willa and a boy who died in infancy, decades ago."

"That must've been difficult." A twinge of grief tugged at my heart. Who had Jack Daggitt been, really? Had he always been an ornery, outspoken crank? Or had life's challenges and disappointments, along with the terrifying changes in the world, pushed him to be abrasive?

"You ever wonder how people become the way they are?"

"Nah. I try to take people at face value. If they're kind to me, I'm kind right back. If they're jerks, I'm a jerk. I don't need an explanation of their backstory, traumas, and history. I meet people where they are."

"Maybe I overthink everything. Including people," I said.

"You? Overthink? No way." Erica snort-laughed.

"How did Jack get to be bitter? Don't you wonder that?"

She shook her head. "Maybe he was a born bumberclat."

I tipped my head back, chuckling. "Where do you get these words? What is a bumberclat?"

"An a-hole."

"Ah. What do we do with this information about Willa?"

Erica pulled the straw out of her drink. She reused the same stainless-steel straw for all of her personal drinks. She looked at it as if she was contemplating the meaning of the universe. "Your dad was right. We need to piece together Jack's final days, and Darla and Willa's, as well. Was she staying with him?"

"Dunno."

"When's his funeral?"

I lifted my shoulder. "Dad probably knows. Let me text him."

My text to dad was succinct. He responded quickly, which probably meant it wasn't busy downstairs. I read it aloud to Erica.

"'I meant to tell you. It's next week, on the beach.' Wave emoji."

"Peter's getting better with the emojis. Have you even told Darla we're officially taking on her case?"

I rolled my eyes. "I don't think it's that formal. It's not like we have a PI office with clients lined up outside the door."

"Not yet. If you and Sheriff Cupcake pooled your resources, the two of you could have something serious."

I snickered, thinking how Noah would look adorably exasperated at the thought of us opening a private investigating firm together. "You've been spending too much time with Dad."

"Seriously, you should call Darla. She's probably still worried as all heck that she'll be hauled to jail any minute. Did she ever get back to you about the bag?"

I slapped my hand on my forehead. The bag. I'd forgotten all about that and glanced over. The cream-colored canvas tote bag sat wedged between the sofa and the wall. "I'll call her now and tell her we're officially on, and maybe she can come by to pick up her tote. I hope she won't mind that things will be slow for the next few days. I really, really, really need to prepare for this dinner. Oh, and what do you think about a small redecoration project before Saturday?"

She stood up and tapped her fingers on the desk. "Why not? What's a little more chaos? Lana, heck no. We need to focus."

If Erica was telling me to focus, I was in big trouble.

Chapter Fourteen

After Erica left the office, I checked on Stanley. Still snoozing like a champion. Now I had to phone Darla, a conversation that I knew was necessary, but it weighed heavily on my mind.

It wasn't that I didn't want to help. Or that I didn't like her. I did, quite a bit. She was quirky and smart, and made me laugh almost every day she came into Perkatory. She was one of those people I'd met since coming home that I'd always wanted to hang out with, but it never quite came together.

I'd hoped to get to know her better at the community garden, but that hobby seemed to be on hold, since Peas on Earth was sealed off by police for the foreseeable future.

But helping Darla clear her name of a murder—one she hadn't even been formally accused of—was a lot to ask of a virtual stranger. Especially since I wasn't fully convinced of her innocence. But the prospect of her being wrongfully accused was a worse outcome than my own misgivings.

Plus, I was intensely curious about Jack's death now that I knew more about his daughter and the people he surrounded himself with.

There was no shortage of suspects in my mind. Eight, at last count. Way too many.

There was his daughter, who acted oddly at the dog park and who had medical knowledge that likely included a familiarity with fentanyl. Her behavior at the park could have been grief, though. It was a feeling I was all too familiar with after Mom died—for months after she passed, I'd sometimes walk away from conversations that were too heavy, overwhelmed by sadness.

Then there was Clay the littering surfer, who didn't want to discuss the case when Lex called. Beau, the dog groomer who didn't like how Jack cared for his puggle. I couldn't forget about Bill the contractor, either, although I knew little about him.

There was Rose, his friend, but she had an alibi and no apparent reason to kill Jack. After all, she was the only person I'd talked with who actually liked the guy.

Two other women who had gotten into disputes with him—Olivia the Dylan-hating neighbor and Joanie the developer—both had alibis, or at least claimed to. Anybody could lie about an alibi, though, or pay someone to kill another person. I'd learned as much as a crime reporter in Miami.

And then there was Darla, who arguably had the biggest beef of all with Jack. Getting a restraining order against someone was no small matter, and she had sent him a mildly threatening text. I glanced at her weathered tote bag with the words "Salem, Massachusetts" on the side, with a cute graphic of a witch's hat.

Sighing, I dialed Darla on speakerphone, wondering if she was working today at Ye Olde Taffy Towne, the candy store down the street. It occurred to me that I didn't even know where Darla lived.

She answered on the first ring and said, "Hello" in a brisk, breathless tone.

The click and snick of what sounded like a door lock filled my ear.

"Darla? It's Lana. You busy? You sound busy. I can call you back. Oh, I do have your bag. It's here in the office."

"Oh, hey, Lana. Thanks! That's good to know. I was worried I'd dropped it somewhere. And no sweat about calling right now. Just unlocked the store after taking a fifteen-minute break. I like to power-walk around the block a few times a day when it's slow. Gets the blood pumping, you know? It's hard on the legs, standing around, waiting on customers, and making taffy for eight hours a day."

"Working retail is unforgiving on the body, that's for sure. My feet are killing me by the end of the day after a shift at Perkatory." This had taken me some getting used to after years as a reporter, where I'd mostly sat in my car, an office, or on a hard bench at the courthouse, watching legal proceedings.

"Amen to that. You should try some shoe inserts. That's what I did." Darla seemed to enjoy giving people helpful life tidbits like this, and I found that endearing.

"Good to know. Listen, Darla. I wanted to let you know that Erica and I, well, and my dad, too, are going to investigate your case. We have been looking into it a bit. Found some pretty interesting stuff."

I heard a gasp on the line. "Oh, Lana, this is the best news I could've hoped for. Thank you. Oh gosh. I'm going to cry."

"No, no, don't cry." The thought of such emotion right now was too much to handle. "I am going to need to ask you more questions, though."

"Sure, go for it. Or you can come over to the store if you're not busy at Perkatory. I'd love to give you a pound of my new taffy. Made it today, in fact. You're going to love it. Get this, it's fruity cereal flavor."

I pressed the heels of my hands into my eyes. The thought of fruity cereal taffy made me want to hurl. "You don't have to do that. That's sweet, though."

"Welcome to Ye Olde Taffy Towne. Oh, hi, Moose!" Her voice was loud, and I winced. "Lana, hang on, I'm going to set the phone down, someone walked in."

Before I could protest or tell her that I'd walk the few blocks to her shop so we could chat in person, I heard the tha-thunk of a phone being set on a hard surface.

"I'm glad you came in because I wanted to continue our conversation. You want to try my new taffy flavor?" I heard her call out, probably to the mysterious Moose. Clearly it was someone she knew, and I could almost hear the happiness in her voice. Who was Moose? Her boyfriend? A regular taffy customer? What kind of a name was Moose, anyway? Was it short for something?

Who knew how long she'd be talking. Darla had a tendency to ramble. I pondered whether to hang up and walk over. It wouldn't take but a few minutes, and she might not even realize if I hung up. My eyes went to the legal pad, and I scanned the notes that I'd made. If I brought that to the taffy shop, I could show her everything we'd gathered so far. Plus I could return her bag.

As I closed the notepad, I heard a commotion on the speaker. It sounded like shuffling, or possibly something hitting a durable surface. Perhaps a box of the dreaded taffy.

Darla's voice broke through the noise. "Hey, what the he—"

I couldn't quite make out the sound that came after. It was either a yell or a laugh, and I bent over the phone, speaking about two inches from the screen.

"Darla? You okay?" I said her name a few more times, then paused and looked at the screen.

The call had been disconnected.

I dialed her back, and it immediately went to voice mail. I rang a second, third, and fourth time, and every call went to a recording of Darla saying, "Hey, you crazy cats and kittens! Leave a message."

"Super weird," I muttered aloud.

In the corner, Stanley opened one eye. I drew in a breath. "Buddy, you're going to stay here for a little while, okay?"

I had bowls of water and food for him in the office, and he seemed content in his cozy bed. It wouldn't be a problem to leave him in here for a half hour or so, and I kissed the top of his head then grabbed my purse. Something about that call didn't sit right with me, and I wanted to check on Darla.

After carefully locking the door to my office, I went down the hall and out the back stairs, into the alley. I didn't want to alarm Dad and Erica about what I'd heard. It was probably nothing—Darla talked about her foibles with taffy all the time, and probably knew as many people on the island as I did. Working in retail on Devil's Beach meant you got to know everyone, whether you wanted to or not.

Surely, she'd dropped the phone on the floor or fumbled a sample. Or perhaps the customer had been difficult. Goodness knows I'd had my fair share of those kinds of people in the café.

I power-walked down Main Street, hoping I didn't run into anyone I knew along the way. Probably I was paranoid about Darla's well-being. Sometimes I had an overactive imagination about things, and some (like Erica) have said that because I'd surrounded myself with crime for so long in Miami that my mind automatically went to dark places.

Oh, crap. I forgot her tote. Whatever, we could get it later. The urgency I felt in my gut overrode any desire to return to Perkatory for her stuff. It obviously wasn't something she desperately needed, otherwise she'd have returned my text yesterday.

On the second to last block of Main Street, I took a left onto Palm Way. There were a cluster of small wooden homes that had been turned into businesses, and that's where the taffy shop was located. It was the final building on the block, right after a jewelry store and an art gallery selling tropical paintings.

The taffy joint was in the smallest home of all, not more than an oversized shed. The exterior was pink and adorable, and normally it was a top tourist draw. Today, however, there was no one on the street.

It was eleven in the morning on a Wednesday, though, and that was prime beach time for tourists in April. Stores had their rhythms, usually in the mornings, at lunch, and after dinner.

I bounded up the three stairs and yanked open the door, calling out Darla's name.

But when I got inside, I stopped. The place crackled with an ominous, heavy vibe. Normally Darla played pop music at a near ear-splitting volume because she claimed the tweens who loved taffy were more likely to drag their parents inside if the place felt, in her words, "hip."

Today, the upbeat music played softly, almost too soft to hear. It was eerie.

"Darla? You okay? Where are you?"

I glanced around the small space. The walls were painted a light blue, with a mural of white, fluffy clouds and wrapped pieces of taffy with happy faces soaring in the heavens.

There was a register atop a tall, white desk, and I tallied six barrel-shaped bins placed around the showroom, all filled with colorful, wrapped taffy. Behind the register was a counter, and that's where Darla wrapped and packaged boxes of taffy for tourists to ship. A swinging door nearby led to the taffy-making area. I'd been back there once, at Christmas, when I stopped by to give Darla a gift card to Perkatory since she'd been one of our top regulars at the café.

I knew the back room had a large, stainless-steel machine that pulled the taffy, stretched it between four rods until it was the proper consistency. I could barely look at the stuff without getting nauseous.

Today, as in December, the entire store smelled sickeningly sweet, as if sugar molecules infused the air. While calling out her name again, I took a step behind the desk, because I spotted something atop the counter.

A syringe.

No no no . . .

My heart was now beating in my throat. I yelled her name two more times, expecting—no, hoping—that she'd burst from the one door leading to the kitchen prep area.

That's when I heard a groan. It was coming from the direction of the door. It was only audible because the pop song had ended, and there were a few seconds of silence before the next song, which I identified as "Watermelon Sugar" by Harry Styles.

The things one remembers during the strangest moments.

"Are you in there? Darla?" First I took my phone out of my purse so I'd have it in hand in case something was amiss. Then I rushed to the door and eased it open.

The sight that greeted me made me cry out and press my hands to my face. Darla was lying in a slick of blood, half under a stainless food prep table. She moaned while slowly turning her face toward me.

"Lana," she whispered, and I went to her side. Every part of me was trembling.

Chapter Fifteen

"What happened? Oh my gosh. Oh gosh. Oh. Gah." I was hyperventilating from the terrible scene. "It's okay. I'm calling for an ambulance. It's okay."

It very much was not okay, nor was it going to be, from the looks of the wound on her head. While kneeling and grasping her hand, I shakily called 911.

This time, Bernadette didn't answer. I didn't recognize the voice, and I shouted, "Taffy shop! Someone's hurt badly! Come quick!"

The phone slipped from my grasp onto the floor when Darla made another death rattle.

"Hang on. Please hang on, Darla," I pleaded. She seemed semi-conscious, but barely. "Can you tell me what happened? Who did this?"

"Lana," she murmured, her eyes fluttering.

"Yes, talk to me. Stay with me." I leaned in, squeezing her hand that was growing colder.

"Mushrooms are fungi and four plants." I could barely hear her, she was speaking in such a low, gravelly voice.

"What?" I blinked.

Darla's eyes fluttered shut. Her head flopped to one side, and her hand went slack in mine as I begged her to stay awake.

It didn't take police long to arrive. Maybe only five minutes, but those minutes seemed like a lifetime. All I remember was hearing that "Watermelon Sugar" song bounce off the walls, and the voice of a paramedic asking me to step outside.

Numb from shock, I slumped on the far edge of the stairs while emergency workers ran inside. I managed to call Perkatory and let Barbara know where I was and asked her to check on Stanley in the office. It was anybody's guess when I'd be back to the café. I also quickly texted Erica to let her know I was okay and what was going on, instructing her not to tell my father yet.

The last thing I wanted was him worrying about me.

When Noah walked up, I stood and collapsed into his arms, sobbing.

"I came as soon as I could. I'm so glad you're unhurt. I don't know what I'd do if something happened to you," Noah whispered into my ear. His words made me sob harder.

He smoothed back my hair and stared into my face. Part of me expected a reprimand, but that was merely my tragedy-warped brain on the fritz. Noah had no idea what I'd been doing here, and for all he knew, I was paying Darla a social call or buying him taffy.

"Can you sit tight out here while I go inside to check on the scene?" His tone was gentle, as if he didn't want to scare me.

I nodded and sniffled.

"Here." He reached into his pocket and pulled out a handkerchief. I pressed it to my watering eyes, and it smelled like his laundry detergent, which made me cry fresh tears.

"Is she going to be okay?"

Noah looked to the door of the taffy shop, then at me, his mouth in a grim line. "Let's find out. I'll be right back."

I sank onto the steps again and shut my eyes. I wasn't sure what had happened to Darla, but one thing was clear.

This attack was no coincidence, four days after Jack's murder. Who wanted both dead? And why? Two violent crimes in less than a week would not only set the Devil's Beach gossip network aflame, but it would also shake the island's tourist industry to its core. Exactly what the town didn't need with the upcoming Funnel Cake Festival.

I stood and paced for a few minutes outside the little pink building. More officers showed up, then the county sheriff's forensics van. Four people in identical, white hazmat suits filed past me.

Whatever was going on inside seemed to be taking a while. Why weren't they carrying Darla out of the store and rushing her to the hospital? Did the emergency workers have the capability of stabilizing her in the store? I watched as one of the paramedics—the guy from Sunday with the mullet and mirrored sunglasses—walked out and shut the ambulance engine off.

"What's going on?" I asked him as he walked back up the steps. "Aren't you going to the hospital?"

He paused and studied me, and something akin to pity flickered in his eyes. "No," he said finally, and went inside.

I rested my head in my hands and folded into a little ball. If they weren't going to the hospital, that could only mean one thing.

Darla was dead.

As I was gulping in breath after breath, Noah came back out. "Why don't we go somewhere to talk? Like my office?"

I nodded and mutely followed him to the cruiser. He opened the door for me, and I climbed in. We were silent the entire short drive to the police station. All the while, I was kicking myself for not calling for help back at Perkatory.

Perhaps if I had—if I'd listened to that little voice of instinct that said something was wrong with Darla—maybe she'd still be alive.

Noah and I nodded at the woman at the front desk, and we walked into his office. He shut the door and paused at a small refrigerator that I'd bought so he could keep his water and tea cold.

He opened it and took out a water, cracking it open. Instead of drinking from it himself, he handed it to me. I shook my head.

"Please? You're probably dehydrated." Noah was big on hydration.

I accepted it and downed half the bottle in one shot. Then I licked my lips. "You want to know what happened, and why I was there, don't you?"

"Well, sure. But I want to make sure you're okay first."

I tilted my head back and forth. "Not sure I'll ever be okay after seeing that."

"Understood." Noah wasn't sitting across from me at his desk. He was next to me on the shiny brown leather sofa that was pushed up against one wall. It overlooked Noah's bookcase, which was filled with police manuals, legal tomes, and the occasional science fiction novel.

"I might as well come clean. I've been investigating Jack's death." There was no reason to keep my sleuthing activities a secret now.

He inhaled for what seemed like a minute while staring at the ceiling. "Go on," he finally said.

I explained everything, starting with how Darla asked for help because she didn't trust authorities after her run-ins with the law up north, and ending with the background check I'd gotten on Willa.

By the time I was finished, I was good and fired up. Darla was a decent person. A hardworking woman trying to get her life straight. And her life had ended in a taffy shop for what? Who wanted her dead? Any shock or fear I'd harbored gave way to anger.

"Darla doesn't deserve this," I smacked my hand on the arm of the sofa.

"No. She doesn't." He massaged his forehead with one hand. "Let's go over your call with her again. Did she indicate who came into the store?"

I shook my head. "She called the person Moose. It happened in a matter of seconds, and I assumed she'd messed up the taffy somehow, dropped it on the floor. I wasn't sure if she laughed or yelled. She has an unusual laugh, that's probably why."

"And you saw no one when you walked into the taffy shop?"

"Not a soul." I took another sip of water.

"Did you touch anything?"

I wrinkled my nose. "The front door, and the door to the back room. And . . ." I hauled in a shaky breath, "Darla's hand. I held Darla's hand as she . . . she . . ."

"Was she unconscious when you got there?"

"Barely conscious. She said my name twice, and then said something super strange. I'm not sure I even heard it correctly. She said, 'Mushrooms are fungi and four plants.' Or maybe she said, 'Mushrooms are fungi and more plants.' I could barely hear her. It doesn't make sense."

Noah reached for my hand and cupped it into his two larger ones. "Sometimes people say things at the end of their life that only have significance to them."

"She did love mushrooms, or fungi. Talked about them a lot." I paused. "I'm going to miss her. She was a regular, and one of the best."

"I know, cupcake. I know. We're going to find out who did this to her."

I shifted in my seat to face him. "Do you believe this has anything to do with Jack's death?"

Noah swallowed hard. "This early in the investigation, it's hard to say. I'm hoping the taffy shop has a security camera."

"It does, but Darla disabled it. She felt like the owners were spying on her. She told me that last month."

He rolled his eyes. "Great."

I scooted toward him and he wrapped his arms around me. We sat like that for several long minutes.

"I wish we could stay like this for the rest of the day," I sighed. Safe in his arms.

"I do too. But I need to get back to the scene. And you need to give an official statement."

"Am I a suspect?"

"Not as far as I'm concerned. I highly doubt you have the upper body strength to give anyone a head injury like that. Darla was pretty buff, and no offense, but she could've easily taken you down."

The image of an injured Darla popped back in my mind, and I shuddered. "Do I have to return to the taffy shop? I'd rather stay here and give the statement."

Noah brushed a lock of hair out of my face and nodded. "I'll make it happen."

* * *

After I recounted everything I'd seen for the official record, I walked home in a zombie-like state, alone. Noah had given the okay for me to leave the police station, and all I wanted was my familiar surroundings.

I'd texted Dad, who had heard the news about Darla from various sources. He and Stanley met me at home, and I was so happy to see them waiting on my porch that I ran up, folding them into a big hug. For once, Dad didn't speak.

I let us inside and Dad unclipped Stanley from his pooch pouch.

"Lana, I'll make some snacks for us. Why don't you go in the living room with Stan and relax." The look on Dad's face was familiar. I'd seen it when I returned home from Miami, depressed and despondent.

I didn't have it in me to argue, so I picked up Stanley and we settled onto the sofa with the remote and a pink fuzzy blanket. When I turned on the television, I was careful to avoid the true crime shows I usually watched.

I'd had enough true crime today to last me a while.

Finally, I found a mindless yet captivating reality TV show about couples on blind dates, and tried to become absorbed in the insipid dialogue to take my mind off everything. Stanley seemed to sense my sadness and snuggled onto my lap. Dad interrupted my mental break when he brought in a tray of tea and chocolate cookies that I'd hidden in the back of the cabinet.

"Surprised you found my secret stash," I joked.

He chuckled. "Your stash isn't so secret. I figured that chamomile tea was better than coffee. Don't need your nerves any more wound up."

Dunking a chocolate cookie into the tea, I blinked back tears. "This situation with Darla is awful. She had her quirks, but she was a good person. Who wanted her dead? I can't help but think it was the same person who killed Jack. It has to be, right?"

Dad pulled at his goatee thoughtfully. "Noah called me."

"When?" I frowned. How long had it been since I found Darla? Time seemed to be slippery this afternoon.

"After he talked with you at the station. He called me from the taffy shop. Asked me to be with you until he could come over."

I sniffled. Noah was a gem. I, on the other hand, was not. Poking around in this case behind his back made more guilt settle heavy in my chest. I possibly could've saved Darla, and I was doing Noah wrong.

"He told me something else." Dad seemed uncomfortable because he was looking everywhere but my face.

"What?" I wrapped both hands around my mug.

"He said the medical examiner found fentanyl in the syringe at the taffy shop."

"Similar to the one found near Jack?" I couldn't believe it.

Dad nodded. "Noah and the medical examiner said they didn't think the blow to the head would've killed her. It looked terrible and resulted in a lot of blood, but probably wasn't what did her in."

I sat back and tried to absorb this information. It seemed incomprehensible that Darla was dead, and that she was killed in the same way as Jack.

For once, Dad didn't say anything silly, and we sat in silence while watching the dating program. After a while, he spoke up.

"Where do they get these people for these shows?"

"Well, half of them seem to be from Florida, so there's your answer."

We looked at each other and grinned. Just like when Mom died almost four years ago, and when I came home after my layoff and divorce, Dad and his goofy smile took the sting out of life's painful moments.

"How's your popsicle business, anyway?" I asked, out of the blue.

Dad giggled. "I've come up with the right mint-to-mocha ratio. In fact, I was thinking about bringing some over on Saturday night for the dinner with Noah's family."

Groaning, I folded over, burying my head in a throw pillow. *The dinner.*

"What's wrong, munchkin?"

"I need to go food shopping for Saturday. I'm so behind with everything."

Dad playfully swatted me on the leg. "Not tonight, you're not. You've suffered a trauma and you need to relax with terrible TV and your dog."

I sat up, hugging the pillow. "You're probably right, but I've only got three days."

"Pfft." Dad dismissed me with a wave. "We'll go to the store together later."

"Tonight? Tomorrow morning, early?"

Dad wiggled his nose. "No, I have a few things going on. My meditation class early tomorrow, and Perkatory."

"Friday?"

"Maybe, or definitely Saturday morning."

I shook my head and gave in to Dad's inertia. I'd go to the store tomorrow. How hard could one tray of lasagna be, when I'd already perfected the recipe?

We sat and cracked stupid jokes while watching a few episodes of the dating show—it was an entire marathon—until there was a knock at the door. Dad stood and announced that he'd get it.

I heard the creak of the hinges on the front door and Dad's voice. "Noah, my man, come on in. Ooh, what did you bring?"

"Lana's favorite." Noah walked into the living room with an enormous pizza box. Smelling food and seeing his favorite person, Stanley rocketed off the sofa while Noah handed Dad the pizza.

"Triple meat, extra cheese, from the Pizza Keg."

I perked up. That was my preferred pizza place on the island, although I didn't tell Erica and Joey that, since Joey's restaurant was also known for its pies. I preferred the thick crust of the Pizza Keg, versus Joey's New York–style thin crust.

Dad left the room and Noah sat next to me while Stanley raced to his toybox. He loved to show off his toys when anyone came over; he grabbed a stuffed dinosaur and raced around the room with it in his mouth.

"You doing better?" Noah rubbed my upper arm.

"Dad made tea, and we watched some trash TV, so yeah, big improvement from earlier."

Dad walked in with a plate in each hand. "Pizza for the hard-working sleuths."

I accepted the plate without commenting on his description of me as a sleuth. "Thanks, dude. Where's yours?"

Dad rubbed his hands together. "I have a dinner engagement tonight, and since Noah's here, I figured I could leave you alone. Unless you need me, and I'll stay."

Why was he being so cryptic? Did Dad have a hot date? I didn't ask because the concept of Dad romancing a woman was too much for my brain to process in the moment. Surely he would've told me if he'd found someone special. "I'm fine. Especially with this pizza that's about to be in my belly."

While I made a little shoo motion, Dad bent down to kiss me. "Call me if you need anything, munchkin. Noah, have a good one. Oh, and let me know if you want to talk with that guy I know who's selling a charter boat. I think it would be perfect for your new business venture."

"Thanks, sir. We'll see." Noah shook Dad's hand.

"Stay safe, kids." Dad smooched Stanley on top of the head and loped out. I inhaled one slice and reached for another while Noah was still working on his.

"Guess I was hungry," I mumbled. "What's that with Dad and the charter boat?"

"Peter has been looking for a fishing boat for me."

"Why? Are you seriously thinking of leaving the force?" Life seemed extra confusing today.

"We'll see, cupcake. We'll see. Today I need to focus on you, and this case."

Noah was probably merely humoring my father, who lived to connect people with homes, boats, yoga classes, and potential suitors. “Hey, why are you taking the time away from a crime scene? Shouldn’t you be investigating, or helping to investigate?”

Noah wiped his mouth with a napkin. “It’s true. I can’t stay long. But I wanted to make sure you were okay.”

An *aww* noise escaped my mouth, and I leaned over to kiss his cheek. “Thanks. I’ll be fine. Honest.”

He swept back a lock of my hair. “I’ve come to a conclusion.”

“Oh yeah? What about?” I carefully picked a tasty hunk of pepperoni off the pizza and popped it into my mouth.

“You.”

Gah. What now? “Okay. Lay it on me.”

“You’ve been looking into Jack’s death—”

“Well, uh, not exact—”

“Don’t try to explain or deny. We both know what you’ve been doing.” Noah smiled. “And I know you’re burning with curiosity about Darla’s death.”

“True.” I wondered where this was all going.

“I’ve decided that I’d prefer to work with you, and hopefully keep an eye on you, than have you out there on your own, winging it. You do that a lot, you know. Wing it. Like a wild, feral bird.”

I chewed slowly and swallowed, unsure if I appreciated that characterization. “What do you mean by that, work with me?”

“I’d like your opinion on these cases. In private. No newspapers, no freelance articles, no chatting with friends or family.” His smile faded, and he stared at me with those dark eyes of his.

“You mean, I can poke around and then tell you what I find?”

He twisted his mouth to the side. “I’d rather you not poke around in person. But if you find anything online, in the safety and privacy of your house, I’d like to know. But you can’t mention the details to anyone else. Like your father or Erica.”

Keeping secrets from Dad and Erica would be difficult, but worth it to help Noah on these two homicides.

"Hmm. Are you joking? Why are you doing this? In the past, you haven't wanted me anywhere near the murder cases."

He huffed out a little laugh and reached for the crust on my plate, which I never eat. Noah loved pizza crust. "Keeping you away from the homicide cases hasn't worked in the past, and probably won't work this time, either. My main goal now is keeping you safe while a murderer is loose. But the truth is, you're a good sleuth. You see patterns. Your mind is open. I need that kind of thinking right now, because I'm damned stumped on these cases, Lana. But make no mistake: I don't want you knocking on doors or interviewing people. You can't put yourself in harm's way. But if you stumble across information online, I'd appreciate if you share it with me."

Things had to be serious if Noah used a swear word. He almost never used profanity, and from the sober look on his face, I knew he wasn't messing with me.

"Of course I'll work with you, and yes, I'll keep everything secret. And I'll only sleuth online. Promise. Pinky swear." I sat up a little straighter and offered him my small finger. He locked his into mine, and we kissed.

As terrible as I felt about finding Darla, the prospect of helping to nab her killer was the only comforting possibility for closure, as far as I could see.

Chapter Sixteen

No sooner had Noah left to return to the crime scene that I realized I was already withholding information from him.

Darla's tote bag.

I'd been so shocked and upset by what I saw at the taffy store that I'd forgotten all about the canvas bag sitting in my office. What was inside? Probably nothing important, but I had a burning desire to check.

After telling Stanley to hold down the fort, I set out to Perkatory in my car. As I parked in the alley, hoping I wouldn't run into anyone while I dashed inside, my phone pinged with a text. It was Erica.

Hey, are you okay? I'm at a dentist appointment but can come by in a couple of hours.

I let out a groan of relief and texted her back. *No worries, we'll catch up later. I'm doing okay. Really!*

FIRE, she responded, in all caps. That was her latest way of saying "cool."

I slipped through the alley door of the building and crept up the back stairs, avoiding everyone inside the coffee shop. I didn't want or need all the questions surrounding my discovery of Darla, and was thankful Erica wasn't around. If she was, I was genetically incapable of not sharing what I was about to do.

Feeling stealthy, I quietly unlocked the office door, then shut it and exhaled. I'd managed to get up here sight unseen by the staff downstairs. I immediately dove for the bag in the corner and sank onto the threadbare sofa. My heart slammed against my chest, probably because I felt like I was doing something wrong.

I extracted three notebooks from the tote. One was an old black-and-white composition book. The other had a cartoon mushroom on the front, and the third sported a pretty Victorian flower print on the cover. I set those next to me on the sofa and dug around the bottom of the bag. There were three ball-point pens, two empty taffy wrappers, one uneaten piece of taffy, and a wad of receipts held together with an extra-large paper clip.

Okay. I formed a plan. My eyes swept around the room and landed on the desk. There. I needed that surface so I could spread everything out.

After clearing a space, I worked methodically, taking photos of everything. I started with the receipts, carefully snapping pictures of each slip of paper. She sure liked the Purple Power drink at the Smoothie Hut, the veggie deep dish pan pizza from a chain pizzeria, and the garden center on the mainland. All of the receipts were dated last month.

Once I was finished with those, I placed all the receipts back into their little stack and clipped them together. Then I started in on a notebook, the one with the smiling cartoon mushroom on the front.

It was only written in about a quarter of the pages, and I tried to be as quick as possible as I snapped photos of every page. What I really wanted was to sit with the words and read everything, but I could do that later on my computer at home. My intense curiosity would have to wait—I wanted to keep my promise to Noah and help him with the investigation.

For the next several minutes, the only sound was my cell phone making the old-timey camera shutter snap sound.

I finished that notebook and went on to the black-and-white book. That appeared to be notes about growing mushrooms, from the few words I read. Then I moved on to the Victorian notebook, which appeared to be more of a journal, with dates.

None of this seemed significant at first glance, but I captured it all anyway. When I was finished, I softly slid everything back into the tote bag and made my way out of the office. I drove over to the taffy shop and pulled up to an officer, who was standing near a ribbon of crime scene tape that prevented traffic from driving down the street.

It was Jorge Aguilar, a guy I'd known in high school. He was a few years younger than me and had been a band geek as well. He greeted me with a sad smile. A memory of him and Kevin stealing a clarinet player's reeds came to mind.

"Can you believe this is happening again?" he asked.

I shook my head. "Devil's Beach used to be such a quiet community."

"You got that right." He patted the hood of my car. "You doing an article?"

I shook my head. "Nope. Done with journalism. I have something to give the chief," I said with a smile, trying to be as friendly as possible. Jorge, like the rest of the force, knew I was dating Noah.

"He's at the victim's apartment. Do you know where that is? Or I can take whatever you have and give it to him. I expect him back in a little while."

"Oh, uh, it's personal. Could I get that address?"

Jorge leaned in and whispered the street address. I thanked him profusely, urging him to come by Perkatory for a free cup of coffee.

Even though I was no longer a journalist, I wasn't above bribing cops with free coffee in exchange for information. It's how I operated while working the crime beat for the Miami paper.

A few minutes later, I arrived at Darla's apartment. The two-story complex was from the sixties, all angular, mid-century modern angles. It probably had been a tourist motel for northern travelers when it was built, but these days, it served as cheap housing for retail workers. I'd heard this was one of the most affordable apartment buildings on the island—and it was still close to two grand a month. I also had no idea that Darla lived here.

Today, there seemed to be more police cruisers and crime scene vans than residents' vehicles. I pulled into an empty space on the far end of the lot and texted Noah.

Hey there. I have something important for you. I'm outside of Darla's apartment.

He texted back. *How'd you know where to find me?*

My excellent sources, I replied.

A few minutes later, Noah walked out of one of the ground floor units. He glanced around until he spotted my car, then strode toward me. I climbed out with the tote and leaned against my car.

"I didn't think I'd see you so soon," he said as he approached.

"I forgot I had this." I handed it to him.

"What is it? Salem, Massachusetts?" He read the words on the side of the tote.

"It's Darla's. She came to Perkatory the other day with a bunch of bags. We got to chatting and she left this one behind. I totally forgot after everything happened, but thought you'd want it."

He opened it and peered in. "Thanks for bringing it over. Have you gone through this?"

I licked my lips, knowing I couldn't tell a lie. "I did, briefly."

Noah glanced up and raised an eyebrow. "Briefly?"

"It's three notebooks and some receipts. I gave them a cursory look. Okay, I also took some photos so I could study the pages later."

He rubbed his forehead. "I wouldn't expect anything less from you."

"I'm going to take that as a compliment. You told me I could poke around safely."

Finally, he smiled.

"How's it going in there?" I gestured to the building.

"Slow, as these things usually are. We haven't found anything major. Yet."

I nodded, thinking of all the times I worked the crime beat and peeked into crime scenes in Miami. "Do you think I could take a quick look inside her apartment?"

Noah blinked at me. "A quick look?"

"Yeah. Used to do it all the time when I was a reporter. I promise I won't touch anything."

His dark brow knitted together. "Well, there is something I'd like your opinion on."

"Great!" I peeled myself off the side of the car and used my key fob to lock the door. "Let's go."

"We'll stop at my car first. You're going to need gloves and shoe covers."

We were silent as we power-walked to his cruiser. He fished something out of the trunk and handed me a plastic bag.

I studied his face. "You're serious about this. You're sure you want me poking around? You won't get into trouble?"

He flashed a dazzling smile. "Trouble? I'm the police chief, cupcake. And as you said yourself, you used to peek into crime scenes as a reporter. As long as you're with me, you're fine. And this isn't an active crime scene, anyway."

We walked to Darla's apartment. It was on the bottom floor, the last unit on the far left. I looked down, and there was a doormat with an image of singer Lionel Richie and the words, "HELLO, IS IT ME YOU'RE LOOKING FOR?"

A laugh escaped my lips and I pointed at the mat. "That's pure Darla. She had a quirky sense of humor."

The door was open, and I could see a handful of people inside. Crime scene techs and officers. It was like any cop show you'd see on TV, a bunch of tired-looking folks going through the stuff of a dead person. In real life it was depressing, not dramatic.

Noah leaned over to slip shoe covers around his shiny black police shoes. "Well, let's see what secrets Darla has inside. Put your gear on."

I complied, stuffing my sneakers into the blue shoe covers, then wrangling on the gloves. Doing this felt official, like we were really making progress—but my mind knew that was a lie. We were no closer to solving Jack's homicide, and Darla's death complicated everything by a thousand percent.

"Here are the ground rules. Keep your gloves on. Try not to touch anything. If you think something's significant, let me know. We're here to look, and only look. When in doubt, follow my lead."

"Got it."

I followed him into the apartment. From the looks of things, the place was quite small, especially for the price I knew Darla had paid. The living room and kitchen were one space, divided by a worn Formica counter made out of beige laminate and particle board. There was a hallway, and I spotted two doors.

The place smelled like laundry detergent, a fruity-floral blend with a punch of citrus. Probably she had to wash her clothes in a heavy-duty load to get that taffy scent out.

Noah reached for my arm. "We'll start with this room first. We'll take it slow." He spoke in a hushed tone, which somehow made the hushed busyness of the crime scene techs in the apartment even louder.

I raised my right hand. "I have two questions."

He nodded. "Yes?"

"What are we looking for? And why are we whispering?"

Noah's brow furrowed. "Dunno. I always whisper at crime scenes. It's a respect thing."

"I see."

"And we're looking for anything that seems interesting. But mostly to get a feel of who Darla was."

"Got it."

We shuffled through the sparsely decorated living room, carefully avoiding the crime scene techs dusting a few hard surfaces for fingerprints. First, I inspected a plant—a large monstera in a pot—and briefly marveled at how she'd kept the thing alive and healthy indoors. Noah stayed by my side, and if any of the police officials in the apartment thought it was odd that I was there, no one said a word or even looked alarmed.

I moved on to the next piece of décor: the bookcase.

It was about my height, painted white, made of cheap particleboard. The piece looked familiar because I think I'd had the same model in Miami. It was packed with books, and sadness washed over me. Darla had loved reading and books so much that she'd arranged each tome by color. Each shelf was its own rainbow hue, which gave the otherwise bleak room a cheery vibe.

Most of the titles were plant reference texts. One entire shelf was devoted to mushrooms, while another held several volumes about poisonous plants. Other books were about gardening in Florida, and she had a shelf just for fiction.

Turned out Darla loved historical romance novels—I spotted a few titles that I'd loved. I wished I'd known this about her, because I would've enjoyed chatting with her about some of these books.

"Finding anything interesting?" Noah said in a low voice.

"Perhaps. Some books on plants and poison."

Turning back to the bookcase, I gave it a quick once-over and glanced at a nearby desk. A crime scene tech was furiously snapping photos of the items on top. Stacks of papers, a mushroom statue, a mug filled with pens. Several saltwater taffy wrappers. Mundane stuff from a regular life.

A life snuffed out.

"There's something I'd like you to see in the bedroom," Noah said. "Follow me."

We took a few steps and turned left into the one bedroom. There were no techs or cops in this room, which made it almost eerie, it was so quiet and still.

"Whoa, look at all this." I hadn't been prepared for how cute it would be. Unlike the living room, which was sparsely decorated, and Darla's clothing style, which was utilitarian and tomboy at best, her sleeping area was awash in pink and white.

It was as if the mural of the pink peony on one wall had exploded into the room. A fuzzy pink throw was on the bed, which was neatly made with a fluffy white duvet. Pillows and a plush headboard matched the pink throw, and the rest of the furniture was bone white—except for a clear, Lucite chair in the corner.

"I'd have never pegged Darla to have this bedroom. Not in a million years."

It was a small space but filled with the fading light of the early evening. Still, there wasn't anything personal, as far as I could tell. No photos, books, or tchotchkes. The place wasn't merely tidy. It was like a high-end furniture showroom, devoid of dust and personality. It was all so odd.

"Check this out." Noah went to a bureau and slid open the top drawer. He extracted a silver-framed photo and held it out.

It was of Darla, wearing a parka and a knit hat. She looked happier than I'd ever seen her. She had her arms around the midsection of a tall, burly man with a scruffy beard and straight, dirty blonde hair that fell into his eyes and over his collar. They were in the mountains somewhere, a place obviously cold and clearly not Florida, from the snow in the background.

"What does this photo say to you?" Noah tapped his blue-gloved finger on the shiny frame.

"It was in the drawer when you found it?"

"Under the socks."

"That tells me that she's either trying to hide something out of shame or anger, or because she doesn't want to look at the person in the photo anymore. She used to have it on display, probably, but something happened with this man in the photo and she couldn't stand seeing it out in the open."

"Good." I sensed that Noah was testing me on my investigative skills. "What else?"

I hovered my index finger over the man's scruffy face but was careful not to touch the glass. "He doesn't look as excited as she does to be in the photo. His face looks . . . bored? Sour? She seems ecstatically happy, and trust me, she never seemed that way in everyday life."

"Really?"

"Darla was something more of an Eeyore. Kind of a low-key, no-nonsense person whose humor tended to the sarcastic and weird. I never knew her to get excited about much, other than mushrooms and taffy. And this photo looks fairly recent, because this is her new haircut. I'd say she got bangs, oh, around the holidays. Before that, her hair was wavy and loose, and she'd put it up while working into a bun. Here she has the new, short cut, with bangs."

"Interesting observation."

He went to put the photo away, but I touched his wrist. "Wait. Look at his body language. His hands are stuffed into his jeans, while she's all over him like a barnacle. Possibly this is the way he is, but most men know to at least act excited when a woman wants to take a photo."

A grin spread on Noah's lips. "Are you insinuating something about me? Us?"

"You're always happy to take photos. Aren't you?" I tilted my head.

"Confession: I'm not actually a fan, but I fake it to make you happy. I act excited."

I fought the urge to playfully swat him on the arm, because we were at a crime scene and supposed to be serious. "See, that's what I mean. The guy in this photo didn't even try to muster enthusiasm. He looks put out. I wonder if this is Moose."

"The name you heard when you were talking to her on the phone today."

I nodded. "Maybe she has photos of this guy in her cell phone. That's the obvious place."

"We didn't find her phone at the shop. We're looking for it here."

This news momentarily stole the breath from my lungs. "I was talking to Darla before this happened."

"Could've been on the store's landline."

I shook my head vigorously. "I called her cell. That means whoever did this took her phone."

Noah groaned.

"Hopefully we can find out this guy's identity, because he might be able to tell us about her life. Maybe it's a brother. Or a boyfriend. Although she never spoke about dating anyone until this week. But . . ." I tapped my gloved finger against my chin.

"But?"

I squinted one eye while trying to remember. "It was a few months ago, right around the time of her new haircut. She told us she would be away for a week, but she never told us where she went. I wonder if she went with that Moose character, and if he's the dude in the photo. Of course, that was right around Christmas, and we were slammed at the café, so I didn't press her. Darla always seemed like someone who was quite private. I try not to pry into my customers' personal lives. That's Erica's job."

Noah slipped the framed photo back into the drawer and shut it. I stood near the bed, marveling at the peony mural on the wall, and all the frothy pink hues in the room.

"It's funny. I never thought Darla was a girly-girl, even a little. I always got an adult tomboy vibe from her. I'm shocked that she lived like this."

Noah turned to the bed and checked underneath the white eyelet dust ruffle, then he flipped the duvet up and ran a palm under the mattress. He stood up, his hands empty.

"Cupcake, when you investigate enough crime, you realize that most people aren't who they say they are. And when you find someone who is, you hold onto them for dear life."

Chapter Seventeen

An hour later, after scrutinizing everything in Darla's small, sparse apartment, we were back at my place. Noah, being the chief, felt that his detectives and officers had everything under control at both the taffy shop crime scene and Darla's apartment.

Stanley welcomed us at the door with the excitement of a dog that hadn't seen his family in years. As usual, he greeted me for approximately three seconds, then threw himself into Noah's arms.

After we got him calmed down with two doggie meatballs and lots of kisses and snuggles, Noah stood in the middle of my living room with his hands on his hips.

"How are you feeling? Are you tired? It's only eight o'clock."

"If you're asking if I want to go to sleep, the answer's no. And I'd rather not be alone tonight." I bit my lip. What I really wanted was to look through the photos I'd taken of Darla's notebooks.

"I wouldn't think of leaving you tonight, but I'm curious if you want to go over the evidence you found in Darla's bag, or if you want to wait."

My eyes widened. "You read my mind. If you're game for that, I'm definitely up for it."

Noah chuckled. "Figured you would be."

"Okay, what do we need? Snacks? Coffee? Tea? My mom's old whiteboard?"

He ran a hand through his hair. "I guess some water. Where's the whiteboard?"

"In the guest bedroom, where Dad left it," I called out while walking away.

First, I went to change out of the clothes I'd been wearing all day—somehow it felt wrong to sit around in the jeans and T-shirt I wore when I found Darla. It hadn't occurred to me earlier to change, probably because I was in shock. I threw on a pair of yoga pants and one of Noah's hoodies that I'd swiped from his house a few weeks ago.

Then I went into the kitchen to pour us two big glasses of water and arranged some Oreos on a plate, since they were Noah's favorite. He rarely allowed himself to have the cookies because he was into fitness and healthy living, but I figured this—our first official investigation together—was a special occasion.

I walked back into the living room to find him staring at the whiteboard. It was filled with Dad's wild handwriting, from his earlier conjectures about Jack's death.

Noah shook his head. "You and your crew, I swear."

"We get the job done."

He pointed the eraser at me. "What's rule number one of this investigation? Wait. Is that my hoodie?"

"Yep. It is. And the number one rule is, don't say anything to Dad, Erica, or anyone else." I pantomimed zipping my mouth.

"Good girl." He erased Dad's words with vigor. "Now. Do you have a printer we could connect to my laptop, or, better yet, a wireless printer that works with your phone?"

I bit my lip and winced. "I have a printer but it might not be working."

"The one near your desk in the bedroom?"

I nodded, and Noah walked out of the room while I sat on the sofa. Stanley was on his bed, watching the goings on.

Noah returned with the printer and a ream of paper, and I sat and snacked while he set everything up on the coffee table. When he was finished, cables were everywhere, and he took two folders out of his briefcase.

"While I write a list of suspects on the board, why don't you go through the public files we have so far on Jack's homicide." He swiped an Oreo off the plate and stuffed the entire cookie in his mouth.

"You got it." I reached for the stack of papers. Although I was thrilled that Noah was sharing paperwork with me, I knew it wasn't that big of a deal—all of this was public record, easily accessible to journalists or anyone who filed a request with the department.

The only sound in the room came from the squeak of the marker on the board and the soft, muffled noise of pages being turned. Jack's case file wasn't large, and I'd seen several like it during my days as a reporter. It was written by the responding officer, in dry, dull language with plenty of police lingo.

"*Your affiant was summoned to the Peace on Earth Garden after a 911 call made by a citizen.*"

"Noah, tell your officers that it's Peas. Like the vegetable. Not Peace. There's a typo here."

He shook his head. "Don't get me started on my officers' grammar. I swear some of them have never read a book."

I chuckled and read on. One of the things I adored most about Noah was that he loved books.

The report was pretty bare bones. "An initial search of the property identified the body of an elderly man lying in the dirt near tomato plants. He was fully clothed and appeared to have been dead for only a short time. No decomposition was present. There were no indications of a disturbance or struggle."

A list of evidence collected at the scene included the syringe under Jack's body, his wallet, his car keys, the gold earring that I'd found, and four cherry tomatoes.

Then I got to the autopsy. It, too, wasn't all that enlightening. It described death by fentanyl injection, the location of the puncture wound, and the overall condition of Jack's body. According to Vern the medical examiner, Jack had been a robust, healthy eighty-one-year-old with no health issues.

"There's not much here," I remarked.

Noah stepped back from the board. "That's precisely the problem. Okay, here's who we've got so far. Am I missing anyone?"

I studied his list and went through it aloud. "Willa the daughter, Clay the surfer, Beau the dog groomer, Bill the handyman, Joanie the developer, and Olivia the Dylan-hating mom. I think that captures it. Unless we're overlooking someone. But wait, these are all suspects in Jack's death. What about Darla? And the guy she mentioned on the call with me today—Moose."

Noah stared at the board while gnawing on his lip. "My gut tells me that if we solve Jack's death, we'll solve Darla's, too."

He added Darla's name, and the word MOOSE in big letters.

I tapped a pen on the closed case file. His logic seemed reasonable. "What's Willa's alibi? Why would she want Darla dead? It doesn't make sense."

"She doesn't have one for Jack's death. Told us she was home watching a movie."

"Seems a bit sketch. Have you contacted Clay?" I reached for my phone.

"Stopped by Clay's house today. He wasn't home, and was on the mainland, allegedly looking for a job. My plan is to hit up his house early tomorrow. Bill seems to be a bit more elusive. He hasn't been home during the two times we stopped by his house, and we haven't reached him on the phone."

"Also a bit sketchy. Clay's a drinker, so there's that, too." I quickly told Noah about my conversation with Lex. "Well, let's check out Darla's notebooks. How about I email you the photos I snapped, and we can look on your laptop? I took a ton of pictures and we'll go blind if we try to read on my cell."

Noah pointed to my laptop, which was on the coffee table alongside his. "It'll be faster if you email half to me and half to you, and we can go through them at the same time on two separate computers."

I smiled. "You always have the best ideas."

"That's me. An idea man."

It took me a solid ten minutes to email the hundreds of photos. Once they'd all arrived in our email inboxes, Noah and I sat side by side on the sofa. The sound of keyboard clicks replaced conversation as we each opened our first file.

"This is cozy," I said, nudging his leg with mine.

He chuckled in response and reached for another Oreo.

I'd sent myself photo after photo of the receipts. None seemed significant. It didn't take long to check my batch of photos, which left me with a burning disappointment in my chest. Meanwhile, Noah printed out several files, and my long-dormant printer whirred to life.

I was shocked it was even working.

"I'm not finding anything so far. Mostly food receipts, recipes for taffy flavors, and a few notes about mushroom growing. You?"

Noah hummed. "Yeah, this is interesting. It appears to be her journal. Here's what she wrote: 'Talk to Lana.' There's even a check mark next to it. See?"

I glanced up from my screen. "That's mildly notable, I guess. Not really, though, if she's a list-maker like me. I write down everything I need to do."

"Oh yeah? Why?"

I lifted my shoulders. "It makes me feel accomplished to check things off my list. I write down things that I know I'll do, like brushing my teeth. That way I can check it off and get a little dopamine hit."

This elicited a snort-laugh from Noah, then he stopped and read aloud, his finger hovering over the side of the screen.

"'Even in death that guy's yanking my chain. It was nothing but problems with him at the garden from the moment I took over. He gave me a hard time about every single thing. Every decision I made, he'd write a ten-page email rebutting it. Every time I asked him to not use certain pesticides, he'd argue like he was going before the Supreme Court.'"

"Wait, what?" I sat up, alarmed, placing my laptop on the table. "Lemme see that. Did she write those words?"

He hovered his finger underneath the passage, which was written in neat, loopy cursive. "Yep. Here. See?"

"No way," I whispered.

"What?"

"She said those exact words to me in Perkatory when she asked me to clear her name. Like, the very same sentences, no deviation."

"That's weird. Who does that?" Noah's dark brow formed a scowl.

"What else does it say?"

"That's all on this page. Here's the next. She's very precise and numbered and dated each page of her journal. And look at this." He clicked to another photo. "These doesn't seem like journal entries. It seems like she's rehearsing conversations."

"Welcome to Ye Olde Taffy Shoppe," she wrote. "We have ten flavors of taffy, including a new flavor, cosmic grape. Please have a look around, and let me know if I can answer any questions."

After that paragraph were several versions of the same information.

"That's odd. She wrote things down before saying them. I wonder why." Social anxiety, perhaps? It was the only thing that came to mind.

Noah clicked out of the photo and opened the next. We both stared at the screen. Darla had written one word on each line. The date at the top read Sunday—the date Jack was killed.

Jack

Is

A

Giant

Jerk

"I'm printing this one out. Seems significant," he muttered.

"What the what?" I sputtered. "Was Jack no longer a problem because he was dead when she wrote that?"

Now I had to consider whether Darla was a killer all over again. Crap on a cracker, this case was confusing.

Noah scrolled down so we could see the rest of the page. There were six letters.

"JIAGJ. What does that mean?"

"Oh, wait," I squeezed Noah's arm. "Erica told me that Darla used mnemonics to remember things. Look. Jack Is A Giant Jerk—JIAGJ. Although why would she need a mnemonic to remember that?"

"Whoa. It would've taken me all night to figure that out. Nice work, Lewis."

I beamed. There was no greater feeling of pride than cracking open a puzzle. Whether it was identifying the murderer in a TV mystery in the first half of the show, or piecing together an investigative news article, I loved the challenge of figuring out obscure information. Doing it to help solve the murder of a friend was deeply gratifying.

And yet, my crack investigative skills had gotten us no closer to the truth. There were pages and pages of acronyms in her journal. Some, like the one about Jack, were explained. Others weren't. It would take a code cracker weeks to figure all this out. Noah peered at the screen intently.

"What's next?" I asked.

"You're already finished with yours?"

"Mmm-hmm."

Noah shifted, stretching his arm around me. Now, this was comfy. Together, we scrolled through several pages of her journal, commenting on her notes about various plants and new taffy flavor ideas.

Strawberry lemonade was underlined three times.

"Barf." I buried my face in Noah's chest and he laughed.

"You really hate taffy, don't you?"

I pantomimed a gag as he clicked to the next page. We were on a new notebook now, dated two weeks ago, before Jack was killed.

"*My beloved says we will prevail,*" began the first sentence on the first page. "*M says we will seek vengeance, and my name will be cleared.*"

"M for Moose," I said.

"Well, that's a big departure from the taffy recipes and the mushroom manure fertilizer," Noah quipped.

"Who is her boyfriend? The guy in the photo? She's never mentioned anyone, not once. And I've never seen her with a guy."

Noah worried his bottom lip between his teeth but didn't say anything. I sensed this case was annoying him, because nothing seemed clear.

We clicked through several more pages, but her writing was all about mushrooms and fungi. Noah let out a long sigh. By this time, I was starting to get sleepy, probably from the excitement and trauma of the day.

"I'm going back over everything," he murmured.

"Mmm. I'm hitting the wall. So tired all of a sudden." I curled up next to him and rested my head on his chest. We were slumped in a weird position on the sofa, and to anyone watching, we probably looked uncomfortable. But being this close to Noah on this particular day was exactly what I needed.

My eyes drooped and my breathing slowed. The sound of keyboard clicks and Stanley's snores from the other side of the room lulled me to into sleep.

The next thing I knew, I felt Noah scooping me into his arms and gently carrying me to bed. He then brought Stanley in and covered him with his fleece doggie blanket at the foot of the bed. Finally, Noah climbed between the sheets himself and spooned me tight. My last thought before I fell into another deep slumber was that I hoped Darla, at least once, had felt the peace I did in that moment.

Chapter Eighteen

I was wide awake at five thirty. Normally I liked to hit the snooze button a few times, but today, I jumped out of bed and went straight to the coffee maker. Noah, of course, had been awake since five, had already showered, and was checking his email.

"Who is this woman and what has she done with my girlfriend?" Noah kissed me good morning as I was preparing a mug of hot water and lemon for him. How he got through the day without caffeine was anyone's guess.

"Lots and lots to do today." I took half of a lemon and nestled it into the squeezer contraption, then aimed it over Noah's to-go mug. "Which brings me to my first question."

"There's more than one question?" Noah's black hair was semi-dry after a shower and had curled into an adorable cowlick.

"Considering everything that's going on with Darla and Jack's cases, do you think it's the best weekend for your mom to visit? It's Friday, so there's still time to postpone." I chucked the spent lemon into the trash.

"Normally I'd agree and reschedule, but she has a three-week cruise coming up with her friends, and she wants to meet you before that. Probably so she can brag to everyone that her son has finally met a decent woman. We can't move it. I'm sorry, cupcake."

I stifled a sigh. Compromise was essential for healthy relationships. "Okay, cool, cool."

"Oh, and I forgot to tell you. My sister's vegan. Is that going to mess you up with your dinner menu?"

"Not at all." I waved my hand as if I wasn't lying like a rug. "I can make the lasagna vegan."

"Or better yet, make a vegan and non-vegan version. The last one you made with that cheese was incredible."

"Oh yeah, that's a great idea." I smiled. What the fluff was I talking about? I hadn't bought the ingredients for anything, and here it was Friday and I was promising two trays of lasagna. The clock was ticking so hard that it was screaming at me.

"Cool. I'll take care of the wine." He kissed my temple and grabbed his mug. "I'm going to stop by Bill's place on my way to the office. I'll be in touch. Remember. No talking about the case, no putting yourself in danger. You can definitely use your ample internet capabilities, though, but no in-person investigation. I'm serious."

I wrapped my arms around his neck. "I'm Lana. Nice to meet you."

"You're so silly." He brushed his lips over mine. "Talk to you soon."

Stanley escorted Noah to the front door, while I stayed in the kitchen drinking coffee and jotting a new list of grocery items. Since it was Friday, there was no way I could avoid the grocery store today. I'd work my shift at Perkatory, then race over the bridge to the big grocery store on the mainland.

I wolfed down a piece of toast with peanut butter, let Stanley in the yard to do his business, then pedaled my bike to Perkatory. That was one of the perks—pun intended—of Devil's Beach, that everything was close to home.

Everything but an excellent and large grocery store.

When I pedaled up to the café, there were two people waiting to be let inside, eager for their caffeine fix. Both were regulars, service workers who were toiling long hours among spring breakers, but still. Fridays were one of our busier days, and I felt in my bones that today would be a doozy.

I quickly made the regulars their double espresso lattes, then turned on the tunes. Lately I'd been relying on a yacht rock playlist on my favorite streaming service, and I turned it up a notch louder than usual. Customers on Fridays generally were in a good mood, and some smooth seventies tunes would help them ride into the weekend.

"Only the Good Die Young" by Billy Joel was the first song, and I stared at the speaker. Perhaps the wrong song for today, considering the news of Darla was surely spreading across the island. I pressed "next song" on my phone, and "Do You Believe in Magic" by the Lovin' Spoonful bubbled up.

Much better.

I was steadily busy for an hour, and right at seven, Erica ambled in, wearing a black Perkatory T-shirt, black jeans, and combat boots. Today was one of our staggered shift days, and she high-fived me when she came behind the counter.

"What's cookin', good lookin'?"

"Oh, not much. Noah and I spent last night—" I winced, because I wasn't supposed to tell anyone about our investigation.

"You what? Got engaged? Played naked Twister?" Her eyes grew wide. "Oh, crud. I totally forgot about yesterday. Are you okay? Aww, did Noah comfort you last night? I'm really glad he was there for you."

Only Erica would forget about an actual homicide down the street. But this gave me an excuse to deflect from my near spilling of secrets. "Yeah, I'm a little shaky today, but overall fine. Noah did come over last night, and, uh. Yeah."

Erica and I nodded at each other. Sometimes she did know when it was time to probe, and when to stay silent.

"Well, I'm glad you're here. Glad you're okay. What would I do without you?" She tied her apron around her waist. "Now let's steer this ship into the weekend."

The pace picked up as the morning went on. Most of the tourists wanted cold, frothy drinks, and to ask about tomorrow's Funnel Cake Festival. Erica answered those questions because she was working the event with Joey.

"We'll be making key lime funnel cakes, and traditional strawberry ones, too." Erica reached for a stack of festival flyers on the counter, handing one to an impressed customer.

When the rush died down, I sidled up to Erica.

"Hold the phone. You didn't tell me you were making key lime funnel cakes." Key lime was one of my favorite flavors.

"It's a last-minute entry into the funnel cake competition. Joey and I came up with the recipe last night. We were eating some key lime pie, then started to experiment in the kitchen, and we were up until two perfecting it. I don't think I can ever eat anything lime flavored again, I tested so many."

I was about to ask Erica if I could snag some key lime funnel cake for the dinner party, when John from Beach Boss, the souvenir shop owner down the block, walked in, looking like he was going to weep.

"I can't believe the news about Darla. I was talking to her the other day in here over coffee, about my bromeliad blooms." He blinked back tears. John was a large-framed, happy-go-lucky guy, and to see him this upset broke my heart.

"Aww, I'm sorry." I walked around the counter and gave him a hug, wondering how he'd feel if he knew Darla might actually be responsible for another person's death. That didn't mean Darla deserved to die, of course. The complexity of it all made me sniffle, too, and Erica came over to us and hugged us both.

As we were consoling each other, I heard the boom of a familiar voice.

"What do we have here? A cuddle puddle?"

It was Dad, and now he was hugging the three of us. Fortunately, the customers at Perkatory took our antics in stride, and one woman asked if she could join the group hug. Dad welcomed her in. That was my cue to break apart from the group, because while it was okay to hug John, Erica, and my dad, I drew the line at random strangers.

A while later, behind the counter, Dad came up to me. "Munchkin, we need to have a talk."

He sounded surprisingly serious. "What's up? You okay?"

Dad shook his head. "Not out here. Can we go into the back room, or, better yet, upstairs to the office?"

This was a shocker. Dad never requested privacy for any of his conversations. Usually, he was a no secrets kind of guy, and didn't care if the entire world knew his business. My stomach tightened, and I racked my brain, trying to recall if he had a doctor's appointment recently. What if Dad was sick? My mind began to race. I thought of Willa and her grief, and my anxiety mounted.

"Sure, let me ask Erica to watch the counter."

She was making a special mocha latte for John, and agreed to hold down the fort. Dad and I trooped upstairs in silence. Once inside the office, he took the desk chair and I sat on the worn sofa that was covered in a colorful batik print that Mom had gotten decades ago in India, or so I'd been told.

Suddenly I felt like I was a teenager, sitting in here doing my homework while Mom or Dad crunched numbers in ledger books. They'd opened Perkatory when I was in high school, mostly because Mom loved great coffee and had traveled the world as a coffee buyer.

"What's wrong, Dad? Why the serious face? Are you feeling okay?" My shoulder muscles tensed.

Dad sipped in a breath and pressed his hands together in a prayer position. He glanced up to a framed photo of Mom on the wall. It was a photo taken long before I was born, at a music festival in Europe. She looked like a young Stevie Nicks, all ethereal and ultra-cool with her long, feathered hair like Farrah Fawcett, tinted round sunglasses, and fuzzy rainbow scarf.

"I never told you about a conversation that I had with your mother in the weeks before she died."

I reared back. "Whoa, I wasn't expecting you to bring up Mom today."

"It's time we talked about this. I haven't wanted to tell you until it's necessary. It's essential that I tell you now."

I sat in mute, confused silence, but finally nodded. "Go ahead."

"Remember that time period between when your mother had the heart attack, and then her stroke?"

I scrubbed at my face and mumbled, "Yeah."

How could I forget? Those were the worst six weeks of my life, going back and forth from Miami to Devil's Beach. We thought Mom was going to recover, which seemed like a spot of good news given her condition—and because my marriage was in trouble.

Then she was gone. One day, I'd been talking with her about coffee; the next, she was dead. Doctors said it wasn't unusual for a person to have heart problems but succumb to sudden strokes.

"Well, when she came home from the hospital the first time, she invited Barbara over for dinner. You know your mother, always wanting to make a good meal for friends and family. You were back in Miami, it was a weeknight. A Wednesday. I remember it clear as day. She made her seafood red sauce with linguini."

A sad smile spread on my face. I could imagine Mom moving slowly around the kitchen at the beach house, boiling water for pasta and breaking up the canned San Marzano tomatoes. She'd perfected a four-ingredient red sauce, then added fresh shrimp, scallops, and octopus. "No, you never told me about this dinner."

For some reason, Dad was looking everywhere in the office but at me. "Your mother sat me and Barbara down before we ate and made us promise her something."

His words hung in the air, and I expected him to go on. He nodded. I blinked. "What did she say?"

"Your mom said that if anything happened to her, she wanted Barbara and me to be together as a couple."

I looked around helplessly. Of all the things he could've told me, this wasn't one I expected. "I see."

"It's taken a while, and now we're dating." He pushed out a breath. "Barbara and I are an item. We plan on making it Facebook official tonight. She's also the silent partner in my Perk Pops business. We came up with the idea together on our first date, which was three months ago."

My eyebrows squished together. He'd been keeping this from me for three months? "I'm sorry, what?"

"I know there's no good way to announce this, but I wanted you to hear it first, before the Devil's Beach gossip worked its way to you. Or before you saw it on Facebook. We've been going off-island for our dates. We discussed telling you together but decided I should talk with you alone. I hope you're not upset, because we really want your blessing. Since it was Mom's idea and all. I never even thought of Barbara that way, but your mom, well, she knew us better than we did."

I stammered for a bit, unsure of what to say. It wasn't that I didn't want Dad dating, or that I disliked Barbara. In fact, of all the single women on the island, Barbara was an excellent, age-appropriate match for him. She'd been friends with my parents for years. She was employed, didn't have a criminal record, and was actually one hundred percent sane.

One of the few people on Devil's Beach who were.

And if Mom suggested it, I was cool with it.

But it still came as a shock. Dad, *dating*? Would they eventually get married? Would Barbara be my . . . stepmom?

"Well. Gosh. That's . . . that's great." I tried to be more enthusiastic, but the surprise of it all left me feeling feverish and uncomfortable, like this office was too small and too hot.

"I wanted to make sure you were okay with it." Dad looked genuinely concerned.

"Oh, Dad, yeah, I am. I love Barbara. She's like family." While I did have complex feelings about him moving on and dating, I didn't want to get into those now. Not while processing Darla's death. It was all too much emotion for one week, and I tended to shut down if I felt overwhelmed.

"Great! It might take you a little while to get used to. Heck, it's even taking me a while." Dad slapped his thighs. "Would you mind if she came to dinner tomorrow with the entire gang?"

I answered without thinking. "No, not at all."

There was no way I could say anything but yes. I'd known this day was coming, but I didn't believe it would be this week, the same as two murders and a big dinner. There was no right time for this kind of news, regardless.

"Excellent. We'll bring some vegan appetizers." He stood up, and I did too. "Munchkin, I love you."

"Love you too, Dad." He folded me into a bear hug, and then asked if I was going downstairs.

I shook my head. "I need to take care of some paperwork up here."

"Cool, cool. See you down below. Oh. We're still on for grocery shopping tomorrow morning, right?"

"Absolutely." The thought of driving to the mainland tonight when traffic was at its worst and the store was crowded seemed too much to deal with.

When Dad left, I sat in the office chair that was still warm from his body and stared up at the photo of Mom. What would she do after the events of this week, with Jack and Darla, and now this news?

Mom would probably say one of her signature lines: "When words don't make sense, a good cup of coffee can make everything clear."

Then she'd laugh and pour another cup, which was exactly what I planned to do.

Chapter Nineteen

Even though I was still reeling from Dad's news, I went downstairs and behind the counter to help out, even though all I wanted was to go home and crawl back into bed with Stanley. It seemed as though life was happening way too fast, and I wanted to hit the pause button.

The café was quiet, with many of the customers tapping away at laptops. The early '80s hit "Key Largo" by Bertie Higgins was like a warm hug in the air with Dad humming along and Erica casually thumbing through the *Beacon* newspaper.

She tapped on the page. "Isn't this one of our suspects?"

I stood next to her and studied the paper. It was two inside pages filled with photos. In journalism parlance, it was called "a double truck," because back in the old days of newspapering, the heavy metal pages for printing were filled with lead type and rolled around the newsroom on carts, or trucks. Two pages for one single project were dubbed "double trucks."

In larger newspapers double trucks were for special investigations. In smaller papers like the *Beacon*, they were showcases for photos, a way for the community to see itself reflected in the local news.

This spread was no different; it was of the island farmers market, held every Sunday in the winter.

There, in two of the photos, was Beau the dog groomer. He was at the Pooch to Perfection booth, selling dog shampoo.

"This might give him an alibi," I murmured. The market's hours were from nine until three, and Jack was likely killed around ten in the morning, according to the autopsy report. The market and the community garden were about three miles apart.

If one was ambitious and didn't get caught in morning beach traffic, they could kill someone at the garden and be at the market within a half hour. There was only one way to find out, though.

I dialed Mike Heller of the *Beacon.*

"Lana Lewis. My favorite reporter." His rich baritone made me smile. "Are you calling to tell me you've finally written that features piece on reasons your barista hates you?"

I winced. Several months ago, I'd written a couple of freelance articles for Mike, and he'd wanted a few features too. But the pay was abysmal, the topic insipid (as many feature stories are, at least the editor-generated ones), and I'd gotten swamped with café business.

"Still thinking about those, Mike," I said briskly. "Listen, I saw the double truck of the farmers market. Nice pics, who took them? I didn't see a credit."

His chuckle wafted through the phone. "I did. Our photographer was out sick and I had nothing interesting or local to put on a couple of pages, so voilà! I played photographer for the day."

"Well, they were excellent. I really loved the one of . . ." My gaze went to the paper. "The organic goat milk stand. But I'm curious about a couple of the photos, the ones of the guy working for Pooch to Perfection."

"Beau? He's awesome. Did you know that he's the only one able to bathe Henry?" That was Mike's rescue pittie. "Henry adores him."

"Oh, cool. He did a great job with Stanley this week, too. I'm curious. How long were you at the market that day? And was Beau there the entire time?"

"I arrived right when it opened at nine. Hmm. Now that I think about it, yes. Beau was there the entire time, because he was giving away samples of dog shampoo, and it was quite popular. He had a line for about thirty minutes straight. Those photos didn't come out so well, though. Why do you ask?"

The last thing I wanted was for Mike to know I was assisting Noah with the murders. "No reason, just curious."

"Lana, you always have a reason for your curiosity. Spill."

I inhaled a thin breath. It was taking every ounce of willpower not to tell him my secret. "Mike, I can't. I'm sorry. Maybe later. Just trust me that this is important and that you've been a big help."

"Does this have to do with Darla's murder? I was going to call to ask you to comment, but honestly, I knew you'd be broken up, considering everything in your past. During high school." His voice took on a soft tone. Mike and I met when I was in high school and he was the new editor of the paper.

He'd taken me on as an intern that summer. My parents had pushed me into the unpaid job because I'd been depressed that my best friend, Gisela, had gone missing.

"You know me too well, Mike. I'm doing okay. Listen, I have to run, a customer walked in. Talk soon." I hung up and drummed my fingers on the counter, watching as a group of spring breakers walked in and gawped at the chalkboard menu overhead. Erica joined me and we waited as the group debated whether to get iced vanilla lattes or Nutella lattes.

I tapped out a quick text to Noah, telling him that Beau was no longer a suspect and why.

Excellent process of elimination, he wrote back. I slid the phone into my apron pocket.

"I overheard you talking to Mike," Erica said out of the corner of her mouth.

I nodded. "I cleared Beau's name." There was no use in denying it, since she'd overheard my conversation. Surely this was innocuous enough news that I could share. "He was definitely at the market the entire time, handing out dog shampoo. Mike saw him."

"Excellent. One down, seven to go. Or is it eight?"

I licked my lips. "Seven. That we know of." Which didn't make me feel better.

One of the spring breakers, a guy shaped like a fireplug and wearing a Hawaiian shirt, neon green shorts, and matching green shades, stepped up. "If we get the Nutella latte, can you put some fireball in it? Like mix it all together in your blender over there? A boozy milkshake."

He set a bottle of alcohol on the counter and gestured to the blender station. Erica looked at him, stared down at the bottle, and sighed. "We were like this once, weren't we?" she asked me.

I snickered. "I'm sure we probably were, and this is karmic payback for our misdeeds."

* * *

Once my shift was over, I booked it home. Clearing Beau's name had lit a fire under me, and hopefully I could knock more suspects off the list. I'd asked Noah if I could poke around on Joanie and Olivia's alibis, and he said yes—as long as I didn't pretend to be a police officer, or didn't tell any of my nosy friends and family what I was doing.

The second I arrived home I fired up my laptop and plopped on the sofa, a half-filled notebook and favorite pen at my side. Stanley stood in the middle of the living room, staring at me.

"Give me an hour, buddy. One hour, and we'll play after that."

As if he could tell time and wasn't pleased with my answer, he heaved a heavy dog sigh and trooped to his bed in the corner of the room. He flopped down dramatically.

Meanwhile, I muttered to myself as I talked. Olivia said she was in the Keys with her family that Sunday, and Joanie was in Miami at a real estate conference. From their ages and overall vibe, I wondered whether they would be eager to post on social media about their travels.

I navigated to Facebook and within minutes, I found Olivia's account. We had several mutual friends on Devil's Beach, including Lex Bradstreet. Interesting. Lex was everywhere, it seemed, but I wasn't here to pry into anyone's personal relationships.

All I wanted to know was where Olivia had been on Sunday. Every post of hers was public, and considering she published photos multiple times a day of her son, it took a while to scroll through. I found myself fascinated by her videos, too: she seemed to enjoy filming making her son's lunches, and I wondered if I was a mom, would I take the time to cut bread crusts off, shape mini sandwiches into flowers, and dehydrate kale parmesan chips.

This made me think of how Dad assembled my lunches when I was a kid. He'd slap together a peanut butter sandwich on wheat and throw a banana in the bag. Sometimes he'd slip a note in, claiming that the Dalai Lama had packed the lunch. That had always confused me as a seven-year-old.

"Aha," I finally said aloud as I reached Olivia's posts from Sunday. Sure enough, there were several entries, all of her family—her husband, her son, and their golden retriever—splashing on a beach in the Keys.

One entry, at nine thirty that morning, was tagged to a restaurant in Key West, with the caption "Last time I was in Key West I was twenty-two and not up at this hour. Now I'm at a kid-friendly restaurant and ready to take on the day! I'm not even hungover LMFAO."

It showed the three of them grinning over Mickey Mouse–shaped pancakes. That was all the evidence I needed to know she was not a suspect. I jotted some notes and moved on to Joanie.

From the little I knew about her, I suspected she'd be more private online. In my time as a reporter, I'd noticed that the richer a person was, the more they protected their privacy. Joanie seemed to be no exception because her Facebook and Instagram profiles were locked down.

I stroked the keyboard with my fingertips. How could I confirm Joanie was in Miami? I typed the words "real estate conference Miami" and the weekend's dates into Google, and within two clicks, found a big one held at the Convention Center in Miami Beach.

The Florida Realtors Trade Expo was the largest in the southeast, I learned. It had its own YouTube channel and a schedule, and I navigated there. It took me a while to wade through the schedule because it was a weeklong conference. Sunday was the final day, and I finally found what I was looking for.

Sunday Morning

Keynote: Women Developers in Affordable Housing. Speaker: Joanie Clarke, of Clarke and Sons Inc.

Aha. There was a link to the YouTube channel, and I clicked over. There was Joanie, giving a forty-five-minute speech on why women were needed in all levels of affordable housing development.

While it seemed darkly ironic that she would talk about this to a crowd of a thousand when her hometown of Devil's Beach had very little affordable housing and folks were struggling to pay rent, I couldn't deny one fact.

She, too, had a solid alibi during the time Jack was killed.

As the video droned on, I sent a text to Noah, updating him on my progress. He returned my message with a thumbs up and the words *Working on Clay now, talk later.*

I wasn't sure if we were any closer to the truth, but it felt like we were making progress. Slowly. It was a frustrating feeling, but I had to remind myself that this wasn't television, and it wasn't news, when things seemed to happen quickly once a homicide was committed.

In truth, I'd come to discover, the investigative process was painstaking and filled with obstacles.

My neck felt achy because I'd been dipping my head to look at my devices—I swear, technology would be the death of all of us—and when I looked up, I spotted Stanley. He was standing in the middle of the living room with one of my sneakers in front of him. The shoelace was frayed and wet at the end, the obvious victim of his mischief.

"What's going on, buddy? Why'd you steal my shoe?" I rose from the sofa, intending to grab it from him, but he latched his tiny jaws on the soft edge and dragged it over to his bed. When I tried to snatch it back, he let out a tiny growl.

I made a clicking noise with my tongue and put my hands on my hips while I looked down at him. The words of the puppy kindergarten teacher echoed in my head: *a bored dog is a destructive dog.*

Although my sneaker hadn't been destroyed, this was Stanley's way of calling for help. He'd been cooped up in the house all day. Now I felt terrible, and although I knew I should be cleaning or preparing for tomorrow's dinner, the thought of my dog being bored and uncomfortable didn't sit well. He'd never chewed any of my shoes before this afternoon.

He placed a paw on top of the sneaker and stared up at me with defiant brown eyes.

"Wanna go to the dog park?"

He sprang to standing and wuffed softly, releasing my sneaker from his little paw. Everything else would have to wait.

Chapter Twenty

Because it was late afternoon, when most people were still at work, the dog park wasn't packed. There were a couple of elderly ladies with their poodles, and a Boston terrier with one eye. Stanley greeted everyone with enthusiastic sniffs, and the pack of tiny dogs collectively trotted off to have dog park adventures.

I perched on a bench, my arms folded, thinking about my ever-growing to-do list. The humidity had settled in the air, signaling that summer wasn't far off. The entire place smelled like sawdust and cut grass, since the town had recently mowed and put down new mulch.

As I was making a mental note of every room I needed to clean, an idea came to me.

What about a catered dinner? How much would that be for six people? Surely worth more than the stress I was putting myself under. It had been a difficult week, with two homicides. Dad's big life announcement had also thrown me for a loop. No one would fault me for mailing it in.

Except me, of course. I'd fault myself, chastise myself, beat myself up. My recovering perfectionist tendencies were showing, and I needed to put on my big girl panties and do what was best for my guests *and* me. Sometimes you couldn't do it all, Mom used to say.

I think she'd agree that this was a week where I wasn't capable of doing it all.

I reached for my phone and called Bay Bay's with the tasty grouper chowder, asking if they could cater a dinner for Saturday. I'd pay extra, I pleaded to the manager.

"Sorry, Lana, too short of a notice. Normally we'd be able to do it, but we've got the Funnel Cake Fest tomorrow," he replied.

I hung up. Undeterred, I dialed several more local restaurants. Their response was all the same. The Funnel Cake Fest was all anyone could focus on since it was one of the island's signature events. No one was taking catering orders, even with the promise of a huge tip. One restaurant suggested I try a few places on the mainland.

While I pondered this, I watched Stanley pick up a dirty tennis ball and take it to one of the elderly dog owners on the other bench. He loved pressing other humans into ball-throwing service. The woman tossed the ball a few feet, and he looked at her with a withering stare, as if to say, *That's all you got, lady?*

Stanley, small as he was, liked to play fetch like a big dog. He was fast, ripping through the grass to capture the ball. The farther the throw, the better the game. He picked up the tennis ball and trotted over to me, obviously knowing I would indulge him.

I did, hurling the yellow ball to the other end of the dog park.

"You've got a nice throw. Were you a softball player in high school?"

I turned in the direction of the woman's voice and was startled to see an impeccably coiffed Willa Daggitt standing there. She wore the same zebra-patterned sunglasses as the other day, along with a pink polo shirt and matching pink pedal pushers, along with crisp white sneakers, looking more like she was headed to brunch on Palm Beach than sitting around a stinky dog park. She even sported a dainty pearl necklace.

The only indication that she wasn't doing something elegant was a simple black fanny pack around her waist.

"Hey there, want to join me?" I moved my leash and purse onto my lap and scooted to the end of the bench, trying to hide my surprise that she'd approached me, given our last interaction at this very park.

She sat on the edge and twisted her body in my direction. "I'm sorry for the other day. I didn't mean to be so brusque. It's just that . . ."

I held up a hand. "I've lost a parent, so I know how difficult it can be. And my mom died under normal circumstances, a stroke. I can't even imagine what you're going through."

Although I sort of did, given the circumstances of my high school friend Gisela's disappearance. The fact that it had never been solved weighed on me, even a decade and a half later. But now wasn't the time or place to bring that up, or even dwell on it in my mind.

Willa shifted so she was staring straight ahead at the parking lot. "I only moved back to Devil's Beach a couple of months ago. I'd left here after high school and rarely came back. Only did to visit my dad over the years. As my career took off, I visited less and less."

"What year did you graduate? I went to Devil's Beach High too." I knew we weren't remotely in the same class, but I wanted her to feel comfortable talking with me. For that I needed common ground.

She told me the year, and I told her mine. "I left as soon as I could too. And now I'm also back. It's not as bad as I thought it would be."

It was way better, in fact.

"They say you can't go home again. Well, Thomas Wolfe said that. But until this week, I was thinking like you. That coming home wasn't entirely a bad thing. Now I'm not so sure."

I recalled her medical disciplinary record and bankruptcy. That and her father's murder had to be a one-two-three punch like no other.

She let out a bitter little snort. "My father was killed with synthetic opioids here. It's so ironic it's almost laughable."

My face contorted in confusion. "Excuse me?"

She huffed a little laugh. "Sorry, I've been spending a lot of time in my own head, even before Dad died. I'm Willa, and I'm a pill addict. That's what I tell people in recovery meetings every day. I've been clean for a year but knowing that my father died from a fatal dose is some kind of sick message from the universe."

Oh, perhaps that was why she lost her medical license. Her raw vulnerability tugged at something in my heart. I sensed that it took great effort to be genuine and honest with me. "I'm sorry, what you're going through sounds incredibly difficult."

"I'm sorry, too. I was recently getting to know my dad on a deeper level. He was a difficult guy. Very opinionated."

"So I've heard," I said, then added quickly, "My own father really liked him, that's for sure."

"Some of the things he used to say, the rants he'd go on. My word, he had so much energy. I'd get annoyed and wonder why he got so worked up about meaningless crap, you know?" She shook her head. "He had the unique ability to get close to people, be extremely friendly, then cut them off ruthlessly if he felt maligned or offended. He even did this to me, sometimes. It drove us apart for a while."

My eyes widened. It sounded exactly like what had happened to Darla.

Willa continued with a palpable sadness in her voice. "And now all I want is to see him again. I miss his chattering and his fire."

We sat in silence for a minute, with me trying not to weep because I was thinking about what I'd do if I lost Dad—and how, even though Dad was a little weird, we had a healthy father–daughter relationship. I was blessed.

Finally, she spoke up. "You know what I discovered after he died?"

I wondered why she was telling me all this but wasn't going to stop the conversation. "No, what?"

"He had a TikTok account." She smiled and unzipped her fanny pack. "Let me show you. Had I known about this before he died, I would've keeled over from embarrassment. Does your dad ever do anything to embarrass you?"

"Well, recently, my father marched through town dressed in a gorilla suit for a protest, then got arrested, so yeah, I'm familiar with fatherly embarrassment. And don't even get me started on how he used to dress like an extra on *Miami Vice* when I was in second grade."

Our eyes met and we both smiled. I liked this woman.

"Check this out." She held her phone screen so I could see it. In the video, Jack was doing a TikTok dance. She pointed at it with a pale, pink-tipped fingernail. "That's a popular dance that all the kids do. Look. He got a hundred thousand likes. I had no idea he was even doing this."

We watched as Jack appeared to twerk robotically to a rap song, and I stifled a giggle. "He's pretty good."

"He used to be a jitterbug instructor when he was a young man."

"Awww." I paused while watching Jack rock his body from side to side and cross his arms over his chest.

"That dance is called the Swagg Bounce. Swagg with two gs. I learned that from watching hours of videos, embarrassingly enough. I don't even know how Dad found out about this, or why he started. I wish I could ask him."

"The things that go through parents' minds," I said, trying not to chortle. Jack was quite hilarious on camera, and he had thousands of comments, many in the "you go, old dude" vein.

"Look at this comment: 'This guy has more energy than I do and I'm a quarter of his age.'" Willa laughed, and I did too.

This was a new and endearing angle to Jack's personality. What a complex man.

Willa grinned. "Half of his videos were like this, of him dancing and being silly. I can't stop watching them, because it's like he's here with me, being goofy, being his best self. He used to be like this when I was little, but after my parents' divorce, somehow the world got to him and made him bitter and angry. The other videos are of him ranting about politics and the environment and life in general."

"Oh, really? Can you show me the last video he did?" I also wanted to make a mental note of his username so I could watch his posts later.

"Yeah, let me see. I'm not too proficient with TikTok. I only discovered it because I was going through his computer after he died and found a bookmark. I ended up downloading the stupid app and I've lost so many hours to it. I've become addicted to this one cute baker from France. But I guess it's a way to pass the time instead of grieving."

She swiped and tapped at her phone. "Here it is. He went on a tirade about the guy who's building the new deck. Totally fair, in my opinion, since that guy seems like a jerk. Hasn't been by in a couple of weeks yet took thousands of Dad's money. Or more. I only know Dad lost money because of what he said in these videos. He didn't tell me any of this."

"Bill?" I asked excitedly.

She frowned at the screen, swearing under her breath. "Do you know Bill, or how to get ahold of him? I'd like to get Dad's cash back, or maybe take Bill to small claims court. I have a half-built deck out back, and it annoys me every time I look at it. Dad would want that to be finished, or for me to get his money."

"I don't know Bill at all, but your father's friend Rose mentioned him as a suspect."

Willa sniffled. "Oh, you know Rose?"

"Yeah. She's an acquaintance of my father's. They're both active in the community garden." Probably it was best if I left out the part about how Erica and I grilled Rose at her home.

"My father had such a crush on her and was trying to work up the courage to ask her out. Can you imagine at that age, being nervous? Check this out."

I wondered if she knew that her father had a dalliance with Joanie Clarke, but figured it wasn't the time or the place to break that particular bit of salacious news.

She swiped at her phone screen and brought up her photos, flipping through several of Bella, then stopping. "He bought this necklace for her. It's actually a set, with earrings. Isn't that adorable? He found it at that jewelry store downtown the day before he died. He showed it to me and said he was planning on giving it to her the next time they had dinner together."

She paused. "They were supposed to have dinner the day he died."

Interesting. Rose hadn't shared that detail. I leaned in and squinted. The photo was blurry, but the shape of the pendant was unmistakable.

It was a watering can, exactly like the earring I'd found in the garden. "That's . . . interesting, considering what I found."

She frowned. "Why would you say that?"

I pulled out my own phone and navigated to my photos. She gasped when she saw the little gold earring in the dirt. "Where did you see this?"

"At the garden, right after we found your father. Now I'm wondering where the other earring is."

She sat back, taking a deep breath. "That's puzzling. I wonder if he dropped the earrings that day?"

"Or did whoever kill him steal the earrings and drop one?" I mused. The discarded earring was bothering me even more now that I knew Jack had bought a matching set for Rose.

Willa nodded slowly and stared into the middle distance, as if lost in thought. I didn't want her to disengage from our conversation, so I cleared my throat.

"When was the last time your dad saw Bill?"

She licked her lips and her eyes focused on me once again. "The day he died. Bill came over to the house, and he and Dad had an argument. I thought it was super sketchy, because Bill was asking for more cash to finish the job. He seemed way too eager to take Dad's money. When Bill left, I asked about it. But Dad refused to tell me anything, saying he didn't want me involved. And yet he made a video! Does that make sense to you? Here it is."

She pressed play and angled the phone so I could watch. Jack was sitting on a lawn chair in what appeared to be a garden, lush and verdant. It definitely wasn't Peas on Earth. The video was pretty shaky, like he was holding the cell phone.

"Where is he sitting in this video?" I murmured.

"Our backyard. Those are all his plants, he loved gardening so much. The video's quite shaky because he wasn't using the tripod like he did when he was dancing."

I leaned in so I could hear his words.

"I am ripping mad," Jack started. "I hired a contractor here on Devil's Beach to redo my deck around the beginning of the year. I wanted an entire teardown and rebuild, with a spot carved out for a hot tub. Here were the plans I drew up."

Jack held up a piece of paper, which looked like a remedial sketch of a box and a circle. Then he lowered the paper. "I met Bill Walker through someone at the community garden and paid him five grand to start work. He claimed the entire thing would cost ten grand, which seemed on the high side, but I let it slide because I needed a special space for the hot tub."

Willa paused the video. "He wanted the hot tub for his arthritis."

"Gotcha." That was interesting, though. Who at the garden had introduced him to Bill? Rose, perhaps? If so, why hadn't she mentioned it?

Willa started the video again and Jack's face filled the screen. He was so animated that spittle sprayed from his mouth.

"This Bill character demolished my existing porch and everything was going well. Or so I thought. He left all of the old boards in my yard and killed a crop of my bromeliads. I called him to complain and he never returned that call. Then he showed up a week later to take measurements and hauled away half the junk. I thought it was a misunderstanding, and I'm a reasonable guy . . ."

"He wasn't a reasonable guy," muttered Willa.

". . . and then he asked me for three thousand dollars to continue the job. Since we agreed on ten, I figured that was okay, and gave it to him. Well, he constructed a base for the porch along with a reinforced area for the hot tub. Then that started to sink into the ground. It's Florida, I told him, the soil is wet and sandy."

The video went on like this for another minute, with Jack discussing every grievance about Bill and the new porch. He paid Bill a few thousand more dollars, and work inched along, never to completion. I could understand why he was upset, honestly. I'd heard horror stories about contractors and wondered if Bill was even licensed.

"In the end, I paid Bill Walker fifteen thousand dollars and the porch is nowhere near finished. Look!"

The camera swung to a half-built porch, a maze of two-by-fours. Jack came back into view.

He brandished a finger in the air. "Bill Walker, you have met your match, and I'll see you in court!"

The video stopped and Willa turned to me. "You're sure you don't know Bill? Everyone here likes to gossip."

"I'm around a lot of people at work but don't know names. Do you know if Bill was a licensed contractor? Where he lived? Anything?"

She shook her head. "Dad chose him. There was a few weeks' gap between him signing the initial contract and the work starting. I remember telling Dad that was a red flag and he should get out of the deal before more money exchanged hands, but Dad was adamant about using Bill. Since Dad was so stubborn, I let it go. My God, I never imagined it would end like this, or I'd have been more vocal."

She inhaled a shaky breath. "Sorry to be so emotional. I told officers all about this and they led me to believe they were going to talk with Bill. But I have no idea how that went. All I know is that it's been almost a week and there's been no arrest in Dad's murder."

"It's natural that you would be emotional. I can't imagine what you're going through. Who else do you consider a suspect? Who wanted your father dead?"

She lifted her hands in the air. "No idea. A lot of people didn't like him, but I didn't think anyone hated him enough to kill him. Maybe that Darla character, but that doesn't make sense either, since she recently passed away. What is going on here, anyway? The island never used to be this strange or dangerous. What did I come home to?"

That was one question I couldn't answer. The weirdness of Devil's Beach was something I'd long since accepted, like death, taxes, and the rejuvenating power of an excellent latte.

"When did your father make that last video, anyway?"

"The morning he died. From the time stamp, it looks like an hour or so after he met with Bill and had that fight, and a couple of hours before he died. Or maybe he made it earlier, but he definitely posted it following that blowup with Bill."

"Did you see their fight?"

She shook her head. "I was at the bakery, getting us breakfast. Those giant bear claws at Pretty Baked, he loved those. By the time I got back, Bill was gone. When I came home, Dad was beside himself."

"What happened when you got home? What did he say?" She didn't seem to care that I was asking questions, so I was riding this train until it stopped.

"I made some coffee and we ate the bear claws. That's when he told me about the fight with Bill. Most of it was stuff he'd already told me, but he said that Bill promised to finish the deck if Dad paid him another two grand. Dad told him to shove it and threw him out of the house."

"Hmm. What I don't understand is why your father went to the garden after that. You know about his fight with Darla, the garden president, right?"

She rolled her eyes. "Yes, he told me every detail about Darla. And he filmed several videos about her, and how mean she was. That's been bothering me as well, considering what happened to her. After breakfast he got a text. Didn't say who. All he told me was that he was going out for a while and he'd be back around dinnertime at the latest. I saw him put his claw in the car."

I blinked. "His claw?"

A laugh escaped her lips. "That's what we called his trash picker. His claw. It's one of those grabber things." She pantomimed squeezing something with her hand. "He'd take that when he would go to the beach. He loved walking up and down on the sand, picking up trash. Said it was like meditating."

"So that's where you thought he was going? To pick up trash on the beach?"

She nodded. "He did that often. Nothing that day was out of the ordinary. Except that text. I remember he angled the screen away from me."

Was that the message Darla had sent him? "And you don't know who it was from? Police never told you?"

"His cell was never found."

"It wasn't?" That was something I'd never thought to ask Noah about.

She shook her head.

"Did you tell police all this?"

"Everything except the TikTok videos. I stumbled upon those only yesterday."

"You should show them to Noah, er, the police."

"Yes, I should. It's just that . . ." Her voice trailed off and she snapped her fingers in the direction of her dog. He was digging a hole in the dirt nearby and trotted over.

"That what?"

"I feel like they're treating me as a suspect. I mean, of course they are, given my background. That's only natural."

I didn't want to let on that I knew about her medical disciplinary record, so I played dumb. "What do you mean?"

"I was a physician up north. But my medical license was pulled." She stared down at her hands, which were resting daintily in her lap. "It all started because of a back problem, and I got addicted."

"That's a common story, from what I understand."

"Sadly, that's true. I thought I could handle it, but I ended up losing everything. I came home to rebuild, and was doing so well, then this happened. Now I don't know what's going to happen."

"You're still clean, though?" I didn't know why I was getting this involved, but something about her sad expression made me want to hug her. Knowing that she'd lost her career on top of all this was like the cherry on top of a poop sundae.

This was a woman who'd had a rough few years. Rougher than I had, and maybe that's why I wanted to extend my empathy to her. I hadn't been able to help Darla, but maybe there was hope for Willa.

"Yes. Still clean. Taking it hour by hour. Thank goodness I was able to get a job working from home in medical billing. That's what enabled me to move down here and still support myself. While living with Dad."

I awkwardly patted her shoulder. "Your father would be proud of you for that."

She nodded but didn't respond.

We sat in silence for a while, watching our two dogs play tug-of-war with a filthy, frayed rope toy.

I summoned all my courage and gently asked, "Where were you when your father was killed?"

With a frown, she studied me. I assumed she was going to tell me to buzz off. "At home, watching a movie. I don't have an alibi, and I know police are looking into me because I was the sole heir of Dad's estate. But I didn't murder him. Dad was annoying, but I loved him."

Maybe it was the sadness in her voice or perhaps it was the way her mouth was set, determined and resolute, but I believed her.

I'd been wrong before about matters such as this, though. What I needed right now was to tell Noah about this conversation. I made eye contact with Stanley, and he trotted over, followed by Bella Pugosi.

"I think they're friends," she said.

By now, several more people and dogs had entered the park. "Stanley loves pugs. They're his favorite kind of dog."

"Perhaps we could arrange a playdate with Stanley and Bella." The two dogs wound their way through her feet.

We both stood. Even though she was a good twenty years older than me, I could see us hanging out over coffee. "I'd like that."

And I would—if she wasn't arrested for murder first.

Chapter Twenty-One

Stanley was much calmer after we left the dog park, but I wasn't. I felt keyed up, antsy, and uncertain.

When I'd felt like this in my journalism days while working on a tough story, there was only one thing to alleviate this feeling: talk to my editor in hopes of finding clarity. But since I was no longer a journalist and didn't have an editor, I'd have to rely on the next best thing.

Noah.

Stanley was still in the mood to walk, and since we were close to downtown and the police department, I kept him on the leash. We moved along at a nice clip, since he'd had enough smelling and rooting around in the dog park. We turned onto Main Street and were only about three blocks from the police department.

As we passed Pretty Baked, the place where Willa had bought the bear claws the day Jack died, I heard a thumping on the window and looked over.

It was Barbara. She was sitting in a seat by the window, and waved me in. In front of her on the table was a bear claw the size of my head. Admittedly it looked delicious, all frosting and swirled cinnamon. I pointed down at Stanley and she held up her hand. WAIT, she mouthed.

My chest tightened as I stood on the sidewalk. Probably she knew that Dad had told me about their relationship, and I wasn't exactly in the mood to discuss that right now. But what could I do? She was my employee, and more importantly, my friend.

I watched as she pushed her way out the door, holding a plate containing the bear claw and a cup.

"I'm glad I ran into you. Do you have a minute to talk?" she asked in a warm tone.

The last thing I wanted to do was chat about Dad's dating life, or my feelings about it. Since I couldn't tell her where I was going or why, I said, "Of course."

Like Perkatory several blocks away, Pretty Baked had a few cute white wooden tables and matching chairs on the sidewalk. Today they were all empty, so we sat at the nearest one. Stanley sniffed her knee, then flopped on his side in the shade.

She set the gargantuan pastry in the middle, then leaned down to offer Stanley the contents of her cup. "It's water," she said.

He lapped it up, and I explained that we'd been at the dog park. When he was finished, she straightened and gestured to the pastry.

"I think I'm going to need help finishing this." She let out a laugh, and that's when I realized she was probably as nervous as I was. "Please, have a little. Or a lot."

My stomach grumbled at the sight of the bear claw, and the cinnamon-butter smell was difficult to ignore. It was incredibly easy when working in food service to skip meals, I'd discovered. "Well, okay. Twist my arm."

I ripped off a hunk and popped it into my mouth. "Oh my goodness, this is amazing." I held my hand up to my mouth. "Sorry. Talking with my mouth full."

There was no way I could eat only one bite of this delectable treat. I took another chunk and savored the soft, melt-in-your-mouth dough. Golden raisins and walnuts were a perfect addition to the drizzle of sweet icing, and I made a soft grunting noise, unable to contain my happiness.

She smiled. "They have the best baked goods here. None of us ever seem to get down this way because we're so busy at Perkatory."

It was true. Although Devil's Beach was walkable, those of us who worked at the café seemed to stay in a two-block radius. That would have to change, given how tasty these pastries were.

"I was going to suggest that we perhaps chat with the owners here about supplying Perkatory with some pastries," Barbara said.

"That's a good idea. I'd love to sell ginormous bear claws." I tore off another piece, obviously hungrier than I thought. There was a time when I'd brought simple baked goods to Perkatory, five ingredient things like Nutella brownies and cake pops made from boxed mix. "I haven't had time lately to bake things for the café, and it would be nice to have a reliable supplier. That baker we've been buying from is excellent but she doesn't have the capacity for large orders. She's more of an artisan baker."

I was babbling, mostly out of nerves. It was as if I wanted to talk about everything but the obvious: Barbara and Dad's new relationship.

"I didn't wave you down to talk business, though. Lana, I know your father told you about us earlier today."

I swallowed a lump of sugar-cinnamon flavored dough. "Yeah. He did."

"How do you feel about it? If you're uncomfortable at all, we can—"

"I'm cool. No. I'm not uncomfortable. Well, I am, a little, at the idea of my dad dating anyone. It has nothing to do with you, it's not because I don't like you or because I don't want you together. It's just . . . a lot. It brings up memories of Mom." I sighed. "I'm sorry. I'll be fine."

She shook her head. "Of course it's a lot, especially after all you've been through. I always felt we should've told you what your mother said years ago. But your father wasn't sure he ever wanted to date anyone. And I wasn't sure I wanted to date your father. He can be a handful, you know. But I find him irresistible in a weird way."

We looked at each other and erupted into giggles. "Irresistible in a weird way does describe Peter Lewis to a T," I said.

"Your mother was quite adamant about this. We talked all night about her wishes, and that evening we tried to insist that her plan wasn't necessary, that she wasn't going anywhere." Barbara plucked a napkin out of a holder on the table and dabbed at the corner of her eye. "Somehow I think she knew she might not have enough time and wanted to make sure your dad would be happy."

I blew out a breath, making my cheeks puff out. "Sounds like Mom."

"Anyway, I wanted to tell you that I hope this won't make things weird for us. That we'll still be friends. I'm not looking to take the place of your mom. She was so proud of you, Lana. She'll always be there for you, but I will too."

Now I felt like crying happy tears. I was ridiculous for feeling awkward about her relationship with my father. This was something to celebrate, not something to overthink. "Of course we're still friends," I cried. "It is a bit weird, but what isn't, these days?"

We laughed for a bit, and she asked me where Stanley and I were headed.

"Going to visit Noah at the police station, to firm up some details for tomorrow."

"Oh, about that. How does stuffed mushrooms sound for an appetizer? They're my specialty."

I tipped my head back. “That sounds incredible. I was worried Dad was going to bring a bag of chips and a jar of salsa or something. Sometimes he’s like a twenty-year-old guy.”

Barbara shot me a knowing look. “Sometimes all men are like twenty-year-old guys. And no, I wouldn’t let him bring a bag of chips. We need to impress Noah’s mom.”

We polished off the bear claw together while talking about tomorrow night’s menu. She gave me some tips on which jarred red sauce tasted the most authentic, claiming I could save time with the lasagna by not making my own from scratch.

“That’s not a bad idea. Maybe it won’t take me as long as I think.”

“You’ve got this. You’re a great cook, and whatever you make, Noah will love. Which means his mom will love. Don’t sweat it. Now, I have to get to the community center because I’m teaching a sea glass class.”

That was Barbara’s true love, sea glass. I had countless pairs of earrings from her, all pretty and beach themed. I’d have to wear a pair tomorrow.

We stood up and embraced. “Thanks for being so accepting,” she whispered.

“I couldn’t think of a better stepmother, er, well. I guess we’re not at that point yet,” I stammered as we broke apart.

“Maybe someday.” She grinned and winked, then walked off.

Stanley and I headed in the other direction, toward the police station. When we arrived, I carried the dog inside, hoping that Noah wasn’t in a meeting or out on an interview.

“He’s here, and last I saw, he wasn’t doing anything special,” griped Bernadette from the desk. She stabbed at the old-school phone on her desk and the speakerphone crackled to life. “Chief? Your lady friend is here.”

“Send her in.”

Stanley lost it when he saw Noah, and I shut the door to the office and let the dog loose. He leaped into Noah's lap, whimpering as if he'd been starved of affection for years.

I flopped onto the sofa in his office.

"What's up, cupcake?" Noah remained behind his desk because of his lovefest with Stanley.

"Well, let's see. Since this morning, I cleared Beau, Olivia, and Joanie as suspects. Had a long conversation with Willa Daggitt at the dog park, and there are new details to share from her. Oh, and my dad has a girlfriend. He's dating Barbara now. Apparently, my mother gathered the two of them together and told them that if she died, she wanted them to be together. I think that's about it."

Noah carried Stanley over to the leather sofa. I lifted my legs and they sat.

"That sounds like a lot to unpack."

"Yeah, where to begin? What do you want to talk about first?" I kicked off my shoes and stretched out, resting my sock-covered feet on his lap.

"I kind of suspected about your dad and Barbara."

"You did?" I blinked, startled. "Did others suspect too?"

"Yeah, a lot of people did. Heidi at the café did, and so did Joey. Barbara and your dad make googly eyes at each other all the time. You haven't noticed?" He smoothed Stanley's lion mane, which made him look like he had a combover.

"Obviously not, because this came as a shock to me. Dad called me into the office at Perkatory and put on his serious face. I thought he had bad medical news, scared the fluff out of me. Then I ran into Barbara at the bakery, and had a heart-to-heart conversation with her."

Noah took one hand off Stanley and squeezed my calf. "You okay with all this? That's a lot to process."

It never ceased to amaze me how much Noah paid attention to my moods and emotional state. My ex-husband would've never assumed that I'd be feeling conflicted about Dad and Barbara, but Noah knew instinctively how I'd react. He did this all the time, checking in with my feelings.

It was one of the things I appreciated the most about him.

"I'm okay, not angry or upset. It's bittersweet because I adore Barbara. I think she's great for Dad. But of course, I'd prefer if Mom was still alive."

Noah shot me a sympathetic smile and patted my leg while also scratching Stanley's back.

"Anyway, we've got quite a party for tomorrow night. Dad's bringing Barbara, so there will be six of us."

"Good deal, cupcake. You all set with dinner ingredients?"

"Yeah, I need to pick up a couple of things, but I've got this." By "got this," I meant that I'd resume calling restaurants and caterers on the mainland when I returned home. That idea wasn't yet abandoned. "Anyway. I mostly came by to tell you about Willa Daggitt. She found some new clues about her father."

I explained to Noah about the TikTok dances, the political videos, and his tirade against Bill.

With a determined scowl, Noah released Stanley from his arms. The dog crawled onto my body and I hugged him while sitting up. Noah went to his computer and tapped at the keyboard.

"What did you say his username was?"

"OldManJack41."

Noah stared at the screen. "Oh, look, he's doing the Swagg Bounce."

I shook my head. "How do you know that? You hate all social media." Noah wasn't even on Facebook, which was now considered a digital retirement home, eschewed by the youths. Or so I'd heard around Perkatory from some high schoolers.

"Two of my young officers were filming themselves dancing the other day. They said they wanted to go viral and that lots of cops dance in uniform."

I heaved a sigh. Maybe Erica was right, that technology was ruining everything—including people's brains. TikTok and these new apps made me, in my early thirties, feel like I should wander out into a field and die of old age.

"Make sure you look at his final video, that's the one where he talks about Bill."

"Got it right here."

The sound of Jack's angry voice filled Noah's office. At this volume, he sounded more combative than he did when I watched the video at the dog park. Threatening, even.

"If what he's saying is true, he had every reason to be angry. That Bill character stole money from him. Lots of it," I pointed out.

Noah shook his head. "We haven't gotten any recent reports of contractor fraud. But sometimes property owners don't call us with that kind of thing, they go straight to the state Department of Business and Professional Regulation."

"Does this mean you haven't found Bill yet?"

Noah shook his head. "Neither Bill nor Clay."

"Gah, this is so frustrating." I tipped my head back and groaned.

"This is police work, cupcake. It's not like you see—"

"On TV. I know. I know. It seems like we're so close, yet so far away. Is this typical?"

He nodded. "As typical as naked men brandishing machetes on New Year's Eve in Florida."

That made me giggle. I climbed to my feet and stretched, allowing Stanley to sniff around his office.

"You headed out? Want me to watch Stanley while you grocery shop? You said you had a few things to buy, and I was wondering . . ."

Noah stood and walked around his desk, meeting me in the middle of his office.

He cupped my face.

"You were wondering what?" I asked.

"If you'd buy that kind of beer I like for tomorrow. The locally brewed stuff."

I knew exactly what he was referring to. "Sure. I can do that. It would be easier if I wasn't with Stanley, and you know how I hate to leave him alone. You're not going anywhere the rest of the day?"

He shook his head. "I'll look at Jack's videos for a couple of hours, then Stanley and I will meet you at home, okay?"

I wrapped my arms around him, pressing myself into his muscular body. Two whole hours to shop alone? Finally, I was catching a break.

Chapter Twenty-Two

I power-walked home, and before I could talk myself out of going, climbed into my car and drove in the direction of the mainland.

For an island resident, going to the mainland was unwelcome and often unpleasant, but a necessity. While we could find most everything we desired on Devil's Beach, from excellent food to hair salons, to bookstores and the perfect café (my own, not the competition), sometimes it was unavoidable to drive ten miles over the causeway bridge and into the suburban sprawl of southwest Florida.

As much as I—and every other Devil's Beach resident—complained about how they hated going to the mainland due to the parking scarcity, the traffic, and the hectic pace of life, there was one thing that made it tolerable.

The drive over the bridge.

It was like something out of a movie, a bird's eye view of soaring over the glittering blue water of the Gulf of Mexico. Today was an especially gorgeous day, with placid water nearly the same color as the clear blue sky. A few boats dotted the glass-like surface, and I cranked my radio up to play Fleetwood Mac's "Go Your Own Way" as I drove.

I was singing at the top of my lungs when I spotted a familiar-looking fin in the water. "Dolphin," I yelled to myself.

That was a tradition in my house, one Dad had taught me when I was small. Whenever someone saw a dolphin, they had to announce it out loud. Totally silly, but I'd done it for decades and wasn't about to stop.

And the fact was, it was heckin' cool to see dolphins playing in the water while driving. It made my hometown even more magical.

That magic ceased when I was over the bridge and absorbed into heavy traffic, however. By the time I reached the fancy organic grocery store attached to a mall, I was second-guessing my decision to come here. Traffic was hellacious, and I steered away from the main entrance, which seemed more chaotic than usual.

"What's going on here?" I murmured as I took a detour. Probably more spring break crowds. People could only go to the beach so much.

Instead of battling even more traffic at a second entrance, I knew to go around to the side and access the parking lot from a street shared by the store and a mobile home park. It was the delivery entrance. Dad had shared the semi-secret access point with me a few months back.

I stopped the car at the far end of the lot. My plan was to first find out if the store could make a couple of trays of lasagna, then I'd return for them early tomorrow. If I was lucky, they had a couple of trays premade. I'd even take frozen. If those options weren't possible, I'd buy the necessary ingredients and scram back to my island paradise.

As I walked to the front door, I made a deal with myself: if I could easily get everything catered, I'd take a stroll around the mall and maybe buy a new outfit for tomorrow. I hadn't been clothes shopping since I lived in Miami, mostly because I wore jeans and T-shirts to work now and had no use for fancy clothes.

I entertained a brief fantasy of buying a cute sundress and greeting Noah and his family at my door, looking effortlessly cool and organized.

If the lasagna situation went as planned, maybe I'd stop at a sandwich shop Noah loved and bring home two authentic Cuban sandwiches. Mmm. That was one of a few things unavailable on the island: hunks of ham, roast pork, Swiss cheese, pickles, and mustard, pressed between two slices of lard-laden Cuban bread.

My mouth watered at the thought of all that salty goodness.

I marched up to the store's front door, which was separate from the mall entrance. There were four people clustered, not going inside. Ignoring them, I looked around for the carts and saw none. Figuring they must be indoors, I breezed past the group.

"It's closed, sweetheart," one guy called out in a Boston accent. His final word came out as "sweet-haaaat."

I stopped in my tracks and looked at the group. "Hunh? Why? It's not even five o'clock. The store doesn't close until nine."

"There was a bomb threat in the mall. Everything's shut down here. Didn't you see all the people standing in the parking lot?" Boston guy said.

I shook my head. "I came in the back way. When's it opening back up?"

Everyone shrugged. "Dunno. We've only been here fifteen minutes, but we're thinking of getting coffee across the street. Want to join us? George here has a deck-a cards." Boston guy pointed at a man in a Hawaiian shirt, baggy shorts, and sandals—with white socks—who was wiping his face with a cloth hanky.

No food. No clothes. No dice.

Glancing across the street, I saw the ubiquitous green sign for a chain coffee shop. Drink that swill with total strangers? No way.

"Have fun, all y'all," I told the group, and walked back to my car.

The interior of my vehicle was already sweltering from the heat even after a few minutes, and I rolled down the window. Luck was not on my side with prepping for this dinner, and now I was on the mainland without a destination, the worst possible scenario here.

I half-heartedly pulled up the maps app on my phone to find out where the closest supermarket was, but it was three miles away in the opposite direction from the island, and in rush-hour traffic, that seemed exhausting.

Undeterred, I called five nearby restaurants to find out if they offered catering. Most did, but said they were unable to make anything on such short notice. One restaurant didn't answer its phone, and the last one quoted me a price that was so outrageous that I resolved to buy my ingredients on the island and bake the silly lasagna myself.

I fired up the car and its air conditioner, battled traffic to reach the Cuban sandwich shop, and parked. There was a line wrapping almost around the building. My patience was being tested today.

The thought of that meaty sandwich sustained me, and I recalled that this shop used a secret ingredient: garlic butter. The entire combination—pork, more pork, pickles, garlic butter, crusty bread—was enough to make me squelch my annoyance, join the queue, and wait a while. This place was little more than a hole in the wall, a former convenience store turned sandwich shop. A mural on the side depicted Cuban hero José Martí on a horse, riding through palm trees.

It was so small inside they didn't have table service, just a walk-up window and a few picnic benches flanking the parking lot. Whenever Noah was missing Tampa, we'd come here and sit outdoors to devour a sandwich. Sometimes he had two.

Friday nights were the busiest, I overheard a woman in front of me say. Made sense, but it also wasn't surprising given my luck today.

We inched forward in line, and I was only one corner of the building away from ordering. The temperature here was hotter than on the island, probably because we were surrounded by asphalt, concrete, and car exhaust.

I passed the time by checking my emails and texting funny memes to Erica. When I heard familiar loud male laughter, I looked up.

"Dude, this sandwich is going to be amazing."

Lex Bradstreet, my sketchy beach bum buddy, was walking in my direction while laughing. He was with another guy. Both wore faded T-shirts, board shorts, and flip-flops. Lex's blonde hair was like spun gold in the sun, and the other man was about his age. He had jet-black tresses pulled back into a man bun. They seemed like they didn't have a care in the world, and knowing Lex, they probably didn't.

I waved at the two of them and took a half step out of line to flag them down.

"Broski," he cried, coming up and giving me a giant hug. He smelled like salty body odor. "We were boogie boarding near the bridge and decided to come here and grab a couple of Cubans for dinner. This place rocks."

I extracted myself from Lex's sweaty embrace. "It does indeed rock."

His friend stood a couple of feet away, unwrapping his sandwich. I could smell the toasted garlicky bread from here. Lex and I chatted about the water temperature on Devil's Beach, and the sandwiches. Lex explained in great detail how he used to live in Tampa and missed the Cuban sandwiches there. Everyone, it seemed, missed the Tampa sandwiches, and Lex launched into a monologue about why Tampa Cuban sandwiches were better than Miami's.

I recalled how Lex was also allegedly involved in the Tampa mafia, but didn't bring that up. The more I got to know Lex, the less likely it seemed he was involved in organized crime.

"Oh. Hey. Did you ever find out what happened to that Jack dude?" Lex asked.

I shook my head. "Not yet. But I'm glad you brought that up. Have you seen Clay? I'd still like to talk with him."

Lex's eyes bugged and he gestured with his hand, as if I was ignoring the obvious. "He's right here, dude."

Clay was in mid-bite. "Hunh?" he mumbled, his mouth full.

"That's Clay?" I pointed at the guy. We'd been standing here chatting for a solid five minutes and even moved a little forward so I wouldn't lose my spot in line, and yet Lex didn't think to introduce us right away?

Lex was not the sharpest stake in the vampire.

"Yeah. Clay, c'mere. This is Lana. The chick from the café where Fab used to work."

Clay chewed while staring at me. "She's not a cute goth girl."

I rolled my eyes. "That's Erica."

"That's Erica," Lex parroted. "Clay, Lana was asking about you because of that mean guy on the beach. What happened with that, anyway?"

I turned to Clay, who, like Lex, was tall and well built but had a certain good-natured vacancy in his eyes. It was best to be direct under these circumstances. "I'm looking into who killed Jack."

"Are you a cop?" Clay looked perplexed and glanced from me to Lex.

"No. I'm . . . doing a podcast."

"Oh, cool." Clay swallowed and grinned. A blob of mustard stained his tanned chin. "I love podcasts. What's the name of it?"

"Ahh . . ." I hated lying. "Crime Time in Paradise."

The two guys laughed. "That's awesome," Lex said, high-fiving me.

"About Jack, I heard you got into a fight with him." I was only five people away from the order window, and I didn't want to lose my place or the chance to pin Clay down on his whereabouts the day Jack was murdered.

"Yeah, I was on the beach swimming one morning. I always bring an orange as a snack. Well, sometimes it's a grapefruit, and sometimes it's a tangerine, but you know, citrus is good for you."

Clay took another bite and I nodded. "Right. Citrus. What happened then?"

"I tossed my orange peels into the water. Figured they were organic material and vegan. Maybe a manatee would eat them. They're vegan mammals, you know."

Lex nodded vigorously.

"I know." Focus, dudes. Focus.

"And then this out-of-control old guy came up, yelling at me, waving one of those trash pickers around. I apologized but he wanted to fight. He even prodded me in the ribs with the trash picker thing. I didn't punch him or anything, just walked to my car. Okay, I told him to mind his own business."

"That's it?" I glanced away nervously. Four people away from the order window.

"Yeah, it was nothing. But he was pretty weird. I heard he was murdered."

"Yes, and you're a suspect."

His jaw dropped, and he looked at Lex. "Me? I've never been in trouble with the law. Okay, I was cited for fishing without a license one time."

"That doesn't count," Lex said, and I echoed him.

"Where were you last Sunday?"

Clay used his thumb and forefinger to pull a pickle out of his sandwich. "That's easy. I was in the Everglades on a python hunt. I have a buddy who signs up for that and I'm part of his team. We left on Friday and came back Sunday night. You know, pythons don't have any predators so they're hella bad for the ecosystem. The state pays us to catch them. We caught two giant monster snakes. I have photos. Wanna see?"

Lex and Clay laughed, and I was reminded of Beavis and Butthead for some reason.

"Yeah, in fact, I do want to see them."

"Cool beans," Lex enthused. "Did you know that pythons sometimes eat gators?"

While I was familiar with the annual python hunt in the Glades, and the menacing snakes' ability to tangle with gators, I wasn't in the mood to have a conversation with these two about biodiversity and non-native species. I was two people away from the window, and the folks in line behind me were getting antsy, talking loudly about how people needed to pay attention to the menu and not hold everyone up at the front by conversing with others.

"This is serious business here," the man behind me muttered.

I pressed my hands together in a prayer gesture and faced Clay. "Can you text them to me? Like right now? Screenshots, so I can see the time stamp?"

"No prob." He handed Lex his sandwich, licked his fingers, wiped his hand on his shorts, then took his phone out of his pocket. I tried not to wince watching this mess unfold.

I gave him my number, and by the time I left the sandwich joint, I had in my possession twelve photos of Clay in the Everglades holding the tail end of a python on Sunday morning, and three delicious Cuban sandwiches.

Chapter Twenty-Three

On Saturdays, the island grocery store opened its doors at nine in the morning.

"Why does it open so late? We should've been here two hours ago," I grumbled to Dad as we pulled around to the back parking lot in his Prius. He'd swung by and picked me up, reiterating his commitment to helping me with the groceries for the dinner that evening.

After I left the Cuban sandwich shop last night, I returned to Devil's Beach and found Noah still in his office. I'd bought him two sandwiches, and the smile on his face when I took them out of the bag was worth every bit of annoyance. We ended up eating in his office while I shared the photos of Clay and the pythons.

I collected Stanley and left Noah in his office because he was headed home to clean his own place in preparation for his family's arrival.

Apparently, I wasn't the only one who left things until the last minute.

Today, I was in full panic mode. Noah had texted an hour ago, saying his mother and sister were on their way. They planned to visit the Funnel Cake Fest, then spend the afternoon at Noah's condo pool. They'd be over at four for appetizers. Dinner, I figured, would be around six thirty.

This meant I had a scant seven hours to cook, clean, and primp. Everything felt like it was riding on this one night. Noah, being the firstborn and only son, likely needed his mother's approval for us to take our relationship to the next level. At least that's what I'd hyped myself into believing.

Dad pulled into a parking space and turned to me. "Lana, you need to get a grip. Your aura is stressful. I can see a muddled red around you." He floated his hand in the air above my head.

"That's the sweat because your air isn't working well in this car."

"It's working fine. Let's do a quick breathing exercise."

"I don't have time for that." My hand found the door handle.

Dad made a tsk-tsk-tsk noise with his tongue. "There's always time to breathe. Come on."

He fiddled with the radio while I rolled my eyes. When the strains of a Hindu chant came on, I stopped arguing. It wasn't worth telling Dad that a few deep breaths wouldn't cure me of my ratcheting anxiety, so I leaned back and shut my eyes.

"Take a deep breath in your nose. Count to one, two, three, four . . ."

I sneezed.

"Do it again. One, two, three, four. Now let it out. One, two, three, four. Do this twice more."

I sneezed again. Either I was getting sick or it was the overpowering patchouli smell coming from the flower-shaped air freshener hanging off the rearview mirror that said BLESS THIS CAR.

Dad chanted an "Ommmmm," and then told me to "visualize experiencing success."

"You can see it. You can smell it. You can touch it. You can taste it. Visualize a successful lasagna," he intoned.

I folded over, laughing. "A successful lasagna will be edible. That's all I'm aiming for. Not to poison anyone."

"Okay, see? At least you're laughing and not complaining. When you laugh, you're not stressed. C'mon. Let's hit the store."

We walked in and Dad grabbed a cart. We didn't get more than ten steps into the store when Dad saw someone he knew from yoga class. As he chatted about the upcoming class schedule and whether he should try aerial yoga, I tugged on his sleeve, feeling like I was six years old.

"I'm going to the noodle aisle," I murmured, and wandered off.

It was way easier to grab things on my list without him. Probably I should've come alone, but it was nice to have help, and more than anything, Dad loved feeling useful. I piled boxes of no-boil lasagna into my arms—I figured I'd need two boxes for each tray—and looped back to the entrance to find Dad.

He wasn't there. Blergh.

Eventually I found him in the dairy aisle, looking at cheese. He held up a package. "Here's some vegan ricotta."

"Great, let's buy that. Two of them, actually." I carefully placed the boxes of noodles in the cart. The last thing we needed was broken lasagna noodles.

"Munchkin, I have an idea." Dad paused at the front of the cart while holding the cheese.

I braced myself. Anything could come out of his mouth.

"Why don't you make only one large tray of vegan lasagna? Who's going to know the difference? I'll love it, Barbara will love it, Noah's sister will love it, you'll love it, and from what I've seen, Noah will eat anything put in front of him. Most lasagna doesn't have meat in it anyway."

"That's not a bad idea." Would his mother be annoyed by fake cheese? Perhaps not, if her own daughter was vegan. "It sure would be easier."

"You have that huge pan of Mom's." Dad's eyes met mine, and I averted them. It seemed odd to talk about Mom now that he was dating someone else.

Dating her best friend. I shook my head to clear the thoughts away.

"True. It would save so much time." Time that I desperately needed to get the house ready. I clapped my hands together. "Okay, executive decision made. I'm baking only one tray of lasagna. Let's get six of those vegan ricotta tubs."

Dad wandered down the aisle and I took my shopping list out of my bag. As I was crossing off several items, I felt the presence of someone close by.

"Excuse me?"

I looked up to see a young woman with rust-colored dreads staring at me. She was pushing a cart and had stopped alongside mine.

"Oh, sorry, I can move. I'm in my own little world here. Sorry." I pushed the cart a few feet, so she had plenty of room in the aisle.

"No, I wanted to talk with you."

I stopped. "Uh, okay?"

"You're Lana, from Perkatory, right?"

I nodded and smiled. It wasn't unusual for people to stop me in public, since they loved our coffee so much. Our customers were truly the best. This one looked to be barely out of her teens, but we counted half of Devil's Beach High as customers, since we sponsored the school's yearbook and newspaper.

"I'm Alexis Dominguez. I work part-time on weekends at the taffy shop. Or did, since it closed down. They haven't opened since, well, you know. I heard you found Darla."

Her large brown eyes skittered to her hands, then to my cart.

"Oh, gosh, I'm so sorry." I clapped my hands to my face. She looked so forlorn that I started to reach for her arm, then paused. "Can I give you a hug?"

She nodded and I stepped between our carts and embraced her. I could feel the sadness coming off her in waves, and my heart was heavy. No one that young should have to deal with something so tragic.

We broke apart and she sniffled. "I'd only worked there a couple of months, and mostly on the day Darla is off. I go to community college on the mainland and thought it would be a good part-time job. I didn't know Darla well, but she seemed super sweet. She made the best taffy I've ever tasted."

I nodded. There was no way I was going to burst this girl's bubble about her coworker. My days of breaking bad news to friends and family were over. She could read about Darla being a suspect in a homicide in the newspaper, if the story ever landed there.

If Jack's case was ever solved.

"Are you doing okay? It's a lot to deal with."

She shrugged. "I've been having a difficult time sleeping, and honestly, I don't want to return to work there when it reopens. The owners are back in town and are keeping the place closed for a week out of respect for Darla."

"I can totally understand why you wouldn't want to return."

"Darla had so much to live for." Alexis scrunched up her face, like she was trying not to sob.

"She had so many hobbies."

"Yes! And she and Bill were planning to travel the country, and she was so knowledgeable about a lot of stuff. Mushrooms and cooking and . . . I don't know." She swallowed hard.

"Wait, what did you say?" My stomach clenched.

Alexis blinked. "Darla loved mushrooms and cooking—"

"No. About her boyfriend. Did you say his name was Bill?" I gripped the handle of the grocery cart so hard that my knuckles turned white.

Dad, who had drifted back to me, was inspecting the ingredients on the side of a tub of cookie dough. He whipped his head around. "Bill? Darla was dating a guy named Bill?"

Alexis nodded enthusiastically. "Yeah. But she never mentioned him. I only knew about him because I heard her talking on the phone a couple of times during shift change. She was secretive about him. I don't know why. I think she only met him a few months ago, because she started being more secretive about her phone calls around Christmas."

My mouth suddenly went dry. This was the missing piece we needed—and Darla's journal entries made so much more sense now.

"Out of curiosity, was Bill's nickname Moose?"

Alexis's face brightened. "Yes! It was! I heard her calling him that on the phone. Once I saw her phone screen and it said Bill Moose on the caller ID."

I glanced at Dad, whose eyes were bugging out at this news, then turned to Alexis. "You told police this, didn't you?"

"Who are you?" Dad blurted at Alexis.

"Who are you, bro?" She gave him a side eye.

"Sorry, this is my father. Dad, this is Alexis and she worked with Darla at the taffy shop." I tried to sharpen my gaze at him, as if to say, *don't speak another word because I want her to keep talking.*

"Oh." She tilted her head back and forth, her gold chandelier earrings brushing against her neck. "You know, I didn't tell police. I only remembered it now when I saw you. Isn't that funny?"

"Funny." I blinked slowly. It was so not funny. The least funny thing I'd ever heard. But she was barely out of high school—how would she know that was an important detail?

I was about to suggest that she head over to the police department this very moment with that detail but was interrupted by my cell buzzing with a text. At the same time, Dad's phone trilled its old-timey ringtone.

"You two seem super busy. I'm sorry to take up your time. Nice meeting you. Too bad it was under these circumstances. I'll see you probably at Darla's memorial service next week. It's going to be held at the community garden." Alexis zoomed away, while my phone and Dad's chirped and beeped in tandem.

Reeling from the news of Darla and Bill, I called out to her. "Wait, can I get your number? Ah, in case I find out any job openings on the island. I'll call you. Dad and I know a ton of people in town."

She stopped and her face lit up. "Would you? That would be incredible."

I handed her my phone and she tapped on the screen. She returned the phone and handed it back, thanking me profusely. As she walked away, I checked my messages. There was a text from Erica.

THE FUNNEL CAKE FEST HAS BEEN INVADED BY GIANT BUGS

What the fluff? I sighed like Stanley does when he's exasperated. There was no time for jokes or nonsense today. I had a lasagna to make, a dining room to clean, and two homicides to solve.

What was I going to do with that information about Bill? I needed to tell Noah, who was probably getting his family settled into his condo. I hated to ruin his free time with his guests, but this was important.

Dad let out a gasp, and I looked over. He was leaning on the cart handle, talking on the phone. With his silver goatee, his medium-length gray ponytail, and his sunglasses, he looked like an extra in *The Big Lebowski*.

"You are kidding me. Lubbers? We haven't seen an invasion of those on Devil's Beach since Lana was a baby."

My face morphed into a mask of horror. Lubbers were giant, disgusting grasshoppers native to Florida. I'd done a story on them once for the newspaper, years ago. They were about three inches long, black, and bright yellow-orange, and could eat through entire gardens or citrus groves in mere hours. When they swarmed one location, the scene was like something out of a horror movie.

I hated them. Most people did. They were also quite common in Florida. But surely a couple of bugs wouldn't cause that much of a commotion at a festival in the park.

"The entire funnel cake festival is shut down?" Dad straightened to standing. "Hang on. I have another call. I'll get back to you."

Dad stared at the phone and squinted over the top of his sunglasses while muttering something about the "caller ID button."

My phone buzzed again. This time, it was Erica sending ten photos from the festival. The pictures were something right out of a nightmare.

"Oh my word, this is wild," I cried out, then made a gagging noise.

Every photo showed an infestation of giant grasshoppers. On the ground. Swarming a tree. *In the funnel cake batter?*

I began to chuckle nervously, then my phone rang.

"The entire festival's canceled." Erica was breathless. "You should've seen the mayor's wife. She got two bugs in her hair and freaked out. It was like a bad 1950s alien invasion movie. People were running and screaming, like the bugs were trying to kill them. I caught some of it on video and I'm trying to sell it to CNN. They only want to give me fifty bucks, but I'm holding out for at least five hundred. You can't believe how disgusting it was out here."

"Oh, I can. I've seen lubber invasions."

"They swarmed a van and it was like the side of it was moving, there were so many. I think this festival is cursed."

I could tell Erica was both repelled and weirdly fascinated by these developments. She wasn't a native Floridian, however, and I knew to take this kind of stuff in stride. It was strange, sure, and gross. But not out of the realm of possibility in the Sunshine State, where once, a giant sinkhole swallowed an entire human sitting in his bedroom.

"Did you and Joey pack up and leave, or are you still there, hoping someone with a giant can of Raid shows up?" I was joking, of course. Insecticide wouldn't kill those bugs. Neither would an atomic bomb, probably.

"We had to. I don't think we brought any back to the restaurant with us. Did you know the only way to get rid of the things is to stomp on them?"

I winced, recalling how my environmental reporter friend Craig Pittman suggested crushing them with a steel-toed boot, or a brick. Every year, when new Floridians posted on Twitter about the giant bugs, Craig would explain in disgusting detail how to kill them.

"Yeah, I knew that tidbit."

"Anyway. Joey and I are free today. Can we come for dinner? I'll help you cook. Or clean."

"Sure. I'd love to have you. Just a warning. The lasagna's going to be vegan." Between the two homicides, the lubber invasion, and the fact that I hadn't cooked one thing yet and the dinner with Noah's family was in a few short hours, what could go wrong with adding additional quirky friends to the table?

"Coolio. I haven't eaten a vegetable in a while. Okay, we're going to go unpack the van. Joey has some cannoli here, and we still have plenty of key lime funnel cake. I'll make sure it's bug free and bring it over. And hey, Lana, you know what they say?"

"What?"

"Florida is for lubbers." I heard her cackle and hang up.

I hung my head and chuckled.

"No, you can't trap and release them. I know, I know it's not vegan to kill them, but you have to. No, you can't freeze them." Dad was talking loudly into the phone, then he paused and yelled, "Do not bring them to the Everglades! Negative, Ghostrider!"

Nearby, I overheard another shopper on the phone, talking about "giant crickets."

"Grasshoppers," a woman cried out.

No sooner did Dad get off the phone than an older woman approached him. "Did you hear about the bugs at the festival?"

The two of them started swapping gossip—apparently the bugs ate an entire crop of shrubs within an hour—and I knew we weren't leaving the store anytime soon. So I dialed Noah.

"Chief Garcia," he barked. "Ah, crap. Sorry, Lana. I'm up the creek without a paddle this morning."

"Because of the lubbers?"

He groaned. "You wouldn't believe how many people at the festival dialed 911. Bernadette's pulling her hair out in dispatch. Like there's anything the police can do about an insect swarm. What am I going to do? Make the officers chase them with nets?"

A giggle slipped out of my mouth, but it ceased when Noah sighed impatiently. "Sorry," I muttered.

"I called the ag department and they're sending a team down from Tampa. They're our only hope, because if these things leave that park, they could defoliate the entire island in a matter of days."

That seemed a little alarmist to me, but what did I know? The lubbers had never defoliated an entire community before. At least I didn't think so. "What a mess. Did your family get in okay?"

"Yeah, they got caught in traffic, with all the people trying to flee the lubbers at the festival. But they're here, relaxing downstairs at the pool. Needless to say, we won't be getting funnel cake today."

"Erica's bringing some over tonight. Listen, I got a tip about Darla while at the supermarket."

"Cupcake, I can't right now. I'm juggling a million calls, the media's swarming me about the bugs, and I have the governor's office upset because he was supposed to swing by the festival during a campaign stop. Oh, jeez. That's his office now. Tell me later, okay?"

"Wait—"

Noah hung up. This was too important to let go, so I switched to text.

I ran into a taffy shop employee at the grocery store. She said Darla was dating a man named BILL. Who went by the nickname of MOOSE.

My phone buzzed with a call seconds later. It was Noah. "What?"

I explained everything that Alexis had said. Noah's only response was a long groan.

"What can we do about this?" I demanded.

"*We* aren't going to do anything about this. I'm going to divert an officer from the lubber situation and have him look for Bill so I can bring him in for questioning. You're going home to cook. I'm officially giving you the day off from the case."

Clearly Noah was in take-charge mode. I had no choice but to let this investigation go, at least for the afternoon.

Chapter Twenty-Four

Hours later, I stepped out of the bathroom and smoothed the skirt of my dress. It wasn't a new outfit, more like a long, sleeveless tunic, but it was comfortable and the pale blue hue was flattering.

I'd managed to clean house with Dad's help, assemble a ten-layer vegan lasagna, and in my opinion, look cute. Pausing in front of the full-length mirror in my bedroom, I nodded at my reflection. Not bad at all, given the recent circumstances.

It was four in the afternoon. I could hear Dad and Barbara in the kitchen, giggling as they transformed the breakfast nook into a bar. They were actually pretty cute together, I had to admit.

I walked out of my bedroom in time to hear the knock on the door. Stanley, likely sensing Noah was nearby, let out three short, sharp barks. Not wanting him to maul Noah's mom or sister, I scooped him into my arms and opened the door.

Noah and two women stood on the other side.

"Hey, cupcake. Wow, you look gorgeous." He leaned in and kissed my cheek. "This is my mother, Ileana, and my sister, Jess."

"Come in, come in." I handed Stanley to Noah as they entered. "It's so good to finally meet you."

"I have heard so many wonderful things about you," his mother gushed. "Come here."

She embraced me, then held me at arm's length. "Look at you. So beautiful. Noah, I can tell you've hit the jackpot this time."

"Not like the other time, she was a real piece of work," his sister quipped. Eek. I didn't want to get on the topic of Noah's ex—mostly because I knew very little, and wanted to keep it that way.

I laughed nervously and turned to his sister. "Hi. Welcome to my home. I'm glad you're here, and sorry you all got caught up in the lubber invasion."

"The ag department team from Tampa's here. They're hand picking the lubbers out of the foliage and are going to take them off island, where they can be exterminated," Noah said. "It might take all night to grab them, but thankfully, the bugs aren't fast-moving."

"That sounds like a gross job," I said and everyone laughed.

We all stood in the foyer chatting about the lubbers for a few minutes. It gave me time to size up Noah's mother and sister. They were both gorgeous humans and shared his expressive dark eyes. His sister was closer to my age—Noah was eight years older than me—and she gave off a sassy vibe.

His mother's gaze fell onto Stanley, who was licking Noah's face. "Look at that little lion dog," she cried.

Finally, someone who didn't think Stanley was a poodle.

I herded everyone into the living room and urged them to sit. "I'll be right back. I'm going to grab my father and his, ah, girlfriend."

Just then, the doorbell rang. "That's probably Erica and Joey. I'll let them in and we'll have drinks and apps after, okay?"

Everyone beamed at me, and my muscles started to soften. I could do this. They were friendly and warm. The smell of lasagna wafted through the air, and all this party needed was some tunes and we'd be golden.

I opened the door and Erica breezed in. Joey carried two oversized aluminum trays.

"Dessert delivery," he said.

"Thank you so much for bringing that. You're a lifesaver."

He asked me where I wanted them, and I gestured to the kitchen. He wandered off.

Erica leaned in. "Are they here?" she hissed.

"Yeah."

"Are they cool?"

"They seem super nice. I'm much calmer now."

"Good. If they don't like you, they're going to have me to deal with."

I watched as Erica, wearing combat boots and a black dress that involved taffeta, swaggered into the living room. I followed.

Erica plopped on the sofa next to Noah and his mom. His sister sat in the recliner. Dad and Barbara were also here, holding silver trays unearthed from the black hole of my garage.

I looked at Noah. "Did you do the introductions?"

He nodded, and his mother and sister were peering at what was on the trays.

"Is that Mick Jagger?" Mrs. Garcia asked, her head tilted to the side. Dad was standing over her like a butler, offering her something on the tray.

I froze. "Dad, what are you doing?"

"Look at this coffee," Jess squealed. Barbara was near her, beaming and holding the tray. Jess held her hands in the air, waving them excitedly. "Is that Noah?"

I peered over Barbara's shoulder. A photo of Noah in uniform was printed atop the coffee.

"Wait. Mrs. Garcia was supposed to get this one," Barbara said, looking to Dad.

"Oh. Sorry. Hang on," Dad responded. He and Barbara exchanged places.

"Dad?" I asked.

"Lana, I brought the coffee printer over. Barbara and I learned to use it, and I thought our guests would be entertained."

Jess took the coffee from Dad's tray. "Mick Jagger. Interesting."

Noah's mother laughed when she saw her son's image on a latte. "Can I take a photo?"

"Of course, but if you put it on social media, please tag Perkatory."

"Dad," I whispered. "Please."

Dad mouthed the word WHAT at me. Erica rose and motioned for me to take her spot between Noah and his mom.

Noah, who was still holding Stanley, buried his face in the dog's mane to keep from laughing.

Dad and Barbara went back into the kitchen and brought out two coffees for Erica and me. Mine had a photo of Stanley, and Erica's had a monkey. Jess took photos and we chatted about the latte machine. Joey emerged from the kitchen with his own latte adorned inexplicably with the words "HAPPY BIRTHDAY" in foam.

"It's not his birthday," Dad explained. "That was a mistake."

Conversation returned to the lubber invasion, and Mrs. Garcia told us how one year in Tampa, the bugs had claimed her croton shrubs. Erica passed photos of the ruined festival around and entertained everyone by telling them how she sold her video to CNN.

"Five hundred smackeroos," Erica crowed.

Noah and I smiled at each other. "Can I talk with you in private?" he asked in a low voice.

"Let's go into the kitchen. I need to check on the lasagna anyway."

We excused ourselves. Noah let Stanley down, and he immediately went to look for his tennis ball because there were new people to play with.

In the kitchen, I pulled open the oven door.

"It smells amazing," Noah said. "Looks amazing, too."

It really did. Emotion filled my chest as I shut the door. "I'm sorry. I only had time to make one giant lasagna, and it's vegan. I hope that's okay, but I had so much to do this week . . ."

My voice trailed off, and for some reason, I felt choked up, like I was about to cry.

"Hey. Sweetie. It's okay." Noah reached for me and drew me into a hug. "Whatever you do today is perfect. You don't have to do anything special to impress my family. They already love you."

I shook my head against his broad chest. "I feel like a failure."

"Why?" He pulled back to look at me.

"We didn't solve either homicide and I didn't make everything I wanted for tonight, and . . ." I sighed.

Noah took my face into his hands. "Goodness, cupcake. That's not all on you. Homicide cases sometimes happen like this. Real life isn't *The First 48*. We have some solid leads. In fact, I have two officers out right now, looking for Bill."

"You do? You think he's the killer?"

"Possibly. He must know something. If he's Darla's boyfriend, why hasn't he contacted us? My money's on him. Or the daughter. We're still collecting evidence on her, though. One of them will slip up soon. Criminals aren't as smart as they think they are. You know that."

I'd learned as much as a crime reporter and nodded. "I'll keep telling myself that."

Noah pressed his lips to my forehead and I shut my eyes for a second, reveling in happiness. When I heard the commotion and conversation of six people headed in our direction, I pulled away from Noah to arrange the potholders on the counter.

"Your kitchen is gorgeous, Lana," Mrs. Garcia said, running her hand over the granite countertop.

Noah sidled up to Dad. "Can I chat with you outside?"

Dad clapped him on the back. "Sure, dude. C'mon. Do you want something a little stronger than coffee?"

"For this conversation, maybe I do."

Noah and Dad went to the makeshift bar and concocted what looked like mojitos.

"I wonder what that's about," I muttered to Erica, who was arranging my fridge to make room for the cannoli and funnel cake trays.

While Dad and Noah were outside, the rest of us stayed clustered in the kitchen, talking about my mom's great decorating taste, since she'd been the one to renovate this place years ago.

Jess went to the bar and announced she was making a Hemingway daiquiri, since we had white rum, grapefruit juice, lime juice, and maraschino liqueur.

"That's what I'm talking about," Erica said, and stepped in to assist with a stainless-steel shaker. She knew my kitchen well since she'd stayed with me for several weeks while her boat was under repair.

Erica and Jess ended up making a pitcher of the drinks, and we all had a glass, toasting to an excellent night.

* * *

There's usually a point in every party where the guests gel, where things seem effortless, when it's obvious the evening is a success. Usually that point comes after dinner or following many drinks.

Tonight, that point happened early on, an hour in, right as I was about to take out the lasagna. Dad and Noah were still outside for some reason, but I wasn't paying attention because I was having such a good time inside with his family and my friends.

We moved from the kitchen back to the living room, talking about everything and nothing. The conversation was casual, filled with laughter and interesting details. Noah's mom was a gem, and she insisted that I call her Ileana. She also kept beaming at me, which made me feel better about, well, almost everything.

Everything but the homicides, that is.

I figured that if Noah wasn't worried, then I wouldn't be, either. The smell of the baking lasagna permeated the entire house, and I announced that it was time to take dinner out of the oven so it could rest for a few minutes.

We all trooped into the kitchen.

I opened the oven door. The giant tray of lasagna looked incredible. Bubbly and delicious, like something out of a glossy food magazine.

"Do you want me to take that out?" Joey asked.

"Nah, I've got it. I sure hope it's done in the middle," I said to no one in particular. It had been in the oven for the proper amount of time, and the more I studied it, the prouder I was.

Joey peered into the oven. "Dang, Lana, maybe you should come work for me."

I smirked triumphantly, slightly tipsy from the daiquiris.

Noah's mom and sister, Joey, Barbara, and Erica, stood behind me. Everyone oohed and ahhed at my creation. It looked exactly like the real thing, browned on top, with the tomato sauce burbling up around the edges.

"It smells like heaven," Erica said, and everyone murmured in agreement. "Makes me want to become a vegan. I probably would if it wasn't for bacon."

"My mouth is watering," Ileana said.

Between that statement and her love of Stanley, I was acing this meeting-the-mom thing.

"Here goes nothing." I slipped on two oven mitts and leaned into the stove, grasping the sides of the pan. It felt like it had gotten heavier while cooking, which was an impossibility.

Gingerly, I slid it toward me, an inch at a time. I was about to ask Erica to grab a large cooking sheet so I could slide it on that, when Jess edged closer to me.

"Are you sure that's vegan?" Jess asked. "It smells suspiciously like real cheese."

"A hundred percent vegan." I eased the tray half out and slid one mittened hand to the side.

The only way out of this situation was through, and I had to do my best to get this bad boy out of the oven. I paused, assessing the situation. The half that was out of the oven sagged on the bottom, probably from the weight of the multiple layers of noodles. This wasn't what I anticipated while assembling it.

"Okay, one . . . two . . . three."

I meant to whisk it out and onto the nearby counter in one graceful swoop. Instead, the tray's back half collapsed, and I lost my tenuous grip on the entire thing.

All eight layers of lovingly made lasagna, including the homemade tomato sauce, vegan cheese, and fake sausage crumbles, landed on the inside of the oven door with a gooshy-sounding splat. The five of us watched as a sauce-covered noodle slithered off the oven door and flopped onto the floor.

"Oh dear," Barbara murmured.

Unable to respond or react, I wondered if I should run to my room like a five-year-old and fling myself on the bed and weep. That's when Stanley appeared, as if out of nowhere. He did that sometimes when food was around—crept in on little silent dog feet.

He nudged the noodle on the floor with his nose. I hauled in a deep breath, scooped him up, and looked at my guests. They stared in dismay at the ruined dinner. Erica broke the silence by ripping into a fresh pack of paper towels.

"It's only a minor setback. Maybe we can salvage it." Erica could be the biggest optimist.

I would not be defeated by this and smiled tightly while reaching for a napkin to wipe the tomato sauce off Stanley's mane. "I think pizza's a great plan B, don't you?"

Chapter Twenty-Five

Joey took pity on me and saved the evening. First, he suggested he cook pasta, then suggested we could eat at his Italian restaurant for free.

Although I put on a brave face and joked about my fumble on the short drive to the Square Grouper, inside I was mortified. Humiliated, even.

Noah put his arm around me as our group walked in. "I'm sorry, cupcake. I know how hard you worked on dinner."

"You should hear the story of how I ruined Thanksgiving the year Noah was five," his mother chimed in. "I accidentally used cinnamon instead of sage and the turkey came out tasting terrible. I didn't think Noah's father would let me live it down. We all make mistakes."

That made me feel marginally better. Joey sat our group in a back room that was low-lit and looked like it was something out of a mafia movie, with the ancient red leather chairs, heavy wooden tables, and faded framed paintings of Naples (Italy, not Florida). I wondered if this was where his father—who had served time for mafia-related activity in New York before he moved to the island and opened his restaurant—did other kinds of business.

Since Joey's dad passed years ago, I figured it wasn't polite to ask. While we were all staring at menus and debating what to eat, I leaned into Noah.

"Want to split the mushroom and sausage pie?"

"Absolutely. And some calamari for an appetizer?"

"Let's do it. I'm going to use the ladies' room, but make sure you get the parmesan bread sticks for the table." That was one of the Square Grouper's specialties.

I slipped away from the group. It wasn't that I had to use the facilities, but I wanted a moment alone to gather my thoughts in peace. Being an only child meant I loved others' company, but when things went sideways, I needed time to recompose myself.

Winding my way through the restaurant, I went toward the deck. A waitress stopped me. "We're not seating anyone out there tonight because of the lubbers."

"Oh, I only want a bit of fresh air."

She waved me toward the door. "In that case, go ahead. But if you see any bug swarms, I'd advise you to come inside."

Obviously.

As I opened the door, the humid air hit me in the face. I was immediately overcome by a feeling of both comfort and discomfort. The smell of briny air was familiar, like it had been a part of my life since birth. But the moisture at this hour was annoying, reminding me that the brutal summer wasn't far off.

The deck overlooked a swampy area on two sides, and I studied the tangled mangrove roots that were barely visible in the darkness, looking for any signs of lubbers. I saw none and hoped that meant the state agriculture people had corralled most of the bugs. Then again it was pretty dark out here, and who knew what was lurking in the shadows.

Normally there would be tiki torches blazing on the deck, but there was only one lamp illuminated near the door. It cast a wan yellow glow, one that was almost eerie.

The other side of the deck faced the parking lot, a point that wasn't in the location's favor. But it was Florida, and when the weather was nice, tourists would sit just about anywhere to soak up the sun.

I tipped my head back and closed my eyes. The day had been a whirlwind, starting with that strange conversation with the taffy employee at the grocery and ending with the ruined lasagna. It was only seven o'clock, so there was plenty of time left for additional weirdness.

Probably I stayed outside for too long, but I needed more than a minute to myself. I couldn't shake the crushing feeling of failure this evening, and it was annoying. I'd struck out miserably at dinner and hadn't helped Noah much with the homicide investigations. Somehow, I also felt like I'd let Dad and Barbara down by not being more enthusiastic about their relationship.

As I thought about it all, tears welled in my eyes. I got like this sometimes, emotional when I was alone and feeling overwhelmed. This wasn't the time for that, though, and I had to get over myself and move on. I'd never been like this in Miami, probably because I never sat still long enough to process my feelings.

I wiped away the tear that had trickled down my cheek and started to head inside. Something in the parking lot caught my eye—a green Kia that looked like a box. It was backed into the space and sported a bumper sticker for the taffy shop.

This made me think of Darla, and my chest grew heavy again. Could I have saved her had I called police immediately after our final phone call? That question would haunt me for the rest of my life.

Then my gaze went to the license plate. MAF A4P, it read.

Something clicked in the recesses of my brain.

"Mushrooms are fungi and four plants," Darla had said during her dying breath.

MAF A4P.

I gasped aloud. Darla used mnemonics to remember details, and perhaps she was giving me one final clue. If that was the case, then her killer was potentially inside this very restaurant.

"Holy crap," I whispered aloud, pressing my fingers to my mouth as I stared at the car.

I needed to tell Noah right away. I made a beeline for the door and pulled it open. The main dining room was packed with people, and I paused to study the faces. But who was I looking for?

A thousand questions raced through my mind as I slunk through the dining room, hoping that whoever killed Darla didn't recognize me. When I arrived back at the table, a cheer went up.

"We got pitchers of margaritas!" Erica cried.

"Um, great. Noah, can I talk with you in private?"

He looked up at me, uncertain. "Sure, I guess?"

I tugged at his sleeve and pulled him to the far corner of the room. Without stopping to take a breath, I told him what I'd seen outside and my theory on Darla's final statement.

Noah stared at me like I was speaking an alien language. "You think Darla's killer's here because the words she spoke that day match a license plate?"

"She remembered things with mnemonics. Yes!" My voice was a touch too loud and I saw his mother staring at us with a pinched, worried expression.

Noah rubbed his neck with his hand and swore aloud.

"You're swearing a lot with this case," I said. "Do you think it could be Bill? Or Moose?"

"I'm going to call my officer who was looking for Bill and ask him to run the plate and find out if it's his car. While he's doing that, I'll take a look out in the dining room and the bar."

"I'll come with."

"Like hell you will."

"Do you remember what the guy in the picture looks like?" I put my hands on my hips. "The two of us have only seen that photo. You're going to need help."

He pushed out a breath while shaking his head and staring at his phone. "Fine."

He tapped out a quick message and I tried not to meet his mother's gaze. Erica also was studying us and held up her glass of margarita. I nodded, and she poured one into a plastic cup and walked over to us.

She handed me the drink, but I shook my head. "What's going on, lovebirds?"

"I think Darla's killer's here," I hissed.

"Whoa." Erica's eyes and mouth opened wide.

Noah started for the door but I reached for him, pulling him back. "Shouldn't we tell everyone what we're doing?"

"And cause a commotion? Everyone will want to help us look for . . . whoever it is we're looking for. No way. Let's go, Lana. Erica, make sure everyone stays in here after we leave. I'm serious."

I scurried after Noah, who paused inside the doorway of the main dining room. We looked like security at a club. Or people who were lost.

We each scanned the crowd. "Do you see anyone who looks like the guy in the photo?" I asked in a low voice.

"No." The muscle in Noah's jaw pulsed. "Let's go check the bar."

He grabbed my hand and pulled me into the dining room so we could walk through. On the way, a horrible thought came to me.

I assumed we were looking for Bill. But what if the owner of the car with that license plate—and Darla's killer—was someone entirely different?

Also, what if I was totally off base about Darla's final clue?

Noah and I made it through the dining room, dodging waiters with platters full of stone crabs, kids flailing in highchairs, and tablefuls of tourists downing colorful tropical drinks.

The bar area was large, and similarly crowded. A band was setting up on a low platform at one end of the room. To the casual observer, Noah and I looked like any other couple on a Saturday night, him dressed in jeans and a polo shirt, me in my casual sundress.

We stood at a small opening at the bar, between two groups of chattering people. Noah leaned into my ear. "Order us two waters."

He kept his back pressed against the bar while I tried to flag down the bartender. When it was clear that the bartender, a young woman with pink hair, was paying more attention to a group of spring breakers, I gave up and surveyed the people standing around the horseshoe-shaped bar.

And then I saw him. The man in Darla's photo with the scruffy beard and floppy, dirty blonde hair.

He was bigger than he looked in the photo, more menacing. So big that he almost took up two spaces at the bar. His face was in profile, and as he shifted in the direction of the bar—and me—I quickly averted my eyes and turned. Now I was standing in the same direction as Noah with my back to the guy.

"I found him," I murmured.

"What?" Noah said.

It was exceptionally loud in here, with the group of college kids nearby laughing and shouting about starting a game of beer pong.

I hopped up on the empty barstool next to me and swiveled it to face Noah. Not wanting to make it seem like we were casing the joint, I threw my arms around him, pretending that I wanted a hug.

"Erm, what . . . Lana?" Noah stammered.

I pressed my body into his, wrapping my arms around his neck and nuzzling the side of his face so I could speak clearly into his ear. "The guy in the photo is at the other end of the bar. If you turn around, he will be on your right, kind of near the door to the bathrooms. He looks exactly the same as in that photo. Same haircut, everything."

Noah nodded and slowly embraced me. "This is a delicate situation, Lana. The place is busy, and this guy's a suspect in possibly two murders. There's no telling what kind of weapon he has on him."

"What are you going to do?"

He inhaled sharply. "Ideally, we'd nab him as he leaves. It's easier to stop a vehicle than to haul someone off in the middle of a crowded restaurant."

"Okay." I snuck a glance at the guy, who was guzzling from a beer bottle. His hands seemed to dwarf the brown bottle.

"Let's go call my officer. Get some assistance."

"Wait." I pulled back and looked at Noah, still with my arms around him. "You want us both to leave here, and take our eyes off the guy?"

"We'll see him if he walks out. There's only one door to the parking lot."

I shook my head. "No, there's a back door to the porch, too. Let's not chance it. You go call, I'll stay here, then you come back and we'll continue to monitor."

Noah touched his nose to mine. "Okay. I don't want you to move from this spot. Don't talk to anyone, look at him directly, or cause any kind of scene. I'll be back in under five minutes. You hear me?"

"Loud and clear."

He brushed his lips over mine and turned to give the guy a glance. He then shifted back to me, while hiking up his jeans. "Yep, that's definitely him. I'll be right back."

Noah slipped away. I pretended to casually play air bongos on the bar, attempting to keep in time to the reggae music playing on the sound system.

Out the corner of my eye, I saw the bartender on the mysterious guy's side of the bar. He raised his index finger and she took a couple of steps toward him. I watched her nod, her long, pink ponytail bouncing up and down her back.

It appeared that he was ordering a drink, which was a good sign that he was staying for a while. I reached for a menu and pretended to study it.

"Excuse me. This is for you."

I looked up to see the bartender standing in front of me. She slid a glass mason jar full of purple liquid and a black and white straw my way. "From the gentleman over there."

She pointed at the guy, and my eyes bugged out. Oh no . . .

"It's our signature Demon Juice drink. He said he wanted you to have one because it looked like you were bored with your man and you needed to get wild."

"What?" I blurted.

"He said, he wanted you to have a Demon Juice—"

"I heard all that. Ah, thanks?" I wasn't sure what the etiquette was in this situation, but knew I needed to stall until Noah returned. "Did he tip you?"

"Fifty bucks," she said with a laugh, and walked off.

I stared at the purple drink, then glanced up. The guy's gaze was fixed on me. I expected him to look threatening, or angry. Instead, he had the smug, arrogant look of a dude about to score with a woman. He winked and held up his own glass in a toast. That's when I noticed that his dirty blonde hair was in a ponytail.

Omigosh. This couldn't be happening.

With a shaking hand, I raised my glass in his direction and mouthed *thank you*. Wait, why was I saying thanks to a possible murderer?

Out of instinct, I attached my lips to the straw and was about to suck in the liquid when I froze. I hadn't seen the bartender make the drink. How did I know he hadn't poisoned it? With my heart thrashing in my chest, I pretended to drink, but didn't.

I snuck a glance, and to my horror, he was still staring at me. He pointed and gestured a thumbs up. For a second I didn't know what he was referring to, then I realized he was asking me how my drink was.

I nodded and returned the thumbs up. Where the heck was Noah? I didn't have my phone on me, or a watch, and it sure seemed like a lot more than five minutes had passed. Needing something to do with my hands, I reached for the cocktail napkin and tried to wrap it around the cocktail glass.

Because I was so focused on that, I didn't notice that someone had slipped into the spot where Noah had been standing.

The guy.

"Hey, cutie." He grinned, revealing a set of straight, white teeth. They were almost a shock compared to the rest of his rumpled, oversized appearance. Everything about him, from his messy hair to the deep creases in his button-down shirt, looked disheveled. But he had great dental hygiene, from the looks of things.

"Oh. Oh! Hello!" I forced a smile. There was no precedent for this situation, but I knew I shouldn't do anything to upset him.

Because he'd either kill me or leave, and neither of those options were great.

"You didn't look like you were enjoying your boyfriend much. Where'd he go?"

My mouth opened and closed and opened again as I formulated something benign to say. "He went out to the car for some . . . business." Goodness, that sounded ridiculous.

He leered at me, his alcohol-tinged breath hitting me like air from a furnace. "Business, huh? If you were my date, you'd be my only business."

Was I supposed to be flattered? Under any normal circumstances, I'd leave. Maybe even throw a drink in the guy's face. There was simply no way I could do that now, not with a murderer standing next to me. I had to keep him talking until Noah got back.

Wait. What would happen then? Would he be confrontational with Noah? Obviously, this guy didn't give a fluff that moments ago I'd been hugging and kissing my boyfriend. But why would he? The man was a giant, and had no conscience, if past events were any indication.

My upper lip broke out into a sweat. A sweat-stache, Erica called it.

"Where are ya from, anyway?" He took a sip of his drink.

"Around." The smile remained pasted on my face, but I felt a little trickle of sweat on my hairline.

"Yeah, me too. Around. I'm outta here tomorrow, though. Wanted to have a little last fun here for one night. What do you say we leave your boyfriend and his business in the parking lot and blow this pop stand?"

I giggled nervously.

He leaned closer, his hand now on my knee. I wanted to gag, to scream, to flee. His eyes were a faded gray blue, like storm clouds.

"I know what you're thinking." He smiled, but it was a dark and sinister expression, one that sent chills through my body.

"Wh—what?" I whispered.

"Maybe I can give you something you won't find with that geeky guy you were with."

Again, I laughed. Maybe I could play coy until Noah returned.

"You sure are pretty. What's your name? Hey, why you breathing so fast?"

"No reason. It's kind of stuffy in here." I fanned my face with my hands. Probably best if I didn't give him my real name, in case Darla had told him about me.

He looked around and squinted. "Yeah, it is, isn't it? Well, I'm Bill."

Everything inside me seemed to expand and fill me with certainty. This was our guy. "Uh, I'm Stevie."

He tilted his head. "Stevie. As in Nicks?"

"Yeah, that's it."

"Well, Ms. Stevie, how do you feel about leather and lace?"

It felt like I was glued to the barstool. What a jerk. "You mean, the song Stevie Nicks did with Don Henley, or . . ."

The alternative was horrific. He chuckled. "You're a real comedian, you know that?"

"I've heard that before." I stared at my drink.

"Why aren't you drinking that? Doesn't taste good? I'll buy you another."

The guy's arrogance grated on me. Maybe it was because my ex had a similar, yet less lethal, arrogance, or because I was simply over men who thought they could do no wrong, but something in me snapped.

"Tell you what," I said. "I'll let you buy me a drink if you answer a couple of questions."

He chuckled darkly. "Sounds like a good deal to me."

This time I took a real sip of my drink. It tasted like grape juice, sickly sweet. "Where do you work?"

He smirked. "I'm a handyman. I do a little of this, and a little of that."

"Why are you leaving town tomorrow? Why not stick around a while?" I gripped my glass.

He affected a sigh. "It's time I move on. I got nothin' here for me."

"Hmm. I see. I'm surprised a big, handsome guy like you isn't taken." Barf. "You don't have a girlfriend?"

He stroked his chin and blinked rapidly a few times, a sure sign that he was trying to conceal something. "I did, but she's gone now."

"Oh yeah? She from around here? Maybe I might know her." Where the heck was Noah, anyway?

"She was, but she didn't get out much. Spent most of her time gardening."

"You talk about her like she's dead." I looked him straight in the face. His eyes widened for a split second. *Gotcha*. "You're Moose, aren't you? Darla's boyfriend."

The look of shock on his face was replaced with a skittish, suspicious gaze over my left shoulder. I turned to find Noah and five officers storming inside the bar and heading right for us.

I leaped off the barstool, noticing that the guy's eyes shot around the room, as if he was looking for an exit. "Noah, it's him," I cried. "It's Darla's—"

Before I could say any more, Bill grabbed my arm, hard. That's when I knew that I would be in serious danger if I didn't do something fast.

"Bill Walker, let her go," Noah boomed. "You're under arrest."

People in the bar gasped and oohed.

When Bill yanked me toward him, police closed in. Landing in the middle of potential crossfire or being taken hostage were two things I wanted to avoid, so I reached for my Devil's Juice mason jar and smashed it into Bill forehead. It didn't break like in the movies, but the blow was forceful enough to stun him for a few seconds.

Purple liquid ran down his face as he cried out, but he let go of me. By now, the people in the bar were either watching or shooting video, and I stumbled over the stool and into Noah's arms.

* * *

An hour later, I was finally calm enough to stop pacing. I was back in the special events room, where we were supposed to have our family dinner. The family was still here, except for Noah, who was in the bar with his officers processing the scene.

Or perhaps he was in a police cruiser, driving Bill—or Moose, or whatever his name actually was—to jail.

"Dear, you really need to eat something." Noah's mom sank into the chair next to me. "The bread really is delicious. Here, Joey brought us a fresh basket, nice and warm."

She held the food out for me, and I hesitated. "Thanks. And, uh, sorry tonight didn't go as planned. I'd really hoped to impress you with my cooking, not get into a bar brawl with a murderer."

Ileana tipped her head back to laugh. "Oh, Lana, if you only knew what my husband put me through. One night on our tenth anniversary, we were at the nicest restaurant in town. He left me there for a double homicide. That's the way of life for an officer's wife. You'll learn."

She leaned in and placed her hand on my cheek. "I got to know you better tonight than at any dinner. I think you're wonderful and I'm thrilled my son has met such a good-hearted person."

For some reason, this made me tear up. Maybe it was the emotion of the evening, or Ileana's motherly tone—something I didn't know I was missing until that moment.

"Thanks." I screwed up my face, trying not to cry. I'm sure I looked like I was about to fart.

"Aww, m'hija. Don't cry." She folded me into a hug and I sniffled on her shoulder. She smelled like bread and Chanel No. 5. Now I knew where Noah got his kindness, and it made my heart melt.

"Are we having a cuddle puddle?"

I looked up and there was Dad. I finally laughed. "Not exactly."

As Dad explained what a "cuddle puddle" was to Ileana, I munched away on the bread, only now realizing how famished I was.

I was on my third piece of bread when the door to the room flew open. There was Noah. Everyone in the room, from Erica, to Barbara, to Joey, clapped and hooted.

Noah waved them off and came over to me, pulling up a chair. He took my hand.

"If you had any concerns about that not being Darla's killer, erase them from your head. We found fentanyl tablets in his car, Darla's credit cards, and notes written by Jack about his deck. I'm sure we're going to find more evidence with all the junk he has in the car. We also located Jack and Darla's phones in a bag in his trunk. And this, too."

He reached into the breast pocket of his shirt and pulled out a small plastic baggie. It contained a gold earring in the shape of a gardening water can.

I gasped. "The other earring!"

"It was in his cupholder. I suspect he stole the necklace and earring set, and Jack's phone after he killed Jack, then dropped one of the earrings on his way out of the garden."

I let out a huge breath. "Wow. It's all coming together."

Noah kissed my palm. "And get this. His name is Hudson Bill Walker. He has two different driver's licenses on him, and a passport in a whole other name. We found a criminal record in Georgia for one of his names. It's going to take a while to sort through everything, but I'm confident we got the guy who killed both Jack and Darla."

I threw my arms around Noah, who returned the embrace with a tight hug. His mom, my dad, and Erica all patted and rubbed my back as Noah held me. Finally, I was able to relax, and the wheels of justice could begin to churn. Unfortunately, it would be too late for Darla and Jack, but at least the rest of us would be spared from Bill's criminal mind.

When I started to sniffle, Noah spoke soothingly in my ear. "It's all okay now, cupcake. We've got you. You're safe with us."

Epilogue

"Noah. Two o'clock. Someone's walking a tiny pig. Oh my goodness, it's adorable. I want to squeeze it. Maybe we should adopt a pig."

Noah squeezed my hand and shifted his head ever so slightly. "Whoa. It is a small pig."

Sure enough, a woman was tottering next to her potbellied pig on the sidewalk near the beach. The cute piggy had on a pink dog harness and seemed to be living its best life. It was one of many sights this Saturday evening, a month after Bill's arrest.

"If dogs are doggos, are pigs piggos?" I mused aloud.

He snickered and slid his arm around my shoulders. "You know what I love about you? Your mind. It's constantly surprising me with its absurdity and its brilliance, often simultaneously."

This made me cackle as we strolled. It was about an hour before sunset, and it seemed like everyone was out tonight. Rollerbladers, dog walkers, people juggling what looked like batons, a group of people doing yoga on a patch of grass. The weather was excellent, one of those rare moments in Florida where the temperature didn't feel like Hades, and the humidity was low.

In other words, a perfect evening.

We were coming from the Funnel Cake Festival, which had been rescheduled after the lubber invasion. It was the first time that Noah and I had been alone in a long while. Bill's arrest kept him busy, and when we installed the latte art machine, Perkatory experienced a crush of customers like never before.

We had lines every day for two weeks. The café attracted so many people wanting photoprinted lattes that I and my entire staff worked seemingly nonstop. And I'd hired a new barista: Alexis Dominguez from the taffy shop. She was a Devil's Beach native whose mother owned a hair salon on the island. Alexis was twenty and going to school for Afro-Latino studies.

As it turned out, she knew quite a bit about coffee because her grandfather had owned a coffee finca in the Dominican Republic, and she'd spent summers there as a kid.

I'd also hired Alexis because Dad was trying to wind down his time at Perkatory so he could concentrate on the two new loves of his life: Barbara and the Perk Pops. When he was finally able to get back into Peas on Earth after the investigation concluded, he discovered that his mint had overtaken several plots.

Erica and I spent two whole days helping him harvest and tame the crop. Then he and Barbara got to work on making the popsicles, and we added those to our offerings, much to the happiness of our customers at Perkatory. The local paper had done an article on the treats, and they were now also in the local grocery store.

Dad was working on his popsicle cart, with Barbara's help.

I was still getting used to the two of them together. It was odd seeing him hold hands with her or kiss her on the cheek like he used to with Mom. But I caught many glimpses of his happiness shining through, in ways I hadn't seen since before Mom got sick. He laughed a lot now and seemed more relaxed.

That, in turn, made me happy, if not a little bittersweet.

We all deserve love, Noah had gently told me. He'd gone through this with his mom, who started dating a couple of years after his father died, so he knew why my emotions were all over the place.

Erica had been more blunt about the news: "What? Did you want your father to be celibate the rest of his life?" That question had made me both cringe and laugh, and I figured that was the best thing I could do under the circumstances.

Laugh, and love, and let go.

Mom used to say that the world would be a better place if everyone would just live and let live, and I was trying to follow her lead. After all, she was the one who got this ball rolling with Dad and Barbara, and more than anything, I trusted Mom's judgment, even in the afterlife. If she thought Dad and Barbara would be a good pair, I couldn't argue with her logic.

Noah and I walked for a good half mile along the beach, taking in the sights and breathing the briny Gulf of Mexico air. We were on our way to a new restaurant called Moonwater, and it felt like this was the first night I'd relaxed in weeks.

The aftermath of Bill's arrest had been a wild ride. The day after the showdown in the bar, Noah and a detective had interviewed Bill, and he confessed everything, touching off days of local, state, and national news coverage.

According to Bill, Darla was completely innocent. The two had met on the mainland shortly before Christmas, in the garden center of a big box hardware store. They'd gone on vacation almost immediately, and Bill said she'd fallen for him hard and fast. He'd fallen for the fact that she had a few thousand in the bank. She also hooked him up with a customer for his handyman business.

Jack Daggitt.

But then she started to complain about Jack and his social media posts about her. Bill—a guy with a long criminal record in other states—decided to steal Jack's money, then silence him for good with the lethal dose of fentanyl. He had a stash of fentanyl pills from his late mother's cancer treatment, and ground up the pills into a liquid substance, then sucked them into a syringe.

When Jack arrived at the garden, Bill was there waiting behind Dad's large mint patch. When he confirmed that no one else was around, Bill stealthily crept up on Jack, who was a bit hard of hearing for his age, and stabbed him in the back with the needle. Wearing gloves so he wouldn't leave fingerprints, Bill injected the lethal dose of opioids into his system and ran. That was his first mistake, leaving the syringe behind.

He insisted Darla knew nothing about the murder.

Darla's mistake was asking me to investigate. She did that on her own, but then told Bill about our conversation. In his twisted, paranoid mind, that meant she needed to be eliminated.

So he killed her.

The only reason he hung around Devil's Beach afterward was so he could sneak into Darla's home after police had cleared the scene. She apparently had a stash of cash hidden in a wall safe in her closet, and he couldn't leave without making sure it was still there.

Now Bill was sitting alone in county lockup on the mainland without bail, awaiting trial and conviction. Darla, who was valiantly trying to rebuild her life, was dead. All because she trusted the wrong man.

Love hurt if you picked the wrong person to love.

Fortunately, I hadn't. I looked over at Noah as we walked to the restaurant. The soft light of the sun near the horizon made his skin look extra soft, and I fought the urge to kiss him right there. We finally reached the restaurant, and we were whisked to our table on the deck overlooking the shimmery blue water.

On the other end of the deck, a guy with a guitar and a harmonica crooned acoustic cover songs. When he struck up a nasally rendition of Dylan's "I Want You," I started to snicker, thinking of the woman next to the garden who hated Jack's music.

"What are you laughing about?" Noah asked as we opened the menus.

"Nothing." I grinned at my handsome boyfriend. Sometimes life handed you serendipity in the strangest moments, and this was one of them.

It was our first sit-down dinner together since the night Bill was arrested at the Square Grouper. Tonight, however, there wasn't anything coming between us. Not our families, not giant grasshoppers, not homicide.

Tonight was all about us. Well, and my perfectly cooked Key West mahi mahi piccata. Every bite was incredible, juicy, and bursting with flavor. Noah, who had ordered a simple, wood-fired grilled grouper, snuck his fork onto my plate and speared a hunk of fish.

"Holy cannoli, that is amazing," he said after chewing and swallowing.

I carefully carved out a portion and put it on his plate. We ate mostly in silence, soaking in the ambience, and the guitar. The sun dipped below the horizon, leaving a fiery orange sky behind. A reggae band struck up at the bar next door, and the strains of Bob Marley's "Is This Love" wafted through the air.

When we were finished, a waiter cleared our plates and asked if we wanted dessert, or after-dinner drinks.

"I was thinking of a piña colada for dessert. You?" I asked Noah.

"Make that two."

When the waiter left, Noah reached across the table and held my hands in his. "I asked you here for a reason tonight."

My eyes widened. His serious tone and the way he was nervously licking his lips had me thinking he was going to either propose or break up. The idea of both made me break out in a sweat behind my knees. Maybe this night wasn't as perfect as I'd thought.

"Okay?" I squeezed his hands and took a deep breath.

"I've come to a decision, one that I've been thinking about for a long time. Well, several months now, but in some ways, I've been thinking about this when I was at the Tampa Police Department."

I nodded, urging him to go on. Was he going to say he was applying for a job somewhere else? Would he ask me to move with him? Would I?

"I'm planning to give my notice to the mayor on Monday. I wanted to tell you first, though."

I sat back, allowing my hands to slip out of his. "What? You're quitting the department?"

He beckoned with his fingers. "Hold my hands."

Letting out a lungful of air, I did. "Why? Where are you going?"

"I'm going nowhere, cupcake. I'm taking your father's advice and starting a fishing charter business here on Devil's Beach. It's what I've wanted to do for a long time, and in four months, I'll have worked as an officer long enough to get a pension. I'm close to forty. I've been in law enforcement almost twenty years. It's time to step down. I don't have the passion for it anymore, and I don't want to continue in a job that depresses me on the regular. Policing is tough, you know that."

My mouth opened and closed several times, until I finally squeaked out a few words. "Really? This isn't a joke?"

He shook his head. "The other night, at your house, before the lasagna disaster, I pulled your father outside and talked with him about it. That's what we were doing outdoors for so long. Peter's become kind of a father figure to me, you know. I respect his opinion a lot. Even if he's a little wacky sometimes. And high. I think he was high when he told me to name my boat the *Liquid Limo*."

"Yeah, don't name it that."

We both shook our heads.

"You're not going to be the police chief anymore." I said this as a statement, not a question. It was taking a few minutes for this monumental news to sink in.

"I'll be a fisherman, hang out with tourists and people who want to see the best of Florida, not someone who routinely dives into the worst of Florida. I have a couple of leads on boats. It's going to be several months before I can take my first charters, because I need to build a website, get proper state licenses, insurance, all that. I figure I'll leave the police department in four or five months, around September. That way I'll be able to open the business in time for the high season in the winter."

"Wow. I never imagined you'd leave law enforcement."

"I didn't either, but it feels right."

I threaded my fingers through his. I'd be lying if I said I wasn't worried about him while he was at work. Devil's Beach was a sleepy town, but you never knew what danger lurked in the shadows. Too many people were armed, and far more were mentally unstable.

We knew that all too well, after the recent saga with Darla and Bill.

"I'm glad, Noah. More than glad. Ecstatic. Are you going to keep your condo, or live on the boat like Erica, or . . ." We hadn't yet discussed living together, but I felt like we both knew it was on the horizon.

He chuckled. "Since we're on the topic of big life changes, ahh, how would you feel about sharing a home?"

A grin spread on my face, so big that my cheeks hurt. "Your place or mine?"

"I like your place better. Stanley's settled there, and I've always thought your backyard would be great for a garden. I wouldn't mind growing some tomatoes in the winter."

With a little squeal, I rose from my seat and went to his side of the table. He opened his arms and I plopped on his lap, wrapping my arms around him, not caring who saw us or what they thought.

"I love you, Lana Lewis," he murmured into my ear. "We make an excellent team."

"Yes, we do. And I love you."

I imagined us playing with Stanley after work, reading the paper in bed on a lazy Sunday, or growing something beautiful in the yard.

Like tropical flowers. Or vegetables in the mild winter. Or, perhaps, coffee.

Acknowledgments

I'd like to thank my agent, Jill Marsal, not only for helping me with this book, but for her invaluable advice.

My amazing husband, Marco, deserves my gratitude for not only putting up with my writerly quirks but also for carrying the load at home. I love you.

And last but not least, my friend Margaret Lashley, who has given me much-needed moral support, laughter, and chocolate pudding.

To my readers who have joined me on this writing journey, thank you for believing in me and my weird sense of humor. This book would not have been possible without your love and encouragement.